ERIN MCKNIGHT

Batter Days

For Eva,

I love you to the moon and back. Thanks for being a part of my "framily."

Erin McKnight

First edition

ISBN: 978-1-7376582-0-7

Editing by Dori Harrell
Editing by Erynn Newman
Proofreading by Katie Donovan
Cover art by Daniel Lunsford

This book was professionally typeset on Reedsy.
Find out more at reedsy.com

For my mom, thanks for always encouraging me to be myself and go after my dreams.

Contents

Chapter One

I HATED POWDERED sugar. Okay, I didn't hate it exactly. Without it, buttercream frosting would taste like flavorless goop—nobody wanted that on top of their wedding cake—but as I looked around my now snow-white work space, I was starting to rethink my position.

Everything from the stainless-steel worktables to the concrete floor was covered in powdered sugar. Sugar I would have to clean up before I could get any more work done.

"Stupid piece of crap." I tossed the hand towel on my shoulder at the mixer, the god-awful mixer that was the source of my latest problem.

I'd been telling my boss, Toni, for months that we needed a new industrial mixer. But did she listen? Hell no! Instead, I was stuck playing a game of Russian roulette every time I used it. The faulty speed controls made the thing go from a low hum to an all-out urban assault in less than a second. I'd actually taken to using a small hand mixer for the majority of my work, but that wasn't going to cut it today.

A scream of rage and frustration boiled up inside me as I looked at the mess. "Just great!"

Blowing a lock of my strawberry-blond hair out of my face, I tightened my ponytail and grabbed the broom to clean up the colossal mess my workspace had become.

I'd been working as a baker and cake designer at Toni's Tasty Treats for three years now. Scratch that. I'd been working as a baker and *decorator*. I couldn't tell you the last time I designed anything other than a child's birthday cake. I'd made so many ice castle decorations in the last year that I was pretty sure I would die happy if I never made anything out of boiled sugar again.

Making fancy cakes for kids' birthday parties was great, don't get me wrong. You could pay your bills with that. But the thing every baker wanted to be known for was their wedding cakes. They were the status symbol of the baking world, and I, for one, was dying for an opportunity to show what I could do. Re-creations were fine, but I longed to design and showcase my own work for a change.

It took me an hour to whip everything back into some semblance of order so I could get back to the cake that had been plaguing my nightmares for the last few weeks. Just thinking about it made me shiver. It wasn't that it was another re-creation. That was par for the course. What bothered me about the Schumacher cake was the less-than-adequate reference materials I'd been given.

Half the time brides brought in a photo of a cake they'd seen in a magazine or online and asked if we could make one just like it. Most of the time, I could take a quick look at the picture and figure it out. But this? This cake was a monster from the bowels of Pinterest hell that refused to let me rest. I was sure the original cake was lovely, but the black-and-white photo was so grainy that the majority of the details were lost. I'd called the bride a half dozen times to ask her what website she found it on, but all I ever got was her voicemail. I tried to blow up and enhance the image on a computer, but it didn't help. Ninety percent of the detail was still a blur, and it was frustrating as hell trying to figure it out.

"Ally?"

I finished the border I was piping and paused to look up at Brooke. She covered the shop front five days a week and would even come in early on Tuesdays and Thursdays to help me with cookies and other simple treats that didn't require decoration. She was a riot. The stories she told about her family and the crazy stunts she pulled growing up in Mississippi made me laugh so hard I cried.

"Yeah?"

Brooke pushed open the heavy metal door that separated the baking floor from the storefront and stepped into the doorway. Her dark skin and long braids stood in sharp contrast with the white apron Toni made her wear.

"There's a phone call for you, babe," she said in her heavy Southern accent.

I put my piping bag on the table. "Thanks. I'll be there in a sec."

Brooke gave me a quick nod before disappearing back through the door.

I reached my arms overhead and pushed my chest forward to stretch out my back before rising to my feet and heading toward the small mirror we kept near the back door. Sighing, I raised my eyes and squeaked in fright at my appearance. White powder covered my face, and enough strands of hair were sticking up across my head that it looked like I'd stuck my spatula in a light socket instead of a bowl of frosting. I grabbed a cheesecloth to clean my face and used some water from the handwash sink to pat down my hair. The last thing I wanted was to go out front and have a customer see me looking like a monster from another dimension and flee in terror.

I pushed the door open and waltzed into the main storefront. Everything about the utilitarian design said this was a serious business. We didn't have time to waste on people who didn't know what they were looking for. It was all clean right angles and sparkling glass. A few standing tables were positioned in the far corner for cake tasters and customer meetings, but there was nowhere to sit and chat.

Brooke leaned against the display case of miniature cakes and treats, with the ancient rotary phone pressed against her chest to mute it. She took one look at me and threw a hand over her mouth to hold in her laughter.

"Don't start," I warned her. The water had done little to tame my wayward locks, and I was certain nothing short of a shower would rid me of the powdered sugar covering me from head to toe. "I've already had a hell of a day. Who's on the phone?"

"Kyle."

My spirits lifted in an instant.

I'd met Kyle when I was working for a catering company to help pay for culinary school. I'd been serving drinks at a fancy fraternity party when one of the drunken frat boys knocked a tray of Irish car bombs all over me. Kyle had been the only one not to laugh. He showed me to one of the bathrooms upstairs so I could clean myself up and gave me one of his shirts to wear so I wouldn't have to spend the rest of the night looking like a wet T-shirt contest reject. By the end of the night, he had my phone number and a date for the following Friday. It'd been five years, and I still got the bubbly happy feeling in the pit of my stomach whenever he called.

Brooke extended the phone to me. I took it from her with a smile. She picked up a nail file and shaped her nails in a thinly veiled attempt to make it look like she wasn't eavesdropping.

I scoffed and shook my head at her before raising the phone to my ear. "Hey, babe."

"Hey, Ally." His voice was as rich and smooth as chocolate buttercream. "You weren't answering your phone, so I figured you were working."

"Yep." I dusted a white, hand-shaped print off my pants. "Same as always. We still on for tonight?"

It wasn't unusual for Kyle to call the bakery if he couldn't reach me. Our other baker had quit last month, leaving me as the only person in the back on a regular basis. The number of hours I worked varied depending on the orders we had coming in, making it harder to track when I'd be working.

"That's what I'm calling about. I had to change our reservation at Le Cirque to eight."

"Oh?" I did my best to keep the disappointment out of my voice, but it must have shown, because Brooke set down her nail file and looked at me with unabashed curiosity.

"They scheduled a last-minute meeting for five thirty tonight. I should be there to pick you up around seven."

"Y-yeah." I cleared my throat. "Sounds great. That'll give me more time to get ready after work."

"Good." A commotion sounded in the background, and I could have sworn I heard Kyle curse. "I've got to go. I'll see you then. Bye."

The dial tone sounded in my ear.

"Bye." I put the phone back on the cradle and glanced at Brooke.

"So?" She plunked her hands on her hips and hitched her eyebrows halfway up her forehead. "What did he say?"

"Just moving our dinner reservation back a bit." I waved a hand dismissively. "No biggie."

I turned and headed for the door. It had barely closed behind me before Brooke came charging after me.

"Oh no you don't. You can't just sit there and tell me nothing happened when you look like somebody just kicked your dog."

"I don't have a dog."

"You know what I mean." She batted a the air like she was swatting a fly.

I couldn't help but snicker.

"Now, what in the world is going on? That boy has canceled on you twice this month."

I rolled my eyes at her. "He's not canceling. Just rescheduling. We've both been busy with work. He's vying for a new VP position that just opened up, and things have been insane here since everyone else left. You know that."

Picking up my piping bag, I tried to focus on my work. Maybe if I ignored her long enough, she'd go back to the front and let me work in peace. At least, that was what I hoped. I probably sat there for two minutes just feeling her eyes bore into me before I gave in and looked at her.

It was moments like these when I would swear Brooke missed her calling as an interrogator for the FBI. The woman was a pit bull. If I didn't tell her now, she would find a way to pull it out of me later.

"It's fine, Brooke." I picked up my spatula and put another heaping scoop of frosting into my bag before turning my attention back to the cake.

"And just how many hours is he putting in?" Brooke asked.

I had to stop and think about it for a minute. "I don't know. A lot?"

Brooke did not look impressed.

"He keeps talking about how important this is for the future. He says he needs this in place so he can move on to the next phase of his life."

"Next phase?" Now she was interested. "Girl, you better start talkin'!"

I pulled my lower lip between my teeth to keep the dopey grin off my face, but it wasn't working. "Well"—I set my tools to the side—"just between us, I think he's gonna propose."

Brooke stared at me with this blank expression on her face. I wasn't sure if she'd heard me until her eyes widened, a grin spreading across her face.

6

"Oh my gosh!" She slapped a hand over her mouth before letting it rest on her chest. "Girl, that is so exciting! When's the big day?"

I flopped back onto my stool and laughed. "He hasn't *asked* me yet."

"True. True. I didn't even realize y'all were talking about getting married."

I hesitated.

Brooke narrowed her eyes. "Ally?"

Oh man. I didn't like that tone. Every time she used it, I ended up telling her more than I intended to.

"Well..."

"Well what?"

"We haven't exactly talked about it."

The way Brooke's face went from excited to skeptical in two seconds flat said it all. I was about to be on the receiving end of one of Brooke Dalton's famous tirades, and trust me, that was the last thing I needed right now. So I picked up my piping bag and tried to make it look like I was too busy to talk with her. Not that it ever worked.

"Not exactly?" she asked in an exasperated tone. She pulled up one of the other stools to take a seat beside me. "What does that mean?"

That settled it. No way I was getting out of this one.

I spun the cake and kept working. "He hasn't mentioned getting married specifically, but every time we've been together over the last few months, all he's talked about is the future and how much more prepared he'll be for the rest of life once he gets this promotion."

"Hmm." She quirked an eyebrow at me.

My pulse ticked up half a beat. "What?"

Brooke crossed her arms over her chest and lowered her chin to glare at me. "So let me get this straight. He's never actually told you he wants to get married? You just assumed that's what he meant when he mentioned the"—she added finger quotes—"'next step in life'?"

All right. I'd admit it sounded ridiculous when she put it like that, but what else was I supposed to think? We'd been together for more than five years now. It was the only logical conclusion.

"What does Derek say about all this?" she asked.

Derek was my roommate and had been my best friend since grade school. We'd met when my mom signed me up for soccer at the local YMCA in hopes of improving my coordination. It didn't work. If anything, it made it worse. I'd ended up falling over every time I tried to kick the ball. The other kids started laughing and calling me Charlie Brown until Derek stepped in and told them to back off. He helped me to my feet and promised he wouldn't let anyone else pick on me. We'd been friends ever since.

"We haven't really talked about it," I said.

"That's a lie! You two talk about everything."

"Well, not about this. You know Derek isn't Kyle's biggest fan."

It was true. Kyle beat Derek at some combat video game the first time they met. He'd rubbed it in for a good twenty minutes, and Derek's never really forgiven him. At least, I think that's what started it. I'm not sure where the hostility comes from on Kyle's end. At least they manage to keep things civil when I'm around.

"Besides." I sat the piping bag on the table. "I haven't had a chance. Derek's been working nights this week to cover for one of the other trainers while his boss is out of town. The only time I see him is first thing in the morning when I'm eating breakfast and he's just getting home. Not exactly a great time to talk about what may or may not be changing in my relationship status."

Brooke opened her mouth to give her rebuttal when the bell over the front door chimed. She glanced at the swinging door and back before pointing a finger in my face. "Don't you think you're off the hook, missy. We're finishing this later."

I snorted. "Whatever."

Brooke hadn't even finished standing before Toni's voice rang out.

"Why isn't anybody here?"

I winced. Dealing with one of my boss's moods was about as enjoyable as a root canal. The swinging door banged off the wall as she barreled into the back room.

She took one look at the two of us and went nuclear. "What is this? Am I paying the two of you to work, or am I paying you to gossip?" She didn't give us a chance to respond. "Get back to work. The both of you. Move it."

In moments like this, it was hard to believe I used to have fun at work. Toni hadn't been quite so grumpy back then. Sure, she'd been demanding, but nothing compared to the mountain of attitude she was now. She spent just as much time in the shop as the rest of us when I started. Now you barely saw her darken the door for anything other than the custom orders she deemed "too important to let anyone else work on them."

She turned her steely-eyed gaze on me, and a cold shiver went down my spine. "That cake isn't finished yet?"

"N-not quite," I stammered.

Her eyes narrowed, and I instantly knew I'd given the wrong answer.

The Schumacher-Randell wedding was one of the biggest social events of the season. Everyone had expected the bride to hire some high-end designer for a custom cake, but when she saw a photo of one she loved online, she'd printed it off and set out to find somebody to re-create it. Part of me still wondered if Toni had even looked at the photos before agreeing to take the job. Then again, maybe she had, and had decided to use this to make my life a living hell. Her "I only do original work, not re-creations" policy ensured it was my problem. Not hers. So why not take the payment and give it to me to figure out?

"So"—the sound of her ire-filled voice brought me out of my thoughts—"what you're telling me is that instead of working on the cake, you decided it was better to spend the day talking?"

"No. No." I ran my hand across my forehead. "It's not that at all. I'm just having a hard time making out the details."

"What details?"

I inhaled a slow, steady breath and rolled my shoulders. If she was finally giving me a chance to say my piece, I needed to make sure I said it right.

"The pictures they gave us are awful." I gestured for her to come look and turned the picture on the stand beside me toward her. "You can't see anything. I even tried to enhance it on the computer, and everything is still too blurry to see what's happening with the design. It's just a big gray blur. They didn't even print the thing in color so I could at least make out the foreground and background details."

Toni picked up one of the enhanced photos and studied it. For a brief moment, I thought she might be coming around. Yeah... I was not that lucky.

She sat the photo back on the table. "The only problem I see is a lazy decorator who spends more time making excuses than working. That blur is a frosting flower bouquet. I hired you because you're good at what you do, but if you can't deliver on your promises..."

I cringed. This was it. I'd finally done it. I'd pushed her too far. She would fire me like she had everyone else the last few years, saying she needed someone dependable. I didn't know what I would do if I lost my job. Nobody would be willing to hire me for the kind of job I wanted without a portfolio of original work to showcase my skills. I couldn't lose this job. I'd have to start all over from scratch, and I'd worked too damn hard to have it all taken from me now.

"I want this cake to be perfection before you leave today," she said. "I don't care how long it takes. Just get it done."

She turned and walked back through the doors toward the small administrative office on the far side of the bakery. Between flaps of the door, I could see her rummaging through the desk before shouting,

"Aha!"

She pulled something out of a drawer and threw it into her handbag before heading back to the front door. She stopped just before she pushed it open, then turned to look at Brooke.

"Make sure to clean out the display before you go tonight. Nobody stops and looks in the window anymore. We need something new to draw attention."

Brooke nodded, a fake customer-service smile screwed onto her face, and watched Toni walk out the door.

The atmosphere in the store eased the moment she disappeared around the corner. I could finally breathe again.

"Make a new display," Brooke muttered under her breath. "I made a new one two days ago!"

I understood where she was coming from. A part of me wanted to smash that stupid cake into a pile of crumbs and leave it there for Toni to find in the morning.

How in the hell did she expect me to re-create something I couldn't even see properly? I wanted to throw my head back and scream, but I didn't have time for that. Not if I wanted to get home in time to get ready for my date. Even with Kyle pushing the time back, I would have to haul ass if I was going to be ready.

I sat down on my stool and looked from the photo to the cake and back again. A sickening feeling took over my stomach. No way could I do this. Even if Toni was right about the bouquet, there was no way to tell what *kind* of flowers they were. The photos were too grainy. I was almost ready to throw the picture across the room when an idea jumped into my head. I might not be able to see the details of the cake, but that meant the bride couldn't either, and since she wouldn't answer her phone… All I had to do was get it as close as possible and use my imagination to fill in the gaps. If I did that, I could get this cake done and be home in plenty of time for my date.

11

I clapped my hands in excitement before picking up the bag and squeezing out a swirling vine of frosting. This would work. I just knew it.

An hour later, I set the bag down. Okay. Sometimes I had to admit that I impressed myself. The cake looked fan-freaking-tastic. I would have dared anyone to take a look at the photo I'd been handed and tell me this wasn't the same cake.

"Damn, girl," Brooke said as she marched into the room. "That almost looks too good to eat."

A burst of pride spread through me. "Thanks. Help me get it in the fridge?"

Brooke moved around the table to grab ahold of the opposite side of the cake stand.

It always made my life easier when Brooke was there to help me move a cake. One wrong step during the transport process could turn all my hard work into a heap of garbage on the floor. The rhythm Brooke and I had developed over the years made the otherwise nerve-racking process easier to manage.

"It really does look amazing." She placed the cake in the fridge.

I cast a look of thanks over my shoulder as I closed the fridge. "I just hope the Schumachers agree with you."

"Are you kiddin' me?" Brooke scoffed. "They're going to love it and you for making it."

Brooke pulled me into a quick hug before gathering her things. The bakery had closed half an hour ago, and it was finally time to go home.

I hung my apron on its hook and snatched my purse from my cubby.

"Oh!" Brooke paused at the door. "And good luck tonight. I want to hear all about it tomorrow. And don't forget to show me that ring."

She winked and headed out the door.

I was smiling so hard my face hurt. I'd been so focused on the stupid cake that I'd forgotten about my date. Now that I wasn't entrenched in flour and frosting, I could let myself feel the excitement I'd been holding back all day.

I glanced at the clock on the wall and let out a curse. I'd have to book it if I wanted to shower and change. Throwing my purse over my shoulder, I shut off the lights and locked the door.

A cab flipped its light on from across the street as I stepped into the cool autumn air. I thought about flagging it down, but I decided against it. It wouldn't take me too long to walk home, and if I wore my hair up instead of curling it, I wouldn't need as long to get ready.

Walking as my main form of transportation was a habit I'd picked up in culinary school. Derek and I had put on a little extra weight from eating my homework every night. His solution was to get in extra workouts at the gym after his shift and drink protein shakes for lunch every day. My solution wasn't as drastic. I walked the five miles to and from class every day. I hadn't lost any weight—I'd still been eating my homework, after all—but at least I hadn't gotten any bigger.

Imagine my surprise when I'd been offered a job just three miles from my apartment. Walking had worked so far, so I hadn't seen a reason to change it. True, the weather could make it unpleasant at times. Winter in New York could be hell, and summer wasn't much better. Even so, it was nothing a few extra layers of clothing or baby wipes and a travel-sized stick of deodorant couldn't fix.

I was a mile from home when I heard the unmistakable sound of Queen's "You're My Best Friend" coming from my purse. I smiled. Only one person had that ringtone.

"Hey, Derek."

"Hey, Als." I could hear the smile in his voice. "You done turning sugar into art yet?"

I shook my head. "Yeah. I'm on my way home. I should be there soon. Why?"

"I was wondering if I should leave some food out for you or put it in the fridge."

"Oh? I thought you were done with your late shifts."

"I traded a few shifts with Ramon so he could go to his son's first communion, remember?"

I smacked myself on the forehead. "Right. Sorry. I forgot."

"It's okay." He chuckled. "So, food?"

"No thanks." I hiked my purse up higher on my shoulder and waited for the walk light to change before crossing the street. "I'm going out with Kyle tonight."

The shift in Derek's tone was instantaneous. "Yeah. Right. Sorry."

There was a pause. Derek must have noticed my unease, because he changed the subject. "What would you say to an old-school movie night this weekend?" he asked. "Just like the old days. Cheap beer. Greasy food. The whole nine. What do you think?"

I smiled into the phone. "I think it sounds amazing."

"Then consider it done." There was a beat where I thought I heard a door open and keys jingle. "All right. I gotta go to work. See ya later, Als."

"See ya."

Chapter Two

MY APARTMENT WAS on the third floor of an old red brick industrial building that had been converted into apartments sometime in the 1950s. It wasn't much to look at, but by New York standards, it was golden.

"Hi, Mrs. Henderson." I greeted one of my neighbors as I came up to the door.

"Hello, Allyson. How was work today?"

Mrs. Henderson was a little old lady who lived on the first floor and was like an extra grandma to everyone in the building. She always had a smile on her face and a plate of cookies somewhere in her apartment for the kids in the building to snack on when they came home from school.

I shrugged. "It was work."

The little Scottie at her side barked.

"Hi, Pepper."

He wagged his little stubby tail.

I gave him a quick scratch on the head before moving on. "Sorry to run, but I've got a date."

Her eyes brightened. "Oh? Is Derek finally taking you to dinner? You know, I've always thought you two would make a handsome couple."

I stifled a laugh. She'd been trying to push my best friend and me together since the day we moved into the building.

"No, Mrs. Henderson. I have a date with Kyle."

She made a face at me.

"My boyfriend?"

"Oh, right." She grinned in embarrassment. "Have a good time, dear."

She walked away, and I just stood there blinking after her. The way she'd told me to have a good time made it sound like she expected me to do anything but. I shook my head to clear the thought from my mind. I didn't have time to worry about what she'd meant.

I raced up the stairs to my darkened apartment. Kicking my shoes off by the door, I fumbled around in the dark until I found the lamp in the living room.

I stubbed my toe on the leg of the beat-up leather couch that faced the entertainment center. "Ouch!"

A string of muttered curses flew from my mouth. You would think I'd know where everything was in the apartment after living there for years, but apparently my clumsy foot wasn't paying attention.

It took my eyes a moment to adjust to the sudden change of light as I switched on the lamp. I looked at the clock in the open-concept kitchen behind me and balked.

"Crap!"

Chatting with Mrs. Henderson had taken longer than I'd thought. No way would I be able to both shave my legs and put on makeup. Oh well. Kyle would just have to deal with my stubbly legs for one night.

I made a mad dash for my room.

Derek had given me the master when we moved in. I'd tried to reason with him about it, but he'd said me having my own bathroom would be better for when company came over. I couldn't disagree with him there. While I might keep the kitchen spotless, the rest of my cleaning skills left something to be desired. So, Derek being responsible for the main bathroom was definitely better.

It only took me ten minutes to shower and put on fresh makeup. I'd decided on the dress Kyle had bought me for a New Year's Eve party at his office the year before. The beautiful velvety green material felt amazing against my skin and hugged my curves enough to flatter my figure without making me feel like a stuffed sausage. The knee-length skirt and long sleeves gave it a feeling of elegance. I twisted my damp hair into a simple updo and secured it with a sparkling clip.

I glanced at the clock. Ten minutes to spare. *Damn, I'm good.*

Since I had extra time, I took off the heels I knew I'd be cursing myself for later and carried them into the living room to wait. I switched on the TV and absentmindedly watched a few minutes of *The Great British Baking Show*. It wasn't until the episode ended that I realized how much time had passed.

I looked at the clock. Our reservation was in ten minutes, and Kyle still wasn't here. My pulse quickened. This wasn't good. Kyle always called me when he was running late. Maybe he'd called while I was in the shower. I pulled my phone out of my clutch and checked the notifications. Nothing.

I pulled my lower lip between my teeth. Had something happened? I didn't live in a bad part of town, but it was still New York City. I gave myself a mental smack upside the head. There was no sense letting my imagination run away with me.

I held out for five more minutes before giving in and calling his cell. I caught myself chewing my nails while the phone rang. I shoved my hand under my thigh. No answer. I ran to the window to see if his car had pulled up outside. Maybe he hadn't answered because he was driving? I peered through the kitchen window. Nothing.

Now I was worried.

"The hell with it," I said to the empty apartment before calling his office.

Kyle didn't like me calling him at work, but my anxiety level was racing toward panic at the speed of light. The lump in my throat made it hard to breathe. I felt like I might pass out by the time I reached the fourth ring.

"Masters."

I breathed a sigh of relief. "Kyle? Oh, thank God. I was losing my mind. Are you just now leaving?"

"Shit," he hissed. "Dinner."

I heard what sounded like a room full of people followed by the click of what had to be a door, because the voices suddenly grew quiet.

"I'm sorry, Ally. I got held up at the office and lost track of time. My boss threw this giant presentation at me in the meeting, and I have to be ready to pitch this to a client first thing in the morning. I'm so sorry, baby."

I tried to hide my disappointment. We'd already had to reschedule this dinner twice because of his job. How many times would we have to change it before we made it to dinner?

"It's okay." My voice came out strangled and thin. "I understand."

"Why don't I take you to lunch tomorrow?" Kyle offered. "I'll pick you up at the bakery, and we can go to that place around the corner you like so much."

I rubbed my forehead to ward off the oncoming headache. "Yeah. That sounds good." *If I get a lunch break.*

Kyle apologized for canceling again as the voices in the background grew louder. Someone yelled at him to hurry up, and he promised to see me at lunch before abruptly ending the call.

I tossed the phone onto the counter with a growl.

I knew I shouldn't be so upset. His boss asking him to do a special project was a good thing. It put him one step closer to getting the promotion he was working so hard for. I should be happy for him, but I wasn't. I was sad and tired and pissed off because I'd raced to get ready for no reason when I could have just put on my pj's and called it a night.

Making my way over to the fridge, I grabbed a container of leftovers and threw it into the microwave before settling in for a few more hours of mindless entertainment.

Chapter Three

THE DOOR HAD barely closed behind me before Brooke barreled onto the floor. I didn't even get a chance to put my coat on a hook before she bombarded me with questions about how my night had gone.

"Can I put my things down first?" I teased.

Brooke rolled her eyes and waited for me to get a move on so she could hear all the juicy date details, but I wasn't in the mood to talk about my nonexistent date. So I put my things in my cubby and sailed past her without saying a word.

Yeah. I should have known that wouldn't work.

"Oh no you don't." Brooke followed hot on my heels. "You don't get to play coy with me. Now, where is that ring? Come on. Let's see it."

I kept my back to her so she couldn't see the disappointment on my face and snatched a mixing bowl off the shelf. "No ring."

"Say what?"

I wiggled my left hand at her to show off my lack of sparkly jewelry.

Brooke gave me a sympathetic half smile. "I'm sorry, Ally. Did you at least have a good time?"

My mouth tightened into a hard line.

"You didn't have a good time?"

"We didn't go out." I looked up from the batch of cookie dough I was mixing to see Brooke staring at me like I'd grown another head.

"What do you mean you didn't go out?"

I sighed. "Something came up last minute, and Kyle's boss needed him to stay late."

"Then he needs to tell his boss to shove it."

I frowned. She knew as well as I did that that was never happening. It would be like me telling Toni I couldn't do something. It wasn't an option.

"Well, he should make it up to you." Brooke threw her arms across her chest.

"He is. We're going to lunch today."

"That doesn't count."

"Sure it does." I gestured to the rack of baking sheets behind me. "Now, either help me bake cookies or stop pestering me. I've got to get this stuff done so I can start on a cake."

Brooke pursed her lips in thought before picking up a baking sheet and helping me roll the cookie dough into balls.

"Just because I'm helping doesn't mean this conversation is over."

"I know." I shook my head at her before reaching over to turn up the volume on the little radio we stashed in the back. Maybe some music would help clear away some of the funk I suddenly found myself in.

* * *

I WAS JUST putting the last touches on an action-hero birthday cake when Brooke stuck her head through the door. "Hey. Kyle's here."

A wide smile spread across my face. "Okay. Thanks. Tell him I'll be right there. I just need to put this away."

Brooke nodded and stepped back.

21

I fluttered around like a madwoman, grabbing a box and putting the cake inside as quickly as I could without messing it up. I was practically buzzing when I slipped off my apron. Giving myself a quick once-over in the mirror, I was shocked to find I didn't have flour all over my face for once. I tucked a loose strand of hair behind my ear and made my way to the front.

I spotted Kyle in his tailored navy suit the instant I came through the door. He was facing away from me, but his angular features and short jet-black hair made him look like a Roman statue. It wasn't until he turned and smiled at me that he even looked real.

"Hey. You ready to go?" he asked.

I came around the counter and took his hand. "Yeah. See you later, Brooke." I threw her a wave over my shoulder and followed Kyle out the door.

Around the corner was a bistro Brooke and I hit up for lunch at least once a week. Their croissants and pasta salads were the stuff of legend.

The bell over the door chimed, and the owner, Sal, stopped wiping down the counter to greet us. A wide, infectious grin took over his face when he saw me. "Hey, yous guys. Sit anywhere you like."

"Thanks, Sal." I held up two fingers. "Can I get two usuals?"

"Sure thing, sweetheart. I'll bring 'em right out."

I thanked him and followed Kyle to a booth by the window in the back. He waited for me to slide into my seat before positioning himself on the opposite side of the booth.

"So," I asked once Sal had brought us our waters, "how was the presentation this morning?"

"It was fine." He waved his hand in dismissal.

The clipped response made me frown. Kyle normally couldn't wait to tell me all about his latest boardroom triumphs. He loved talking about his work. Instead of looking at me, he kept checking his watch and rubbing his hand along the back of his wrist.

I forced down my rising panic and reached across the table to take hold of his hand. "Are you sure?"

His dark eyes locked with mine, and for a moment I could have sworn I saw him panicking.

"You seem a little off," I told him.

He opened his mouth to say something but was cut off by Sal bringing us our food. Kyle pulled his hand away, and I reluctantly leaned back against the booth. Maybe once Sal was gone, we could pick up where we left off? No such luck. Kyle just picked up his panini and went to town. I did the same.

I was about halfway through my meal when Kyle cleared his throat to get my attention. I glanced up to see a crease forming between his eyebrows.

"You okay?" I wiped a stray spot of chipotle ranch off my face.

He leaned forward in his seat. "Ally, there, uh, there's something I need to talk to you about."

His face flushed, and he rubbed at his wrist again. My eyes went wide when he patted his breast pocket.

He was going to do it. He was going to propose right in the middle of the bistro! I sat up straighter and tried to pull myself together.

"Yes?"

I hoped I didn't sound too eager. After all this time, he was finally asking me to marry him. Sure, it wasn't the romantic setting I had expected, but it was happening. I wondered what the ring looked like. I could feel myself vibrating from excitement. Each second that ticked by ratcheted up my pulse until I felt like my heart would explode. When Kyle pulled his hand away from his pocket, I frowned. Instead of a ring box, he was holding a key. My key.

I looked up at him, and he said the last thing I expected to hear.

"I think we need to break up."

Chapter Four

MY BRAIN STRUGGLED to catch up with what my ears were telling me. There was no way I'd heard him correctly. It wasn't possible. He wasn't breaking up with me. He couldn't be.

"W-what?"

Kyle's shoulders rose and fell with his breath. "Ally." He raised his head to look at me. "This just doesn't work anymore. It hasn't for a while, and I think you know that."

"Doesn't work?" I blanched. "I know we've both been busy lately, but that doesn't mean we have to break up. We can just move some things around. Start making our time together more of a priority. I can talk to Toni and…"

Kyle shook his head. "Things have changed. We just don't work like we used to."

"What about that future you were talking about?" I asked. "The plans we've been making?"

He didn't say a word. His eyes dropped to where his clasped hands rested on the table.

My heart felt like it was about to beat out of my chest. I clenched my hands around the edge of the bench seat until my knuckles turned white.

Kyle's eyes lifted to meet mine. "I'm sorry."

All the air rushed out of my lungs in a single breath. I couldn't believe this was happening. I watched unblinkingly as he rose and pulled his wallet out of his pocket. He tossed enough bills onto the table to cover both of our meals, then grabbed his coat off the back of his chair and headed for the door.

"Take care of yourself, Allyson."

I tried to speak, but my mouth refused to form words. I watched Kyle through the windows until he disappeared around the corner. Still, I didn't move. I just sat there staring after him like a zombie. I didn't even notice when Sal packed up what was left of my lunch and put it in a to-go box. He put his big meaty butcher's hand on my shoulder and gave me a sympathetic nod, which I returned with one of my own before gazing back out the window.

Had I missed something? There must have been some sort of sign, an offhand comment here or there that I'd overlooked. I could kick myself for being so stupid. Kyle was one of the best things that had ever happened to me, and I'd screwed it up without even knowing it.

The shrill ringing of my phone jolted me out of my daydream. I fumbled through my bag. My heart sank further when I saw the caller ID.

With a shaking hand, I pressed the ANSWER button and brought the phone to my ear. "H-hello?"

"Where the hell are you?" Toni bellowed.

"At lunch."

"For two hours!"

I glanced at the clock behind the counter and silently cursed myself.

"Did you forget that you have a job to do? The Schumacher cake is supposed to be delivered in less than an hour, and you decided that taking a long lunch is more important?"

I scrambled to my feet. "I'm sorry, Toni. I-I'm on my way."

Toni was still mid-scream when I hit the END CALL button and dashed for the door.

My lungs burned, and my legs ached with the effort of running the five blocks to the bakery. Toni had never yelled at me like that before. Sure, she'd raised her voice a time or two, but she'd never gone off like that.

I burst through the door like a whirlwind. "I'm here," I panted, tossing my things into a cubby and grabbing my apron.

"Where have you been?" Toni screamed, her plump face flushing redder by the second. "Don't you know that you have a job to do? I swear, you are the most—"

"I'm sorry, Toni." Maybe if I stopped her before she picked up a head of steam, I wouldn't get chewed out as bad. "I lost track of time. Let me just grab Brooke, and we'll get everything loaded up."

Toni was still screaming like a banshee when I stuck my head through the door to holler at Brooke. "Will you come help me for a minute please?"

She set down the rag she'd been using to clean the counter and followed me to the back.

We moved the cake with our usual practiced ease. Heaven help me when we delivered it, and I'd have to move it with Toni.

"Hurry up!" Toni grumbled, holding the back door open to let Brooke and me shuffle past. "We're running late as it is."

Brooke waited until her back was to Toni before doing a dramatic eye roll that was no doubt intended to make me laugh, but I just shook my head and focused on making sure the cake was secure.

"So," Brooke drawled as she slid out of my way, "how was your lunch?"

The look on my face must have said volumes. The corners of her mouth turned down as her eyebrows drew together. My mouth opened and closed a few times while I searched for the words, but I didn't even know where to begin.

"We don't have all day!"

I looked over Brooke's shoulder to see Toni storming toward us.

"I'll tell you later," I said just above a whisper.

Her brows knit together, and she placed her hand on my shoulder in concern. I knew Brooke meant to make me feel better, but it just made the pit in my stomach deeper.

"I...we..." The words lodged in my throat like a giant boulder. I couldn't force them out.

Without saying a word, Brooke pulled me into a tight hug. I closed my eyes and leaned into her.

"We do *not* have time for this!" Toni barked.

I let go of Brooke and stepped toward the passenger seat.

"I'm holding you to that conversation when you get back," she told me.

I nodded before climbing into the van.

Every muscle in my body tensed as we drove. I kept expecting Toni to light into me like she had at the bakery, but there was just silence. No radio. No incessant yelling. No nothing. Just an ever-thickening tension that had me bracing for impact.

When the venue finally came into view, I could see Mrs. Schumacher standing at the curb with her arms crossed over her chest. She kept tapping her foot and checking her watch like the White Rabbit. The instant she spotted our van, her arms went up in the universal gesture of annoyance.

"Thank God! You're finally here," she said as she stalked toward us. "I was afraid I was going to have to tell my Melissa that she wouldn't have a cake for her reception."

Toni soothed the high-strung woman while I readied the cake for transport. I'd just finished positioning the cart when she came around the side of the van and started squawking at me to move faster. It was everything I could do to keep from snapping back. *Could this day get any worse?*

Once we settled the cake on the cart, Toni moved to the front and pulled it along like a piece of carry-on luggage instead of a delicate sugary confection. I had to make continual adjustments to the back end of the cart so the cake wouldn't topple over. Every time we went over a bump, I pictured the cake smashing to the ground in my mind's eye. The topper would go first, followed by three layers of lemon and buttercream perfection that made me want to rip out my hair every time I looked at it.

Caterers and hotel staff alike were scattered throughout the ballroom when we entered. They were hanging decorations and adjusting table settings while Toni barreled through them like a steam engine. I wasn't sure how we managed to get the cake in place without a disaster, but somehow we transferred it from the cart to the table without anything collapsing.

Toni went to settle accounts with Mrs. Schumacher while I took a moment to enjoy the fact that I never had to deal with this nightmare of a cake again. I took a deep breath, allowing my muscles to release for what felt like the first time in days. When I opened them again, a pop of color on one of the tables caught my eye. I moved around the long dining table to get a better look at the centerpiece. It was a beautifully arranged bouquet of cream and peach roses, but what had caught my attention was the blood-red orchid sitting in the middle. It was breathtaking.

I let my eyes wander the room as I took in the rest of the decorations. There was no denying the place was stunning. The scent of the dozens of flowers scattered around the room filled my nostrils. It was exactly what I had always imagined my wedding reception smelling like.

I felt my heart dissolve into ash. Looking around the room, I let myself imagine what it would look like filled with my family and friends. I could almost hear Lonestar playing for the first dance. I closed my eyes and willed the images away.

"Allyson!"

I flinched. The only time Toni ever called me by my full name was when she'd been trying to get my attention and failing. Spine stiff, I turned, painting what I hoped didn't look like a completely fake smile onto my face.

Both Toni and Mrs. Schumacher were staring at me. Well, staring wasn't exactly the right word. Trying to set me on fire with their eyes was more like it.

"This is not the cake I ordered," Mrs. Schumacher proclaimed.

It might have just been my imagination, but the activity in the room ground to a halt. My mouth fell open. My eyes shifted to the cake and back. It was definitely the right cake. So what was the issue?

"My daughter's cake had a floral design in the background." She pointed to one section of the cake that had been impossible to make out. "That is a vine."

Oh God. I gulped and looked to Toni for help, but it was clear from the daggers she was shooting me that I was barking up the wrong tree if I expected any help from her.

"Ally," Toni said in what had to be the calmest voice I'd heard from her all day, "care to explain why you changed the design?"

It felt like every eye in the place was on me. I licked my chapped lips and shifted my weight from foot to foot. This was it. I would finally have a chance to make my case about the reference materials they'd given me, and this time, Toni would have to listen.

"Umm…" I swallowed. Now was not the time to be a stuttering mess. "Mrs. Schumacher, I did the best I possibly could. The photo was just too grainy. I couldn't make out the exact details on the cake. I called your daughter several times, but she never returned any of my messages. So I took the basic shapes I *could* see, and..."

"I don't care about your pathetic excuses!" she screamed. "How am I supposed to tell my daughter that the cake she has been dreaming about for the last three months is not going to be here because you were too incompetent?"

My mouth hung open. *Who does she think she is?* I'd worked my butt off on that cake. I'd been handed one of the biggest batches of lemons on the planet and turned it into some damn good lemonade. Why was I the only one who could see that?

My hands shook as Toni pulled Mrs. Schumacher aside. The shouting and screaming eventually stopped, but the tension clung to the air.

Toni might have been a horrible boss, but she knew how to handle irate customers, I'd give her that. After a few minutes of discussion, Mrs. Schumacher huffed and walked to a small table in the corner, then wrote out a check before handing it to Toni.

* * *

THE SILENCE ON the drive back to the bakery was even worse than the trip to the reception hall. The rigid way Toni held herself told me just how furious she was. I half expected steam to start coming out of her ears from the way the vein in her forehead was sticking out.

She pulled up to the curb, slammed the van into park, and headed for the back door before I could even reach for my seat belt. I hesitated. Maybe if I gave her a minute to cool off, she wouldn't be quite so angry with me.

Who was I kidding? She would unload on me the second I walked through the door, and I knew it.

"You are by far the laziest, most pathetic excuse for a decorator who has ever worked here!"

I'd been expecting the tirade, but that didn't make it hurt any less. It took all my strength to keep my shoulders from bowing while she cut me to pieces with her words. Toni's screaming was so loud that Brooke popped in from the front to see what was going on.

"If I had anyone else here who could do your job, I'd fire you right now," Toni went on, "but as it is, I don't. So I'm just going to give you one last chance. You pull another stunt like that, and you will be fired."

Every cell in my body wanted to run from the room, but I made myself stand still. I forced down the nauseous feeling that had suddenly come over me and kept my expression neutral.

"Get out of my sight!" she yelled. "I don't even want to look at you. Just go home. We'll deal with this tomorrow."

Toni pivoted on her heel and stormed out. The air rushed out of my lungs as my legs gave way beneath me. I didn't even realize I'd been holding my breath until I heard the bell over the front door signal her exit.

Brooke was beside me in an instant, holding me up and telling me not to listen to a word that "madwoman" had said. "She's just a hateful old biddy that wouldn't know what a good cake looks like if it hit her in the teeth."

I tried to give her an understanding smile, but I wasn't sure my face muscles moved. I just wanted to go home. I longed for the comfort of my fuzzy pajamas and a hot shower to wash away the day.

"Do you want me to call Kyle to come get you?" Brooke asked.

Just the sound of his name had my heart landing in my shoes.

"No." My voice squeaked out, barely more than a whisper.

"Are you sure? Would you rather I call Derek? I don't want you walking home alone."

I shook my head. "It's fine. I'll text you when I get home, okay?"

Brooke wasn't happy, but she didn't fight me. She waited quietly while I picked up my purse and walked out the back door, hoping another disaster wasn't waiting for me outside.

Chapter Five

I PULLED MY COAT TIGHTER around me and tucked my chin toward my chest to ward off some of the cold as I slogged down the sidewalk. The steadily increasing rain made me thankful I'd decided to wear my boots instead of my usual sneakers. Having wet feet would not make this day any better.

As I passed the bistro, the image of Kyle's retreating form filled my mind. I racked my brain for some sort of explanation, but I couldn't come up with anything. Just thinking about it made my chest hurt. His eyes had been completely hollow when he told me, like he was talking to a stranger. It was like the last five years meant nothing. Every memory the two of us shared was pointless. Every talk about the future. Had it always been like this, or had something changed without me noticing?

I pushed the thought to the back of my mind. *I can't do this right now.* Shoving my hands in my pockets to keep my fingers warm, I picked up my pace. The sooner I could get home, the better.

Stopping at a crosswalk, I looked over and saw the little market Derek and I went to for late-night snacks. The crosswalk light changed, but I didn't move. I stared at the door for a moment before making up my mind and heading inside. A day like today called for comfort food. I passed a row of snack cakes, but the stale chocolate and sweet lard filling wouldn't be enough to satisfy me this time. I gave the extra-large bag of barbecue-flavored potato chips a once-over before deciding against those too. I was just about to give up and buy a container of frosting and some cookies when I rounded the corner and came face to face with a wall of paradise.

"This is more like it." My eyes drifted back and forth across the pints of ice cream, reading the labels like I didn't already know which flavor I'd pick. I grabbed one for myself before snatching a second for Derek. There was no way I was in the mood to share mine tonight.

* * *

WHY DID STAIRS seem to multiply when the last thing you wanted was to walk up them? All I wanted was to curl up in a ball and sleep for at least a year. Maybe then I wouldn't feel like the earth was imploding.

I sighed in relief when my door finally came into view. Fishing my keys from my bag and unlocking the door, I stepped into the dark apartment.

"Son of a..." A string of curses filled the room when my knee bounced off the corner of the couch. I clicked on the lone lamp in the room. *We need a light closer to the door.*

The kitchen clock on the far side of the apartment said it hadn't taken me as long to get home as I'd expected. Derek normally beat me by a good half hour, but he wasn't even off work yet. Good. I didn't want to see anyone. Not even my best friend.

Kicking off my shoes, I padded to the kitchen and put the two pints of ice cream in the freezer before heading to my room. I shut the door and took a moment to look around the space. My bed was still unmade. Clothes were scattered across the floor. My eyes drifted to my vanity and the velvety dress I'd thrown there the night before. Tears started building behind my eyes. I slammed them closed in a piss-poor attempt to keep myself from crying.

I needed a distraction. Maybe a shower would help me feel better. I peeled off my work clothes, stepped under the spray, and let the droplets rinse away the day.

I'd expected it to relax me, but the longer I stood there, the more I felt myself beginning to crumble. Everything felt so hopeless. The future I'd been dreaming about was gone. The little family Kyle and I had once talked about having had evaporated. There would be no white picket fence. No dog. No two-car garage with a basketball hoop mounted over the carport. Nothing. I didn't even know if I would have a job come morning.

A sob worked its way past my lips. I put my hand over my mouth to hold in the sound, but there was no use. I collapsed against the tile wall and let the tears roll. I cried for the end of my relationship. I cried for my job. I cried until I was too tired to cry anymore.

Shutting off the water, I wrapped myself in a large fluffy towel and went in search of my comfort pj's—hideous pink fuzzy pajamas with little yellow duckies on them. Derek had given them to me as a gag gift for Christmas one year, but the joke had been on him when they became my go-to bad-day wear.

I retrieved the ice cream from the freezer and debated grabbing a bowl from the cabinet before just picking up a spoon and heading for the couch. There was no point in pretending I wasn't eating the whole thing tonight anyway.

The next half hour passed with me mindlessly shoving ice cream into my face and staring at the TV. I'd put on *Steel Magnolias*, one of my favorite movies, but I wasn't paying attention to it. My mind and body had gone numb. My only goal was to make it to a reasonable bedtime so I could crawl under the covers and try to forget this day ever happened.

A jingle of keys and rolling of tumblers reached my ears just before Derek came through the door, bobbing his head along to whatever indie rock song was playing in his earbuds. How could men be so good looking when the weather wreaked havoc on them? It wasn't fair. The rain outside had plastered his light brown hair to his head, but instead of looking like a drowned rat, he looked like he was ready for a beach photoshoot.

Derek had played football for a while in college until he hurt his knee, but his work as a trainer meant he stayed in pretty good shape. His broad-shouldered frame topped out at just over six feet. He would have been downright intimidating if the kindness in his blue eyes didn't soften his angular features.

He tossed his keys on the table by the door. He sent a casual glance my way as he took out his earbuds, stopping dead in his tracks when he saw what I had on. His happy gaze morphed into a frown as he honed in on the half-eaten carton of ice cream in my hand.

"Cherry Delight?" he asked, gesturing toward the carton.

I shook my head. "Triple Fudge Brownie."

Derek sucked in a breath through his teeth and winced. "That bad, huh?"

I nodded before shoving another spoonful into my mouth. Derek knew just as well as I did that only the day from hell would have me reaching for the chocolate overload.

He put his phone and buds on the coffee table before taking a seat on the couch beside me. I'd tucked myself into the corner with my feet drawn up underneath me. He placed a hand on my knee and gently ran his thumb back and forth in a show of comfort.

I kept my head down, poking at the last of the ice cream with my spoon. I could feel Derek's eyes on me, but I refused to look up.

The hand on my knee gave a squeeze, and I lifted my tired, red-rimmed eyes to look at him. Derek's mouth twitched into the barest hint of a reassuring smile, and that was all it took for me to cave.

I wasn't sure if I leaned in or if he pulled me toward him, but the next thing I knew, Derek was placing my ice cream on the coffee table and pulling me against his chest. He ran his hand up and down my back. I fisted my free hand in his shirt and pulled him closer.

I didn't know what I'd done to deserve someone like him. He always knew exactly what I needed, even when I wasn't sure myself. Derek was able to make me feel loved and cherished regardless of what was happening around me. It was the reason I was so comfortable around him and why I found myself wanting to confide in him now.

"Kyle broke up with me," I choked out.

Derek went board stiff. I pulled back far enough to see his face. His brows were knit together, his mouth hanging open as his eyes searched mine.

"He *what?*"

I pushed myself into a seated position. Derek's arm fell from around my shoulders and slid down my arm until he was able to take hold of my hand. He gave it a gentle squeeze while I sniffled. I grabbed my pint from the table and looked down at my melting ice cream.

"He took me to lunch and told me he didn't want to see me anymore." I dug around in the carton and brought another spoonful to my lips. "There's Rocky Road in the freezer for you if you want some."

"Thanks." Derek gave me a warm smile, but it only lasted a second before he was frowning again. "Is that really what he said to you?"

I could hear the disbelief in his voice. I'd been thinking about it all day and could hardly believe it myself.

I shrugged. "Does it really matter?"

I could see the gears in Derek's head turning. He was trying to find the words to make everything okay again, but we both knew there wasn't anything he could say to make it better.

"You know what the funny part is?"

He shook his head.

"I thought he was going to ask me to marry him. How pathetic is that?" I chuckled mirthlessly.

"Hey. Hey. Hey." Derek took the ice cream from my hand and placed it on the coffee table before taking both my hands in his. He waited until I was looking him square in the eye before he continued. "You are not pathetic, Als. You love the guy. It's normal to think about that stuff. Besides, you make wedding cakes for a living." He snorted. "Hell, I'm surprised you didn't have a date picked out already."

He wiggled his eyebrows and crossed his eyes. It was a face he knew never failed to make me laugh. I chuckled and rolled my eyes. He was right. I was surrounded by weddings and couples on a consistent basis. You could only make so many wedding cakes for other people before you started designing your own.

I threw myself back against the arm of the couch. *Why did I have to think about wedding cakes?*

"What?" Derek asked, his voice just above a whisper.

"That wasn't all that happened today."

He raised his eyebrows and waited for me to continue.

"Toni ripped me a new one for a cake we delivered today."

I launched into my story about the disaster that was the Schumacher cake. I told him about the horrible source materials, the absentee bride, and the brilliant idea I'd had to fix it.

"Then her mom saw it and flipped out. 'This is not my cake!'" I said in a shrill voice.

His attention never waned as I vented my frustrations about how Toni seemed more interested in stabbing me in the back than helping me hone my craft.

"What if somebody had been in the shop?" I asked, flailing my arms like I was trying to land a 747. "They would have heard her. Hell, I wouldn't be surprised if they'd heard her on the street, she was being so loud." I deflated against the arm of the couch. "I just don't understand how she can be like that."

"She's a bitch." Derek shrugged. "Seriously, Als, I don't know why you keep working for that woman. She treats you like shit."

"Because I don't have anywhere else to go," I reasoned. "My portfolio is practically nonexistent. Nobody outside of a supermarket bakery wants to see princess ice castles and soccer balls on a cake."

Snatching my empty pint from the table, I rose to my feet and made my way to the kitchen. I tossed the container in the trashcan and dropped the spoon into the sink. I turned to go back to the living room, but I didn't feel like staying upright anymore and found myself leaning against the eat-in-kitchen island. Derek followed my lead and took his usual seat opposite me. The stubborn set of his jaw told me he wasn't finished.

This was a conversation we'd had more than once. Derek would tell me I needed to quit my job, and I would tell him I couldn't quit until I had something else lined up. We'd go back and forth until one of us gave in and decided to drop it for the time being. I prepared myself for whatever argument he was about to send my way, but the loud rumble that erupted from his stomach stopped him before he could get started. There was a brief pause before we both erupted into laughter.

"As much as I know you liked that ice cream," he said, "I'm sure you could use some real food." He came around to stand beside me. "How does pizza sound?"

"Pepperoni and pineapple?" I asked.

"Make it stuffed crust, and you've got a deal."

I held out my hand and gave Derek a firm handshake before he pulled me into another hug.

"Thank you," I said. "For everything."

"Anytime."

He held me for a few more minutes before retrieving his cell phone and ordering the pizza. I resumed my spot on the couch.

Half an hour, one large pizza, and the better part of a six-pack later, my eyelids started getting heavy. I curled into the corner of the couch and used the armrest as a pillow.

"Want me to change the channel?" Derek asked.

I shook my head without lifting it from the armrest. I didn't care what was on the TV. I just didn't want to move. As long as I didn't move, I could pretend it was just another night at home with my best friend. I didn't have to think about the fact that my life was spinning out of control. As long as I didn't move, I could pretend everything would be all right tomorrow.

"Why don't you go to bed, Als?" He gestured toward the abandoned pizza box and beer bottles on the table. "I'll clean this up."

The whirlwind of emotions had finally taken its toll on me. Maybe, with a good night's sleep, everything would be better in the morning.

Chapter Six

BEEP! BEEP! BEEP!

I slammed my hand down on the alarm clock, cursing whoever invented it for disturbing my sleep. I peeked my eyes open and groaned when I saw how dark it was outside. Getting up before the sun should be considered a crime against humanity in my book. Still, I did it every day. The joys of being a baker.

I pushed myself into a seated position and started the long process of resetting my brain for the day. I would normally crawl to the coffee pot for some much-needed caffeine and start mentally running through all I needed to get done. Instead, I found myself imagining the myriad of things I could be facing when I walked into the bakery.

I ran a hand through my horribly tangled hair and forced myself out of bed. The smell of bacon and coffee filled my nostrils the instant I cracked my door open. I let my nose lead me to the kitchen, where Derek was standing over the stove.

"Morning, sunshine," he said with a smile.

I growled in response.

He chuckled and pointed to a mug sitting next to the half-empty coffeepot. "I've already got some ready for you. Food will be out in a second."

My feet carried me to the steaming mug. Lifting it to my lips, I let the rich aroma push through the layer of brain fog and sighed at the first heavenly sip.

"Bless you," I breathed, moving to stand beside Derek. "What time did we go to bed last night?"

I took another sip, a near-pornographic moan of pleasure passing my lips.

Derek chuckled. "Do I need to give you two a minute?"

I furrowed my brow in confusion until he gestured toward the mug in my hands. I smacked him on the shoulder.

He held his hands up in surrender. "Kidding."

I stopped pummeling his biceps and went back to drinking my coffee.

"I'm not sure what time," he told me in answer to my earlier question. "I think you stopped sleeping on the couch and went to bed around nine or ten. Not sure how long you were asleep before that though."

I found a piece of bacon sitting on a plate to drain and reached for it. Derek tried to bat my hand away with his spatula, but I already had the piece halfway to my mouth before he could reach me. I chomped happily on it while he finished dishing the eggs onto a couple of plates and carried them to the island. I picked up the plate of bacon and followed him.

"Why didn't you just wake me up?" I asked.

"Believe me, Als. I tried. You were just out."

"Yeah. Crying will do that to you."

Derek hummed in agreement. "It'll be okay."

I whispered my thanks before turning my attention back to my food.

"You know," I said, shoving another piece of bacon into my mouth, "for a fitness instructor, you sure do eat a lot of junk food."

Derek put a finger to his lips and made a show of shushing me. He looked around the apartment like he was expecting someone to jump out of the shadows and attack him.

Satisfied that we were alone, he leaned in and whispered conspiratorially, "Don't tell anybody. You'll give away my secret."

He kept his expression serious, but I could see the spark of mischief in his eyes. We only lasted a few seconds before we were both snickering like schoolchildren. I shook my head at his antics and went back to eating my breakfast so I could get ready to face whatever fresh hell was waiting for me at work.

* * *

THE MUSCLES IN my neck and shoulders tightened the instant the back door to the bakery came into view. The thought of being told to get my stuff and get out had played on repeat in my mind on the walk to work. Every time the notion overwhelmed me, I focused on what Derek had told me on my way out the door: *"You've got this, Als. Whatever happens, you've got this."*

It wasn't foolproof, but it helped.

Taking a deep breath, I shook out my shoulders and pushed the door open. I paused just inside the doorway and waited for the yelling to start, but it never came. I breathed a sigh of relief and tied on my apron. Today would be a good day. I would make sure of it.

I'd barely finished tying my apron before Brooke poked her head through the swinging door.

"All right. Spill it."

I frowned at her. "Spill what?"

"You were all in a mess when you walked through that door after lunch yesterday, and it had nothing to do with Toni being an ass. So tell me. What happened?"

And just like that, my good day vanished into thin air. My anxiety at the thought of dealing with Toni had pushed everything that happened with Kyle out of my brain. I'd forgotten that Brooke would be her own special brand of well-meaning torture.

I looked down at the floor and shook my head. A hollowness formed inside my chest. I didn't say anything, just kept my head down and went to one of the shelves to collect the things I would need for the first treat of the day.

"Ally?"

I could hear the clear concern in my friend's voice, but I acted like I hadn't heard her calling me. The last thing I needed was to have another breakdown. I'd done enough of that last night. I was sick of crying.

The light touch of a hand on my shoulder forced me to stop what I was doing and face Brooke. The instant I saw the concerned look on her face, I knew she wouldn't let me stay silent any longer.

"He broke up with me." My voice cracked as I whispered the confession.

The same hopelessness I'd felt when he left me sitting at the table returned in full force.

Brooke pulled me into her arms. "I'm so sorry, sweetie."

I buried my face in her shoulder and sagged against her.

"Want me to go down to his office and kick his ass for you?"

Her deadpan delivery made me laugh. Brooke wasn't being serious, but I didn't doubt she would do it if I asked her to.

"Can I sell tickets?" We started hooting like a couple of screech owls. "I think you may have to get in line behind Derek though."

"I bet." Brooke wiped a tear from her eye. "I bet he could probably lay him out too. Have you seen the size of that man? I know I wouldn't want to mess with him."

I agreed. Derek wasn't one to lose his temper, but I had no doubt he could do some serious damage if he wanted to.

"Well," Brooke went on, a devious little grin forming on her lips, "at least, not if it was anywhere other than the bedroom, that is."

My jaw practically hit the floor. "Brooke!"

She'd never made it a secret that she found Derek attractive, but she usually wasn't so blatant about it.

Brooke put her hands up in the air. "I'm just saying, the man's gorgeous. You can't tell me you've never thought of him like that."

"Oh my God!"

I could feel the blush heating up my face and neck. I wasn't about to lie and say that the thought had never crossed my mind. You couldn't spend that much time with somebody and not have your mind drift that way at some point, but I wasn't going to tell her that. Derek was my best friend. End of story.

I pushed my way past Brooke and started mixing the batter for a batch of dark chocolate and salted caramel cookies for the display case. If I didn't have these ready by the time we opened, Toni would fire me for sure.

"So"—I scooped a bit of batter onto a baking sheet and glanced over at Brooke—"have you heard from Toni yet?"

Brooke shook her head. "The bitch queen is still MIA. Hey! Maybe we'll get lucky, and we won't have to deal with her today."

Brooke's Cheshire-cat grin made me chuckle. "Yeah. Maybe."

Figuring out Toni's comings and goings around the shop was nearly impossible. She'd disappeared for almost two weeks earlier in the year, and when she came back, we found out she'd been on a cruise with her husband and had just neglected to tell us about it. It was like I'd been able to breathe again. The lack of constant tension had made everything smoother. I'd managed to get twice as much work done because I wasn't constantly looking over my shoulder for the hatchet that was about to be buried in my back. It was amazing. Too bad I didn't know when I would get that kind of opportunity again.

* * *

I'D JUST FINISHED putting the final touches on my second princess cake of the day when I heard the bell over the front door ding. It wasn't something I usually noticed. Once I got into the zone, everything else just faded away. The only thing that existed was me and the cake in front of me.

"Ally?"

I placed the cake in the fridge to help it stay fresh before looking over my shoulder to see Brooke sticking her head through the door, her best customer-service smile plastered on her face.

"Can I talk to you for a minute, please?" she asked.

I narrowed my eyes. "Sure." I dragged the word out like it had three extra syllables. "What's up?"

Brooke glanced over her shoulder before stepping onto the decorating floor. She looked over her shoulder again. That was weird. Brooke never looked this skittish. She walked into a room like she owned it, not looking around like something was about to attack her. Something was wrong.

"There's a couple out front who want to order a wedding cake," she whisper-yelled.

I frowned. That wasn't unusual. People came in to order wedding cakes all the time. We just called Toni and… Oh crap! Toni'd never shown up today.

All wedding cake orders went through her and her alone. The last time someone else had tried to process one before checking with her first, they'd been fired.

"Do they have an appointment?" I asked.

Brooke shook her head. "They said it's an emergency. I tried calling her twice, but it just goes straight to voicemail."

"Crap."

This wasn't good. Toni would flip her lid if she found out one of us took this order without running it by her first. The last thing I needed was for her to come unglued on me again, but turning away business wasn't going to get me any brownie points either.

I drew my lower lip between my teeth and rolled everything over in my mind. Foot traffic had been down recently. I hadn't seen the books, but based on what my days looked like, cake orders were ninety percent of our business. Turning my back on that would be paramount to telling Toni I didn't care if we went under. "All right." I sighed. "Let's do this."

Brooke jerked her head back. "Do what?"

"I'll talk to them. We tried doing it Toni's way, but we can't help it if she doesn't answer the phone. They want to talk to a designer. So, I'll give them one."

"Are you sure, Ally? Toni's already not your biggest fan right now."

"I know. But we have to do something."

Brooke eyed me skeptically. "Okay," she said after a brief pause. "I'll tell them you'll be out in a minute."

"Thanks."

What had I just done? Me and my big mouth. Toni was going to have a field day when she found out I took an order without her okay. Maybe I'd get lucky, and they would just hand me a picture and say "make that." Toni did that to me all the time. This wouldn't be any different. I'd be fine. Right?

"Come on, Ally. You got this."

I shook out my arms and cracked my neck like a boxer getting ready for a fight. With one last deep breath, I squared my shoulders and walked through the door.

The couple's broad smiles and dopey-eyed gazes were almost sweet enough to give me a cavity. The petite, dark-haired woman was leaning against the man's chest as he whispered something in her ear that made her giggle. He picked up her hand and kissed her knuckles before resting their hands over his heart.

I considered bolting from the room. The only thing I could think about was how it should have been me. I should have been the one picking out a cake and giggling with my fiancé. I should have been that happy.

I forced the thought to the back of my mind and screwed my most confident expression into place just as the bride-to-be locked eyes on me.

"Are you the designer?" She grabbed her fiancé's hand and moved toward me.

"Hi, uh, yes. That's me." I held my hand out to her. "I'm Ally. I understand you all have some questions about ordering a cake?"

"Yes. I'm Gina. This is my fiancé, Chris."

Gina's dark brown eyes sparkled as she gazed up at him, and Chris looked adoringly down at her like he worshiped the ground she walked on. Had Kyle ever looked at me like that? I pushed the thought away. Now was not the time to think about my ex.

"We're kind of in a bind," Gina said. "Chris's aunt was going to make our cake, but she fell and broke her hip last night. Our wedding is in two weeks, and the doctor said she may not even be able to come to the ceremony, let alone bake a cake. I know it's kind of short notice, but we were really hoping you could help us."

Two weeks! I nearly choked on my saliva.

"That"—I coughed into my hand—"that's, uh, that's a pretty quick turnaround."

The quickest order I'd ever seen for a wedding cake was two months. There were too many details to worry about. Too much planning. The only way I could see this working was if they asked for something simple. Much more than that, and we would be hard pressed to make it happen.

48

"Do you know what you have in mind?"

The couple exchanged a look. My stomach dropped. I knew that look. That look meant I was going to regret this.

"My aunt found some pictures in a magazine," Chris said.

I breathed a short sigh of relief. This wouldn't be so bad after all. "Great! Do you have the magazine with you?"

Chris looked down at his shoes, and every bit of relief I'd felt flew right out the window.

"She never showed it to us," he said. "She did the cake for my cousin's wedding last year, and it was amazing. So when she offered to do ours as a wedding gift, we didn't push her for details."

My smile hardened into concrete. I wasn't sure if I wanted to face-palm myself for getting into this situation or bitch-slap them both for having no idea what they wanted. Reminding myself to stay calm, I grabbed a pad of paper and pen from behind the counter and gestured to one of the standing tables on the far side of the room.

"Why don't you tell me a bit about yourselves," I told them. "Maybe we can come up with something that will work."

They started with the basics. Who they were. How they'd met. It wasn't until the topic shifted to the wedding that I saw Gina's eyes sparkle like the diamond on her finger. She went on and on about the flowers and colors they'd chosen for the big day, but it was when she told me about her dress that an idea came to mind.

"You wouldn't happen to have a picture of your dress, would you?" I asked.

It was a long shot, but something told me seeing that dress would be just the push I needed to get this design off the ground.

"Yes!"

Gina pulled her phone out of her purse and started rifling through pictures. Chris leaned in to get a look over her shoulder.

"Don't you dare!" She pressed the phone to her chest. "It's bad luck."

He playfully turned his head in the opposite direction. Gina gave me a cheeky grin before selecting a photo and turning the phone toward me.

I gasped. The full skirt and fitted bodice accentuated Gina's figure to perfection while somehow managing to make her look demure. What really struck me, though, was the lace. It ran from the top of the bodice out to form the collar and sleeves. It was amazing.

It was exactly the kind of dress I had always dreamed about wearing. Light. Elegant. I could practically see myself walking down the aisle in it. I tried to imagine the look on Kyle's face when he saw me. Wait. That wasn't happening anymore. I took a moment to compose myself before smiling up at Gina.

"Can I borrow this?" I extended my hands toward the phone.

Gina blanched. "Excuse me?"

"Your phone," I replied. "Can I borrow it for a minute? I think I have an idea, but I'm going to need this photo for reference. It shouldn't take too long. I'll just step over to that other table and draw up a quick sketch. That way he won't see your dress, and you can make sure I'm not snooping."

I gave Gina my most convincing smile. She looked to her fiancé for an answer, but he wasn't helping. He just shrugged and told her it was her decision. Gina looked from me to the phone and back again before sliding it toward me.

"Thank you."

I stepped over to the other table and zoomed in on the lace details on one of the sleeves and started sketching. Nothing too detailed. Just something to give them an idea of what I was thinking. We could always work out more details once we had the basic design figured out.

A grin slid across my face. In the ten minutes or so I'd been sketching, I'd been able to come up with four different designs they could work with. Each one had its own unique features I was sure would spark the couple's interest.

"All right." I handed Gina back her phone. "This is what I have so far. These are just some rough sketches. I can clean up some of them for more detail if you want, but I want to get your feedback first."

I handed them the sheets of paper and waited. They flipped through them all, going back and forth without saying a word. I had to physically hold myself back from rocking in anticipation. I tried to casually wipe my sweating palms on my jeans without them noticing.

Why weren't they saying anything? Didn't they know leaving a person hanging like this was evil?

I watched their faces for any kind of reaction, but all I saw was a couple of blank stares.

Maybe Toni was right to keep me from doing wedding cake designs. *I should just stick to birthdays and bar mitzvahs and let the real professionals handle the big stuff.*

"Oh my gosh."

My eyes flew to Gina's face. Her eyes were wide and glassy, her hand resting gently over her mouth. I looked away in shame. I'd blown it. A golden opportunity to prove what I could do had landed in my lap, and in true Ally fashion, I'd screwed it up.

"This," she said, "is amazing! You can really do these? All of them?"

I might have actually stopped breathing. Had I heard her right? She liked them? I looked up to see her practically salivating over the designs.

"Y-yes." I cleared my throat and tried again. "Yes. I can do any of those designs. I can even incorporate different elements from a few of them into something else if you want. Do you know what you're leaning toward?"

My body hummed with excitement as I picked up the pen to take notes. I hoped they couldn't see my hand trembling. The last thing a bride and groom wanted was a cake designer who didn't know what she was doing, and while I was good at what I did, acting like an overexcited puppy would not win me any brownie points.

Gina and Chris shared a hushed conversation before coming to an agreement. Gina picked up a sheet of paper and handed it to me.

"This one."

I looked down at the paper and beamed. The three-tiered cake was by far the most complicated of the three designs with its multiple textures and colors, but it had an elegance the other two couldn't match.

"Wonderful choice." I grabbed my notepad again. "What changes do you want to make to it?"

"None."

Now it was my turn to look at her like she was the crazy one. Never, in all of my years working for Toni, had I ever seen anyone not want alterations made to their original cake design. That kind of thing didn't happen.

"Come again?"

"It's perfect," Gina said. "I love the way you worked our initials into it, and that bit right there"—she pointed to some of the pale-blue etchings along the side of the second tier—"it looks exactly like the back of my dress!"

There was no way to hide the look of pride on my face. That was exactly the kind of detail I dreamed of my work being known for.

"It's great," Chris agreed. "I can't imagine anything better." He smiled. "So what kind of cake will it be?"

"That's what we get to decide next. Let me get you some samples, and we can go over the different possibilities."

I walked to the back to grab a tray of tasting cakes.

Who was I kidding? I wasn't walking. I was floating. A tiny squeal of delight made its way out of my mouth as soon as the couple was out of sight. Throwing my hands in the air, I victory danced my way to the fridge and started pulling some tasting cakes out. I was finally getting my chance to prove what I could do. This would be awesome.

The next half hour was spent talking about flavor profiles and types of frosting for each decoration. I barely even noticed the chime of the bell over the door.

It wasn't until I saw someone walking up to me out of the corner of my eye that I looked away from the couple. Every muscle in my body froze when I saw Toni looking back at me. Bile rose to the back of my throat. This was it. This was the moment she kicked me to the curb.

"Hello." Toni carefully schooled her features into the most pleasant expression I'd ever seen her wear and snapped her attention to the couple standing across from me. "My name is Toni Alfied. I'm the owner and chief decorator here. Is there something I can help you with?"

"Nah. We're good here." Chris put his arm around Gina's shoulders. "Ally's been a great help."

"She was amazing," Gina gushed. "I just can't get over how brilliant her design is."

"Her design?" Toni's eyes cut in my direction.

I gulped.

Toni held out her hand. "May I see it?"

Gina handed over the sketch willingly. "It's absolutely brilliant. She even worked some of the details from my dress into it. Isn't it great?"

My heart thundered like it was racing a marathon. It was all I could do to remind myself to breathe. Toni looked at me out of the corner of her eye before turning her attention back to the paper in her hand.

"Well," she said, her cool demeanor giving away nothing, "I'm glad we could accommodate you on such short notice. Things like this usually require an appointment. Please don't hesitate to call and ask for me if there are any issues."

"We will." Gina rushed around the table and threw her arms around me in a quick hug. "Thank you so much, Ally."

"You're welcome. Have a great day."

The sick feeling in my stomach intensified the closer they moved to the door. I did my best to focus on breathing through my nose, but I could still taste the bile rising at the back of my throat. I didn't look at Toni until the door closed behind the couple. Anger radiated off her like lava from a volcano, and she was about to erupt all over me.

Except, she didn't say anything. She was as quiet as I'd ever seen her.

She reached for the discarded designs on the table, looking through them one at a time. "Where did you get these?"

I was wrong. I wasn't going to throw up. I was going to pass out.

"I drew them."

I probably should have been insulted by the implication I couldn't design a cake, but I was too busy watching her red puffy eyes to think about much of anything.

"You do not design cakes." Her voice was as hard and flat as an anvil. "When somebody wants a cake, you call me. Do you understand? Under no circumstances do you…"

Why wasn't anything ever good enough for this woman? I could stand on my head and decorate a cake at the same time, but I'd be in trouble because I wasn't singing an aria. Toni wouldn't be happy without her pound of flesh, and my pathetic ass was her favorite source of protein.

"I did call you," Brooke said.

My head snapped toward her, my eyes wide. She could not be doing what I thought she was.

"You didn't answer. That couple wasn't leaving until they'd talked to somebody, so…"

"I didn't ask for your opinion," Toni snapped.

I braced myself for the onslaught. I would not give her the

satisfaction of seeing me cry. The bride had been happy. That was what mattered. I needed to focus on that.

"Next time, you tell them they have to make an appointment." Toni looked down at the design in her hand before throwing it back on the table like it had burned her. "I guess you'll have to do this one. It's not a style I've seen in this shop before. I'd like to tell you to cancel it, but since they already paid for the order, you'll have to deliver. Just make sure you don't screw it up. I have to know I can count on you, Ally. Your stunt yesterday already damaged our reputation enough. I don't want it happening again."

I carefully picked the design up from the table. I should have been outraged, but all I could focus on was that Toni was going to let me do the cake. Finally! After all these years, I would be able to show her what I could do. This was amazing!

Toni glanced over at the display case and grumbled about something before disappearing into her office. My eyes tracked to Brooke. We shared a knowing look before I broke out in a victory dance worthy of a Monday Night Football running back before the office door opened again and turned me to stone.

"I'll be gone the rest of the week," Toni said as she made her way to the front door, "so don't bother calling me. And if anyone *else* tries to order a cake, tell them to make an appointment."

She looked up at me. She looked tired. There were dark circles under her eyes. While they had been a little red and puffy before, they looked almost hollow now as she stared me down.

I nodded my agreement before she turned and marched out the door.

"Bitch," Brooke muttered when Toni turned the corner. "Don't you worry about her. That cake is going to be amazing. Anybody with half a brain could see that."

"Thanks." I smiled gratefully at her. "You didn't have to stick up for me like that."

She waved me off like it was nothing. "Here." She took the design out of my hand and placed it on the table. "Go get yourself some lunch. I can hold the fort by myself for an hour. Just bring me back some pasta salad and we'll call it good, okay?"

"Okay."

I paused at the back door to see her placing my sketches on one of the decorating tables. I wasn't sure what I'd done to deserve a friend like her, but I was grateful to have her.

* * *

I KNEW DEREK was home before I'd even opened the door. The sound of his Thursday night football game was so clear, I could tell you the score and down without seeing the screen. It was amazing we didn't get more noise complaints with these paper-thin walls.

"Hey," I shouted as I stepped through the door. "Turn it down."

Derek pulled his feet off the coffee table and leaned forward to grab the remote. "Sorry, Als. How was your day?"

It took every ounce of strength I had not to grin like an idiot. This day had been amazing! I honestly didn't think I had the words to describe it, but I didn't want to let on just yet. I could feel the corners of my mouth turning upward and clamped my teeth onto my lower lip to keep it in check.

Taking a seat next to him on the couch, I kept my eyes down so he couldn't see the joy on my face. Derek had tortured me enough times dragging out his own exciting news, so I figured teasing him was only fair.

It must have worked better than I thought, because the next thing I knew, he'd turned off the TV and was watching me expectantly.

"Ally, what happened?"

I peeked at him through my lashes to see him frowning. Releasing my lower lip, I let the smile take over my face.

"I got to design a wedding cake." My voice rose in pitch with each word.

The shock on Derek's face only lasted a moment before he pulled me into a bear hug. "That's awesome! Toni's actually letting you do one?"

"Well…" I looked away. I'd known Derek would be happy for me. I just wasn't sure what he would think of me pushing my way into the opportunity. "I kind of didn't get her okay before I took the order."

His eyebrows sprang up to his forehead. I launched into the story about the couple and how Brooke hadn't been able to reach Toni.

"So I ended up talking to them. I gave them a couple of design options, and they absolutely loved one of them."

Derek smiled at me, and my insides melted.

"I'm proud of you, Als."

I stopped flailing my arms in the air and sat up straight. "Really?"

He nodded. "You're finally standing up for yourself. You saw something that needed to be done, and you took care of it. Not even Toni can argue with that."

And just like that, my mood soured.

"Don't be so sure."

I threw myself back against the cushions and began worrying the hem of my shirt. I told Derek about the dressing down Toni had given me. Just talking about it made me want to sink through the floor. Why was it every time this woman opened her mouth, I felt like I was either screwing things up or about three seconds away from being shown the door?

"She's an idiot," he said. "Anybody who doesn't realize how lucky they are to have you is."

Leave it to Derek to know just the right words to make me feel better.

"Thank you."

"No problem." Derek looked at the clock. Half past six. "How does grilled chicken sound for dinner?"

My mouth watered at the thought. "Amazing."

He nodded and turned the game back on, upping the volume the tiniest bit before heading into the kitchen to work on dinner.

I made my way to my room and tossed my phone onto the bed before stripping out of my clothes and heading for the shower. I felt like a new woman by the time I was done. Slipping into my pjs, I noticed the message light on my phone was blinking. I picked it up to see a Facebook notification and responded to the few posts I'd been tagged in before mindlessly scrolling through my feed.

It wasn't until a "memory" appeared on my screen that I stopped to look at anything for more than a second.

My heart gave a painful lurch inside my chest. It was a picture of Kyle and me at some gala event his office had given him tickets to a year ago. We were looking into the camera and smiling with our arms around each other. The couple in that photo had an amazing future stretched out before them.

A knock on my door startled me out of my trance.

"Food's almost done," Derek called through the door.

"Okay. I'll be there in a second." I looked back down, but there was no sense in staring at the photo. It wouldn't change anything.

Derek was already setting two plates of food on the island when I came out of my room. The warm scent of Cajun spices and the sizzle of the grill pan filled the room.

"That smells amazing." I took my seat at the counter.

"Thanks." He scooted in next to me.

We dug in, eating in easy silence for a bit. When we were about halfway done, Derek started telling me about an older man who had come into the gym that morning and grabbed some weights that were far too heavy for him.

"He sets the weight down, and I kid you not, he flipped end over end off the bench." Derek tried to keep his laughter in check so he could finish his story.

I nearly choked on a piece of chicken from holding in a laugh. "Are you serious?"

Derek snorted. "I haven't even told you the best part yet." He put his fork down and turned toward me. "Then he just popped up and looked around to see if anybody was watching before walking off like nothing happened. He didn't even try to put the weights back on the rack."

"That's classic!"

"I know, right?" Derek kept looking over his shoulder every few minutes to check the score.

I shook my head. "Go finish watching the game. I've got this."

"Here." Derek took the plate out of my hand. "I'll dry."

I looked at him for a full minute. The last time Derek had offered to dry while I washed was when he'd needed to talk to me about his decision to become a trainer instead of starting a business.

My suspicions proved to be true a few minutes later when Derek finally opened his mouth. "So…" He let the word trail to nothing.

"So?" I parroted.

"Jeff is talking about opening up a couple new locations."

Jeff was the owner of the gym Derek had been working at the last two years. He was a pretty cool guy who treated his employees well and did his best to make himself available to them.

I handed Derek a plate. "That's cool."

"Yeah."

I gave him a look out of the corner of my eye. At this rate, we would run out of dishes before he told me his news. While Derek was probably the best listener on the planet, talking about the thoughts swirling around inside his own head had never been his strong suit.

"He, uh, he's kind of thinking about putting me in charge of one."

The pot in my hand crashed into the sink, covering both of us in dirty dishwater.

I looked over at him in wide-mouthed awe. "Are you serious?"

Derek wiped the suds off his face and laughed. "Yeah. I thought I'd have to wait another five or six years and open my own place to get this kind of shot, but I think this could really happen."

"That's awesome!" I threw my arms open and launched myself at him. My foot slipped in a puddle on the floor, nearly sending us both crashing to the ground, but Derek managed to hold onto the counter and stabilize us before any damage could be done.

"Where is he opening the gym?" I asked once I'd finished squeezing the life out of him.

Derek shrugged. "I don't know yet. He said he was looking into a few different places and asked if I would potentially be interested in taking over one once it's ready."

"That's so cool. Congratulations!"

I'd just turned back to the sink when what he'd said sank in. I took a step back to look him in the eye.

"A few different places? But they're all here in the city, right?"

His eyes went to the floor, and I felt my heart drop with them.

"I don't know," he said with a sigh. "He's looking all over, but he didn't say which one he had in mind for me."

My heart went through the floor and landed in the basement laundry room.

"Hey." Derek ran his hands up and down my arms. "Breathe, Als. It'll be okay. Whatever happens, we'll figure it out, okay? Just like we always do."

I nodded in agreement, but I wasn't sure this was going to work.

Chapter Seven

QUIET MORNINGS AT the bakery were my favorite. Not having a ton of orders meant I could take my time with what I did have. The only things I had to worry about today were a small order of cupcakes for a kid's birthday party and a sheet cake for a sixtieth wedding anniversary, which wasn't due until tomorrow. Foot traffic was light, so I didn't have to keep stopping to restock the display. *I might be able to get ahead for once.*

My plan was to finish making frosting flowers before starting work on molding the chocolate figures for Gina and Chris's cake topper while I waited for the sheet cake to finish baking. Since his aunt had never given them what she was going to use as a topper, we'd decided to make an edible one. I already had one tray of frosting roses in the chiller to harden. At this rate, I'd have more than enough time to make sure everything was perfect.

"Where is your cake?"

"Ah!" I squeezed the piping bag a bit too hard, and some icing shot into the air and onto my face.

I spun around on my stool to see Toni glaring down at me. Her having been gone the previous week had been heaven. Any hope I'd had for the same relaxed atmosphere this week had just flown out the window.

"Toni." I wiped the frosting from my cheek and placed the piping bag on the table. "You scared me."

"Where is the cake?" she repeated.

I frowned. She looked a bit more worn than usual. The lines on her forehead were deeper, and her eyes were puffy. *What did she do with her week off?*

She spoke again, breaking me out of my thoughts. "The one I let you take the order for. Where is it?"

I gestured to the tray of flowers in front of me. "I'm working on it."

Her eyes narrowed. "Is that all you've got done?"

I bristled. Maybe if she came to work once in a while, she'd know just how much I'd been working on it, but of course, I couldn't say any of that.

"Uh," I muttered, "they don't need it until Thursday. I'm baking the cake tomorrow, and I'm working on the icing flowers now." I held up a flower for her to see. "I already have one tray of them done. We don't have any other major orders due over the next couple of days, so that gives me plenty of time to get what I don't finish today done tomorrow before I start assembling the cake."

I beamed. Most of the cakes I worked on stressed me to the max this close to the deadline, but this cake was different. Even the calls from Gina with a few last-minute notes on changes couldn't shake me. I knew exactly what needed to be done and how to do it. There was no guesswork. No chance for misunderstanding. I just had to get it done.

Toni crossed behind me and picked up a sky-blue rose bud. She held it by the stem of the metal base and twirled it slowly in her fingers, inspecting it for quality.

"Well," she said, carefully placing the flower back on the holding tray, "you'd better make sure you have time. I can't afford another fiasco like the one you caused with our last wedding. Do you understand me?"

I gulped. She might not have said the words, but the implication was clear. One more mistake, and I was gone. The fact I was the only baker she had left had given me a sense of comfort up to that point. I mean, there was no way she would be able to keep everything running without me, right?

I gave a curt nod and watched with wide-eyed terror as Toni turned and stalked from the room. I closed my eyes and took a few deep breaths to center myself. *Focus on the cake.* All I needed to do was focus on the cake.

* * *

WHY DID MURPHY'S Law have to take effect every time I felt like I had things under control?

My day had gone downhill fast after my unexpected visit from Toni. A late-afternoon rush had left us short on tarts and other sweets for the case. Then a rush order had come in for three dozen cupcakes that had to be ready the next morning. That meant my work on the cake came to a full stop. My only saving grace was that I had the whole next day to get it done.

Everything else had been a disaster.

It felt like I was putting out one fire after another. I was exhausted. Curling up in my bed and throwing the covers over my head until the world swallowed me whole sounded like heaven. Even Mrs. Henderson, with her bright smile and glass of freshly made lemonade, hadn't been able to make me feel any better.

Climbing up the stairs to my apartment was like hiking the Rockies. It wasn't until I'd shut the apartment door behind me, effectively cutting off the rest of the world, that I felt better.

I closed my eyes, leaned back against the cool metal door, and let the outside world slip away.

"Rough day?"

Derek was lounging on the couch and had been there for a while by the looks of it. He'd already changed out of his work clothes and had his feet on the table, beer in hand, and a ballgame on the TV.

"You could say that."

I pushed away from the door and flopped onto the couch beside him, tossing my cell phone onto the table.

Derek muted the TV and turned to face me. "Want to talk about it?"

"Not really."

I let my body sink into the couch cushions and shifted my eyes to look at Derek without turning my head. He still hadn't turned his attention back to the ball game. I half expected him to grill me about what had happened, but something in my expression must have told him I was not in the mood.

"Okay." He shrugged and gestured to the TV with the remote. "Wanna watch the game?"

"No thanks." I shifted in my seat and felt my dingy work clothes stick to my skin. "You go ahead. I'm gonna go change."

I shuffled to my room and stripped down to my underwear before throwing myself onto the bed. I didn't realize how long I'd been lying there until a soft knock sounded against my door.

"Als," Derek called, "you all right in there?"

I glanced over at the clock to see nearly half an hour had passed. No wonder he'd come to check on me.

"Yeah." My voice cracked a bit, but I was able to get the words out. "I'll be out in a sec."

My muscles tensed in anticipation. I half expected Derek to open the door to check for himself, but that tension quickly eased when I heard his footsteps carry him back toward the couch.

Moving into a seated position, I let my eyes roam around the room. Mementos and memories of my time with Kyle were tucked into every corner. A voice in the back of my mind told me I should get rid of it all, but I ignored it. I shouldn't toss out the good just because it reminded me of the bad, right?

The longer I sat there, the more restless I felt. All of that pent up emotion was doing me no good. I needed to get it out. I needed to do something. I needed to move.

I went to my dresser and pulled out one of the few sets of workout clothes I owned. Slipping on the yoga pants and tank top, I grabbed a hoodie from my closet before heading to the living room.

Derek was frowning at my cell phone as he read whatever was on the screen.

"Derek?"

He jumped. "Oh, hey."

He gave me an awkward grin as he set my phone back on the table.

"What were you looking at?" I picked up the phone and hit the HOME button to light the screen, thinking there might be a missed notification.

"Weather alert," he said.

I raised an eyebrow. I didn't care that he was on my phone. He used it as much as I did sometimes. His had fallen out of his pocket during a game of basketball with the guys a while back, and the screen had cracked. It had been finicky ever since. So it wasn't uncommon for him to shoot off a text or look something up on my phone when his decided to act up, but there was something about his reaction to being caught with it that struck me as odd.

Pushing it aside as a figment of my overactive imagination, I gave a shrug and reached for the set of AirPods on the side table. "I'll be back in a bit."

"Where are you going?"

"For a run."

I headed for the door and turned just in time to see Derek do a spit-take, spraying beer across the living room. He wiped the back of his hand across his mouth and set the bottle on the table.

"What!" He shook some of the liquid off of his hand.

"I said I was going for a run."

"That's what I thought you said." He reached for the remote and shut the TV off. He squared his shoulders to face me and met my gaze with a critical stare "What's wrong?"

"Nothing."

He tilted his chin down and lifted an eyebrow.

"I run all the time."

He called my bluff. "No, you don't. You walk. You hate running."

Why did he have to know me so well? Just once I wanted him to not be able to see right through me. Was that too much to ask?

"I just need to clear my head for a bit."

He turned to look out the window. Dark clouds were gathering on the horizon, giving the light outside an eerie grayish hue.

"It's going to rain," he said matter-of-factly.

"I like the rain."

"Bullshit. The second it starts raining, you get upset about how your socks are gonna get wet and make your feet cold all day."

I narrowed my mouth into a thin line. Damn his perceptiveness.

"Don't worry about it," I told him. "I'll be back in a few."

I didn't even finish unlocking the door before I felt his presence behind me.

"Bet you twenty bucks you don't even make it one mile without walking."

I turned to face him. A mischievous smirk played on his lips. The smug bastard really thought I couldn't do it.

"Bet you I can make it two," I fired back.

His grin turned into a full-blown smirk. "You're on."

Derek shoved on a pair of tennis shoes and followed me out the door.

The first half mile was good. By the time we hit the one mile mark, a stabbing pain in my right side reminded me why I hated cardio.

"How you holding up over there, Als?"

"Fine," I wheezed.

I sent a scathing look Derek's way when I heard him laugh. The guy didn't even look like he was trying, while I felt like I'd dropped a kidney on the last block.

"Oh, why don't you…?" The sky opened up, and the light mist that had accompanied us since we left the house turned into a torrential downpour.

"Come on!" Derek shouted over the rain.

He picked up the pace, forcing me to practically sprint the last mile. We ducked into our building just as what was left of my lungs gave out.

We stood there, dripping wet and panting. My hands went to my shaking knees. *Note to self: never go for a run with Derek ever again.*

"I'm impressed," my best friend huffed beside me.

"Oh?"

"I thought I was going to have to carry you back." There was a smirk on his face, but it wasn't the bragging kind. There was a hint of pride mixed in with it that made my chest swell.

"Well"—I slowly stood up—"I think you may have to carry me up the stairs. My legs won't stop shaking."

He snorted. Running a hand down his face, he turned his back to me and gestured toward it with his thumb. "Hop on."

My eyes lit up. He really was the best friend a girl could ask for.

Placing my hands on his shoulders, Derek squatted down while I used what little strength I had left to hop up onto his back. I only made it about half way. I smacked into his butt and started to slide before he managed to grab both of my legs and hoist me the rest of the way. He jostled me into position and started making his way toward the stairs.

"My goodness!" I turned my head to see Mrs. Henderson standing beside the wall of mailboxes. "What on earth happened to you two?"

"We got caught in the rain," I offered.

"And he's carrying you because…"

"Oh." Derek chuckled. "Ally tried to run."

Mrs. Henderson tittered at Derek's comment. Pepper gave a bark from beside her.

"I know, right?" Derek replied to the little dog.

Traitor. See if I ever bake you any special doggie biscuits again.

Mrs. Henderson shooed us up the stairs. "You two go get dry before you catch your deaths."

Derek gave her a nod before continuing up the stairs.

"Yes, ma'am," he told her.

I felt bad for him by the time we hit the third flight of stairs. His breathing was becoming a bit more labored, but he kept moving forward at a steady pace until we finally arrived on the third floor.

"You didn't have to do that." I slid down from his back. "I could have made it."

"I know. It just would have taken you fifty years." He returned my playful smack to his chest with a smile.

Unlocking the apartment, I shuffled in and leaned against the entry wall while I tried to toe my shoes off. They clattered to the floor, nearly tripping me when I turned to make my way into the living room. My feet dragged along the floor. *Maybe I couldn't have made it up the stairs.*

I leaned heavily against the back of the couch. That run was by far the worst of the bad ideas I'd had this week.

Derek pulled two bottles of water from the fridge and held one out to me. "Why the sudden desire to go for a run?"

My shoulders fell. Talking about the chaos inside my brain while standing on jelly legs was not on my top ten list of things I wanted to do this evening, but the furrow of Derek's brow told me there was no getting out of it.

I rested against the back of the couch and took a drink of water.

"I just wanted to feel like I could do something," I confessed. "It seems like every time I turn around lately, something else is falling apart, and I just wanted to feel like I had some kind of power."

Derek made his way toward the couch and took a seat on the back of it beside me. He didn't say anything, just offered his quite support.

My fingers found the hem of my shirt and began to fiddle with the soaked fabric. "I'm second guessing everything. Kyle. My work. It's like everything is slipping away, and now with this new cake, I…I just wanted to know I could do something right."

The silence hung thick between us. I could feel the weight of Derek's eyes on me, but I couldn't look at him. I didn't want to. If I looked up, he'd see just how pathetic I really was. What was to say he wouldn't want to leave me too?

"Hey." He placed one of his hands over mine. "Do you think you can do this cake?"

I nodded.

"Then you can. There's nothing you can't do when you set your mind to it, Als. I know it."

Warmth spread through my chest, and some of the weight that had forced me onto the couch lifted. If Derek believed in me, I was going to believe in me too.

* * *

"THAT'S NOT HOW you do it!" Toni barked.

I took a deep breath and forced my jaw to unclench. This morning had been one for the record books. The mixer had decided to blow up. A rush order for that afternoon had been accepted overnight, and my cake was still waiting to be finished. Things had gotten so bad that I'd thrown in the towel and asked Brooke to call Toni in to help because I couldn't keep up.

"This is how I've always done it," I growled through clenched teeth.

I glanced toward the station, where Toni was supposed to be making mini fruit tarts, to see her ingredients laid out but no work. Apparently, yelling at me was more important than doing her own baking.

"And why isn't that cake done? You should be over halfway finished with it by now."

I looked forlornly at my beautiful wedding cake. I'd only been able to add a few bits of piping detail to the base so far. Every time I started working on it, Toni would pull me off to do something else.

I was ready to scream right back at her, ask her how she expected me to get anything done when she kept stopping me to do her work, but I bit my tongue.

"I've been busy." I fought to unclench my jaw before I busted a molar. "That's why I had Brooke call you. If we could just work together and get..."

"I don't want to hear your excuses!"

I flinched.

"If you spent less time talking and more time working, you could easily have everything done. Instead, you spend all your time gossiping and expect me to fix everything for you."

My mouth dropped open. She couldn't possibly be serious. I was the one doing *everything*. She only popped in when she *wanted* to work on something. How could she even pretend to know what I did all day when she was never here?

Toni turned her back on me and stormed to her workstation. My blood was boiling. I clenched my fists at my side to stop them from shaking. All I had to do was keep moving forward. If I could just make it through today, I could get my cake done, and everything would be fine.

Keeping my head down, I focused on my work and tried not to engage the hell-beast. Toni kept stopping every few minutes to tell me what I was "doing wrong." Her lack of progress had us so backed up I was forced to work through my lunch break. We finally caught up enough for me to catch my breath only to have Toni decide it was *her turn* to leave for a break, once again leaving me to handle everything on my own.

I bit back a scream. This was without a doubt the worst day I'd ever had at work. Nothing, not the Schumacher cake, not the other bakers leaving, not even the possessed mixer, could top the mental drain of having to work side-by-side with that woman.

In addition to my brain liquifying, my body was screaming at me. I usually alternated between standing and sitting on a stool when I was working, but I'd been too afraid to sit with Toni in the room. I hadn't wanted to give her more ammunition to use against me, so I'd ignored my aching back and kept hunching over my station.

I forced myself to finish the custard Toni had been working on, then asked Brooke to help me haul out my cake for the third time that day.

"Thank God she's gone!" Brooke said as she carefully sat her side of the stand down. "I can't believe the things she was saying to you. Is she crazy or something?"

"Probably."

"And what's with her being all red-eyed and puffy-faced every day. If I didn't know any better, I'd says she's been drinkin', but I didn't smell any alcohol on her."

I picked up my piping bag and focused on the lace design that would serve as the backdrop for the first tier of the cake.

The bell over the door chimed. Brooke rolled her eyes to the sky and made her way back to the front. She'd only been gone for half a minute before she stuck her head back through the door.

"Ally?"

My shoulders fell. The way she drew out my name like a question told me I didn't want to hear what she was about to say. "They just bought the last of the cupcakes up front."

I was right. I didn't want to hear it. Why couldn't I catch a break? And on today of all days? Every time I thought I would finally have time to decorate *my* cake, something else needed my immediate attention.

I groaned. "Help me put this back."

Once the cake was put away again, I started mixing another batch of cupcakes. I'd just finished frosting the last of them and putting them on a tray to put on display when Toni walked back in. Her expression darkened as she looked from my face to the tray of cupcakes in my hand.

My stomach dropped into my shoes at the sight of her. The vein in her forehead throbbed. She looked from the cupcakes to the fridge, where my cake sat waiting for me. Her eyes narrowed.

"Why isn't that cake finished?" she demanded. "I told you to have it done by the time I got back, and you've barely done a thing!"

I lifted the tray of cupcakes. "We ran out. Let me just take these to Brooke, and I'll be able to get back to work on the cake. It'll be done in plenty of time. I promise."

It wasn't a lie. I didn't know how long it would take me to finish, but having all the sculpted pieces done ahead of time would be a huge help. Besides, there was no way I would let that cake go unfinished. I'd sleep on a workstation if I had to, but it would get done on time.

I was halfway to the door when she spoke again.

"How do you expect to get anything done when you keep stopping for these side projects?"

I stopped dead in my tracks. Side projects? She must have been joking.

I shook my head. "That's not what..."

Toni cut me off before I'd even completed my thought. The longer her tirade went on, the worse I felt. I didn't know if I should be scared or pissed.

"I'll get the cake done!"

Oh my God! I can't believe I just yelled at Toni.

I cleared my throat and tried to pull myself together. "The cake is going to get done. It won't be an issue."

"You're right. It won't. I'm doing it. You're fired!"

The tray of cupcakes nearly clattered to the floor.

"W-what?"

"You heard me." Toni sneered. "You're fired. I have to have someone here that I can depend on. You clearly are not that person, so go."

Every last ounce of breath left my lungs. The room swam in and out of focus. It was like the world was spinning out of control and stopping on a dime all at the same time.

Toni took the tray of cupcakes out of my hand and placed them on the counter beside me.

"Are you deaf now too?" She pushed on my shoulders to get my attention. "I told you to leave. You're fired. Now get out."

I couldn't get my brain to engage. It was like trying to go downhill with the parking brake on. Everything stalled.

"What about the cake?" I managed to squeak out.

"I'll finish it," Toni said. "I'm faster than you. I can get it done and take care of the rest."

I set my mouth into a firm line. How dare she! How many times had she told me I couldn't help with something because it was her design? She always said it was policy. I guess that policy only applied when she felt like it.

"But it's my design! You've always said..."

Toni's eyes narrowed as she took a step closer to me. "You designed a cake that was ordered from my bakery. Therefore, the design belongs to me. I will finish it. Now. Get. Out."

It was worse than being punched in the gut. I tried to stand firm, but despite my best efforts, my shoulders bowed under the weight of her words.

"Get out!"

Everything I had worked for was gone. All the late nights. The endless hours of harassment. They were for nothing. I was nothing.

My arm felt like it weighed a million pounds as I put my apron on its hook. Handing my keys to Toni, I stopped to take one last look at the place that had been my culinary home since finishing school. I caught a glimpse of Brooke staring at me through the small window in the swinging door. I did my best to give her a reassuring look, but I could tell she wasn't buying it.

"Go!"

I flinched at the hostility in Toni's voice before shuffling out the door. I only made it a few blocks before the full weight of what had just happened hit me. I'd been fired. Fired! What would I do now? I didn't have another job lined up. I didn't have any prospects for one either. I had some money in savings, but it wouldn't support me for long. I didn't know what to do.

My chest tightened. I tried to take a breath to make it release, but it wasn't working. My lungs wouldn't expand. I felt my knees begin to buckle and reached for the side of one of the buildings to keep myself from falling. The only thing holding me up was the brick. I couldn't do this. I wasn't going to make it.

Reaching for my phone, I fumbled with the screen before managing to dial the one person I knew would be able to help me get through this.

The seconds ticked by like hours as I waited for him to pick up. I could feel myself shrinking with each ring. Bile rose to the back of my throat. The edges of my vision blurred.

"Als?"

A sigh of relief washed over me the instant I heard Derek's voice.

"What's going on? I thought you were working."

I opened my mouth to speak, but only a tiny squeak came out.

"Ally, what's wrong?"

I tried again to answer, but the words wouldn't come out.

"Ally? Are you there? Say something. Please."

"D-Derek?"

His name came out in a strangled plea.

"Where are you?" he demanded.

"I…"

"Allyson." The authority in his voice brought me back to reality. "Where are you?"

That was a good question. I'd been moving on autopilot. I pushed away from the building, keeping a hand on the brick for balance, to peek at the street sign around the corner.

"Over by SW 18th."

There was a commotion on the other end of the line. A few different voices seemed to be discussing something, but I couldn't make out what it was. My insides felt like they were vibrating, and I leaned back against the wall.

"Derek?" I asked weakly.

"Yeah, Als. I'm here. I need you to breathe for me, okay? Just take a deep breath in and let it all out. I'll do it with you."

I did my best to follow Derek's lead, but my breathing was shaky at best.

"That's good, Als. Do it again."

We followed the same cycle three more times before my lungs started to expand.

"Good," Derek praised. "Do you think you can make it home?"

I nodded.

"Ally?"

"I think so."

"Good. Head to the apartment, and I'll be there in a bit, okay?"

"Okay."

I lowered the phone from my ear and placed it back in my purse as I wandered toward home.

I focused on my breathing to keep the panic at bay. Everything around me was just too loud. I had to block it out. I was so trapped in my head that I didn't even notice Mrs. Henderson calling out to me until I bumped into her on my way into the building. I muttered a quick apology to her and Pepper before shuffling by.

Once inside the apartment, I tossed my coat over the back of the couch, stumbled to my room, and fell onto the bed. I curled my body around one of my pillows.

I wasn't sure how long I lay there before I felt the bed shift behind me.

"Derek," I whimpered, rolling over and burying my face against his chest.

"Shh," he soothed. He pulled me close. "It's okay. I've got you."

Chapter Eight

THE FEELING OF fingers gliding through my hair pulled me out of a restless sleep. Refusing to open my eyes, I turned my head into what I thought was my pillow, only to be greeted with something much harder and warmer than feather down. I blinked my eyes open to see a pair of blue eyes gazing down at me.

"Hey," Derek whispered.

"Hey."

"Feeling better?"

Better? That was not the word I would use. Blah was a bit more like it.

"Not really."

"What happened?"

I turned my face into Derek's chest. Just thinking about it made me want to crawl in a hole and die.

"Would you rather just lie here for a while?" Derek asked.

I nodded against his shoulder.

He settled himself into a more comfortable position on my bed before pulling me in tighter against his side.

We lay like that for a while, neither of us moving, neither of us talking. Derek occasionally ran a hand up and down my arm. My pulse began to slow as I let Derek's calming presence ground me.

"Toni fired me," I said in a hollow voice.

Derek's muscles tensed underneath my fingers.

"She said I wasn't getting my work done on purpose."

Derek gasped. "What?" He pulled away just enough to see my face.

I sighed. "Remember that cake I told you about? The one I got to design? Well, Toni implied the reason I wasn't done already was because I was too lazy and didn't know what I was doing. We were super busy, and I tried to tell her I'd already gotten all the sculpted pieces done ahead of time, but she wouldn't listen. She just kept ranting and raving until she kicked me out the back door."

My voice was little more than a whisper by the time I finished.

"She's a dumbass." The clear, no-nonsense tone forced me to look up at him in question.

"Thank you."

"You're welcome."

I laid my head back down on his chest and focused on the sound of his beating heart, and before I knew it, I'd passed out again.

I wasn't sure how long I slept, but when I opened my eyes, I could just see the barest hint of orange light on the horizon. Derek was sound asleep beside me, his arm draped over me protectively. I glanced over at the clock. Five o'clock. I closed my eyes and went to lie back down. I could sleep awhile longer. It wasn't like I had to worry about getting to the bakery for my nonexistent job.

My head had just touched the pillow when my eyes flew open. I looked at the clock again. This wasn't good.

"Derek, get up!" I shouted as I bolted upright in the bed. I pushed on his shoulder, trying to wake him. His shift started at six. If he didn't get a move on, he wouldn't make it on time.

Derek's eyes blinked open. "What?"

"You're gonna be late. Get up!"

His eyebrows drew together. Why was he looking at me like that? Did he not understand how serious this was? He was our only source of income until I found another job. If he was late after taking off early the day before, there was a good chance he could lose his job too. We would be sunk.

"Go!" I gave his arm another hard shove.

Derek rolled to his side and looked at my alarm clock. He squinted at it, then rolled onto his back and burst into laughter.

Had he lost his mind? I used all my strength to shove his arm one last time, sending him tumbling to the floor with a loud thud.

"Son of a bitch!" Derek rubbed the spot on his elbow where it had collided with my bedside table on the way down. "What was that for?"

"It's already five o'clock. You're gonna be late for work!"

He laughed again.

"What's so funny?"

Shaking his head in amusement, Derek pushed himself up onto his knees and crossed his arms in front of him on top of the mattress before resting his chin on them.

"It's five p.m., Als," he said. "I don't need to leave for another twelve hours."

"What?" I looked back over at the clock. Sure enough, the little red dot indicating p.m. was glowing at me like one beady little red eye. *Crap.*

"Go take a hot shower," Derek told me as he pushed himself onto his feet. "I'll fix us some dinner."

I buried my face in my hands. Just how much did I have to screw up in one day before the universe gave me a break?

* * *

IT FELT LIKE a boulder had settled in the pit of my stomach.

I'd spent the better part of the morning looking through papers and online want ads for every bakery and pastry shop in a five-mile radius. Anything farther than that, and I wouldn't be able to make it to work on time. Public transit didn't run that early in the morning, and my body would only allow me to do so much on the less than five hours of sleep I'd get if I had to make it all the way across the city and back each day.

Seeing the job listing for a decorator at Giovanni's satellite location only eight blocks away from our apartment had been amazing enough. I'd barely expected anyone to respond to my email, let alone call me in for an interview the same day. Standing outside the bakery now, I wondered what I was doing here.

The gold script across the jet-black canopy over the storefront said elegance and sophistication. One look at the place told you to expect nothing less than the highest quality confections money could buy. I was scared shitless.

I told myself I could do this. They wouldn't have called me in if I couldn't.

The bell above the door gave a small chime as I entered. I widened my eyes as I scanned the room. Everything screamed opulence. All the counters and tables were made of wood and polished to shine like mirrored glass. Everything was just…rich, and not in the chocolaty goodness way.

"Can I help you?"

I turned to see a girl in black pants and a matching shirt with the glittering logo on the left breast pocket coming toward me. Her dark hair was pulled back into a harsh bun, and her makeup looked like it had been applied with an airbrush. If I hadn't felt inadequate with my thrift-store slacks and paisley shirt before, I did now.

"Oh, uh, hi." I awkwardly offered her my hand. "I'm Allyson

O'Connor. I'm here for an interview."

The girl gave me a once-over, her upper lip curling into a sneer.

"Right." She pointed to a stark-white leather couch along the far wall. "Have a seat over there, and I'll let him know you're here."

I thanked her and turned to walk toward the couch. For a moment, I thought about turning and heading straight back out the door, but that wouldn't do me any good. My only saving grace was that I didn't have to wait long. A few more minutes of the disdainful look from the girl behind the counter might have had me fleeing into the street.

"Allyson?"

I found myself looking at an old Italian gentleman. I recognized the owner, Palo Giovanni, from a magazine article I'd read a few months ago. He was a tall, gangly man with thinning salt-and-pepper hair. It was the same slicked-back fashion as the men in the old black-and-white movies I forced Derek to watch when it was my turn to pick on movie night.

"You can call me Ally," I said as I rose to my feet. "Pleased to meet you, sir."

The man radiated authority. I stuck my hand out, but he didn't take it. He just gave me this critical, one-eyebrow-in-the-sky look before leading me to his office. He gestured to one of the chairs.

It was everything I could do to keep my leg from bouncing with all the nervous energy coursing through my body. I was liable to vibrate out of my seat if I wasn't careful.

We started with your standard interview questions about how long I'd been a baker, what my availability was like, strengths, weaknesses, yada yada yada. Mr. Giovanni's expression never changed. He sat there like a stone, silently judging me for each comment and weighing my worth against a bag of flour.

"Do you have something you can show me?" he asked.

"Oh-oh yes. Yes. Here." I fumbled through my bag for my portfolio.

I held the small leather binder out toward him. "These are copies of my recent work."

He thumbed through the photos without saying a word.

My portfolio wasn't much. Even though I took pictures of everything I did, the lack of original designs was obvious. I'd nearly burst into tears when I was putting it together that morning. Everything was a recreation or simple design. My only high point was that it was all edible. There were no plastic toppers on anything I did if I could help it. So that was what I focused on.

"Everything you see there is handmade," I said. "Even the sculptures. I'm very good at…"

He cut me off. "Are these the only originals you have?"

Oh hell.

I looked down at my hands and swallowed. "I, uh, don't really have a lot to speak of. You see, my former boss…"

Mr. Giovanni snapped the portfolio closed.

"I'm sorry, Miss O'Connor, but I need an artist, not a simple decorator." He held the portfolio out to me. "I'm sure you're very talented. I just don't have anything for you. Perhaps you can come back once you have a little more to show me, hmm?"

His words were like a slap in the face. Taking my portfolio, I gave him a slight nod and whispered my thanks before heading for the door, ignoring the scathing look from the girl behind the counter as I went.

* * *

"SO IT WAS that bad, huh?" Derek asked between bites of what sounded like an apple. He'd called me while he was on his lunch break.

"It was terrible. Seriously. That girl looked at me like I was covered in flies or something. I don't know what her problem was."

"Well, maybe this is a good thing," Derek said. "I don't think you would have been happy there, Als. Not from what you're telling me."

I hated to admit it, but Derek had a point. As much as I fantasized about working for a high-end place, I wouldn't have fit in there. Everything was too polished. I mean, how could anybody work somewhere where they were afraid to touch anything? I would have spent all my time tiptoeing around trying not to make a mess instead of getting anything done.

"So, what are you going to do now?"

That was the million-dollar question. I'd spent the better part of my afternoon wondering the same thing. I hadn't been able to secure any more interviews, and my conversation with Mr. Giovanni had confirmed what I'd feared all along—without any original work, I couldn't get the type of job I wanted.

"I guess I'll go down to the market tomorrow and see if their bakery is hiring. That will at least get me a paycheck while I look."

"Don't do that, Als," Derek urged. "Just give it some time. Something's gonna turn up. I promise."

I didn't share his optimism. Sure, I wanted to believe him. Really, I did. But with the way my luck had been lately, I wasn't holding out hope for much of anything.

"Derek, I…"

The sound of someone beating on my door stopped me. I wasn't expecting anyone. I didn't have any loud music playing. Everyone I knew was at work, so there was no reason for anyone to be knocking on my door.

I turned my attention back to my conversation just as another series of knocks sounded through the apartment.

"Derek, I've got to go."

"No worries. I'll see you tonight."

"See ya."

The pounding continued. "Hold on! I'm coming!" Could people not wait two minutes for somebody to answer the door?

I practically ripped the door off its hinges to growl at whoever had been trying to beat it down.

"What?"

The irritation seeped out of me the instant I saw the woman standing in the doorway. She looked like hell. Her eyes were red and her skin blotchy from the excessive amount of crying she was still doing.

"Gina?" I asked in bewilderment.

"Ally, oh thank God you're here. I need your help."

I stepped aside and motioned for her to come in. She gave a quick "thank you" before walking past me and taking a seat on the couch. What on earth was she doing here? She should have been out celebrating. The woman was getting married in less than twenty-four hours.

I took a seat beside her on the couch.

"How did you find me?"

"Th-the girl at the store," Gina sniffled. "Brooke. She told me where to find you."

I made a mental note to have a serious conversation with Brooke about boundaries when I met her for lunch later in the week.

"It's awful," Gina said.

"What is?"

"The cake!"

I had to lean back to avoid being hit by one of her flailing arms.

"It's all wrong." She dug through her purse in search of something. "I was double-checking a few things with the caterers at the hotel when they told me the cake had already been delivered. I was so excited that I begged them to let me see it, and when I walked in, this is what I found."

She pulled her phone out of her purse and unlocked it before selecting something and shoving the device in my face.

I wasn't sure what I was looking at. It was a cake. But it looked nothing like what I had designed. My design had been an elegant floral arrangement accented with lace. This looked like a blue-and-green forest had been draped over pastry. There was no elegance to it.

"You see," Gina cried, reaching for the box of tissues sitting on the coffee table. "It's awful."

"Well…" I handed the phone back to her.

I tried to come up with something good to say about the cake, but I came up empty. Maybe because I knew what it was supposed to look like. The cake was still beautiful, but it wasn't what I had designed. I could see where Toni had taken over and veered away from my design. There were traces of what I was going for here and there, but it was so far off the mark that I wondered if she'd even looked at my sketch before starting.

"I marched down to the bakery as soon as I saw it," Gina explained. "The woman who was there, the one who came up and talked to us before, what's her name?"

"Toni?"

Gina pointed at me. "That's the one. I told her I needed to talk to you, but she said you didn't work there anymore. When I asked her what happened to my cake, she had the audacity to blame you. Can you believe that? She said you'd taken the final design with you, and all she had to work from was the rough sketches you did that first day. Can you believe it?"

Took the design? Toni'd acted like I had no right to it. I scoffed. It was more likely that she just couldn't find it and instead of calling me, she'd let her pride get in the way and tried to do it from memory.

"I kind of lost it and demanded a refund after that."

I paled when she told me about the way she had been bragging about my design to everyone in the wedding party. They were all dying to see it. If what Toni put together was what people associated with me, my career in the baking industry was over.

"It's a disaster." Gina dabbed a tissue to her eye. "The wedding is tomorrow, and I'm stuck with a giant pile of crap as a wedding cake."

"I'm sorry you're having to deal with all this," I told her.

Gina's head snapped in my direction. "Can you fix it?"

My eyebrows rose to what felt like fifty feet.

"That's what I wanted to talk to you about. Is there anything you can do? Please?"

My mouth hung open. Was she expecting me to make a three-tier vanilla bean and mascarpone wedding cake with all that intricate detailing in one night? She couldn't be serious!

"I don't think I can," I told her. "Cakes like that take at least two days. Besides"—I gestured to my cramped apartment kitchen—"I don't have the workspace."

"Can you fix this one then?" Gina pleaded.

The look of utter desperation in her big doe eyes was killing me. It was the kind of expression you only expected to see on tiny woodland creatures, not a bride-to-be waiting for her big day.

"I'll pay you whatever you want," she said. "I'll work it out so you can use the hotel's kitchen. I know the manager. All I have to do is let him know you're coming, and he'll give you free rein. If you give me an ingredients list, I can even have them make sure they have everything you need on hand. I promise."

I sat there in stunned silence. This woman didn't know me. She had no idea if I could fix her cake or not—and neither did I, for that matter. Toni could have used the wrong frosting for all I knew.

Gina grabbed one of my hands in a vicelike grip. "Please."

"Okay. I'll see what I can do, but I'm not sure I can help," I said, already regretting my decision.

Her eyes lit up like fireworks. The smile on her face was nearly blinding. "Thank you." Gina pulled me into a hug. "Thank you. Thank you. Thank you." She released me, and I tried to keep my nerves in check as I wrote down what all I would need to make the frosting.

Gina paused at the door. "I'll let them know you're coming."

"Okay. I'll grab my stuff and be right behind you."

I fell against the door the second it closed.

"What have you gotten yourself into, Allyson?"

I glanced up at the clock. Derek was due home in a few hours, and I had no idea how long it would take me to straighten this mess out. I thought about calling him to let him know where I would be, but it wouldn't do me any good since he couldn't have his phone on the floor. So I grabbed the pad of paper I'd been using to write down possible jobs and ripped a page out of the back. I scratched out a quick note so he wouldn't worry and stuck it to the fridge with a random magnet before grabbing my decorating tips and a few piping bags and running downstairs to catch a cab.

Chapter Nine

MY JAW NEARLY hit the sidewalk when I stepped out of the cab. I needed to start paying closer attention to addresses when I took cake orders. I'd known the place wouldn't be a dump based on the dress photo Gina had shown me—nobody who could afford to spend that kind of money on a dress would have their wedding in a trashy venue—but I hadn't expected to be escorted through the front door of one of the swankiest hotels in New York City.

The dark wood and marble used throughout the lobby alone made me feel like I was underdressed. If anyone had ever told me I'd be designing a cake for a wedding at a place like this, I would have told them to go smoke another one.

A skinny older gentleman in a well-tailored suit and a young woman working behind the mahogany welcome desk paused their conversation and turned their eyes to me. The man must have thought I looked as out of place as I felt, because the next thing I knew he was striding toward me with a wary expression on his face.

"Can I help you, miss?" he asked.

I could feel my insides tying themselves into knots. This guy thought I belonged here about as much as I did.

"I, uh…" *Way to sound professional, Ally.* "I'm here to see…"

"Ally! Oh, thank God!" Gina rushed toward me.

Her fiancé, Chris, waved at me from the sitting lounge in the corner Gina had been hiding in. I threw an embarrassed wave in his direction before focusing my attention on Gina's conversation with the gentleman.

"Robert," she said, placing her hand on his arm before turning toward me, "this is the woman I was telling you about. Ally, this is Robert. He manages the hotel. It's still all right for her to use the hotel's kitchen, isn't it?"

Robert's demeanor shifted on a dime. His scowl morphed into what I could only assume was a well-practiced polite expression.

"Of course, Miss Sanchez." He motioned to me. "Right this way, ma'am."

My eyes nearly popped out of my skull. Who was this woman? How on earth had she convinced the manager to let some nobody waltz into the hotel kitchen? This kind of thing just didn't happen.

Gina saw my gobsmacked expression and laughed. "Come on." She took me by the arm and dragged me down the hallway. "I'll show you where everything is."

Robert led us down the hallway and through an EMPLOYEE ONLY marked corridor to a large set of double-hinged, stainless-steel doors. He gestured for us to go ahead. I gave a silent look of thanks before turning my attention to the room. I came to a grinding halt, nearly bumping Gina off her feet. I was standing in the middle of what had to be the most impressive kitchen I'd ever laid eyes on. Every gadget and amenity I could have ever imagined was in this room, sitting right there in front of me. The mixer looked brand new. I doubted its speed controls had any issues. There were even printed rolling pins that pressed a design into the dough. It made the bag of tools over my left shoulder look pathetic.

"The cake is this way."

The staff barely looked up as we followed Robert into a large cool room at the far end of the kitchen that was designed to store flowers and cakes.

I was so enamored with the impressive array of kitchen wares that it took me a moment to realize Gina had stopped walking. I turned my head to follow her gaze, and what I saw made my stomach roll.

The pictures Gina had shown me didn't even begin to do justice to the monstrosity on the table. Toni must have been drunk when she finished this cake. It was so far off the mark that I wouldn't have had any idea what it was supposed to be if I hadn't drawn the design.

"What the…?"

"You see?" Gina struggled to contain the tears I heard in her voice. "I told you it was terrible."

"You're not wrong."

"Do you think you can fix it?"

Yeah. With a sledgehammer and blowtorch. "I can try."

That was the most I was willing to promise her. There wasn't enough time to completely redo the cake. The wedding was in the morning, and trying to do a full reconstruction by myself in that amount of time would have been like trying to paint the Sistine Chapel with a roller brush. There were too many details. My best bet was to salvage as much as possible and try to connect the dots with what was left.

"Thank you." Gina threw her arms around me, nearly knocking me off my feet with the force of the impact. "I'll leave you to it. If you need anything, anything at all, just call me. I'll be sure you get it, okay?"

She was still beaming at me as she backed out the door Robert was holding open for her. I smiled and waved to them both as they left. The smile vanished the moment I turned to face the mountain of sugar on the table behind me. I sighed. It would take a miracle to pull this off.

I grabbed one of the aprons resting on the hook near the door and surveyed the damage with a critical eye. The best thing I could say about the cake was that Toni had completed a design. It just wasn't mine. The base was fine—I'd at least managed to finish that before she kicked me out the door—but the other two tiers were where it fell apart.

The only elements that were in the right place were the sculpted pieces I'd made in advance. Everything else was a mess. The piping was beautiful, but the design was wrong. Swirls were straight lines, and draped frosting was ridged. At least she'd used the right shades of blue and green.

I studied the cake for a few more seconds before picking up the small frosting spatula the staff had so kindly left out for me. "Well, let's see what happens when I try to take some of this off, shall we?"

My hand shook as I scraped at a small patch of blue and green frosting. "Shit."

The frosting was too soft. Toni always used whipped butter in her frosting. It made for amazing flavor and smooth texture, but it meant scraping it off would leave an impossible-to-hide blue and green smear across the snow-white background. I wouldn't even be able to use fondant to save it at this rate.

The spatula clattered against the counter. I put my elbows on the table and stared up at what was supposed to be my masterpiece. I wanted to scream and cry and curse the day I ever decided to take on this cake. There was no point. I would have to tell Gina there was no saving it. I couldn't make another one. Even if I worked all night, there wasn't enough time to redo it from scratch.

My head dropped into my hands as my heart went into my shoes. I'd finally been able to design a cake, and Toni had not only ripped the production of it from me, but she'd also managed to ruin any goodwill my work would have earned me. It was a disaster.

I scanned every part of the cake, hoping and praying there would be some way to salvage it. My eyes landed on the tiny smudge I'd created when I'd tried to remove part of the frosting. The way the blue and green swirled together was sort of beautiful. It was almost like the pad of a water lily.

I shot straight up with my eyes open wide. "That's it."

I took a quick walk around the cake, studying it from every angle. A grin spread across my face. I just might be able to pull this off after all.

* * *

THE PIPING BAG made a small thud when it landed on the table.

"Done," I groaned.

I flopped onto my stool, let my head fall back against my shoulders, and sighed. I wasn't sure how long I'd been working, but I was pretty sure it would have constituted overtime if I'd still been employed. I hadn't stopped for more than a glass of water or a quick trip to the bathroom since I started.

I lifted my head, tilting it from side to side to stretch my aching muscles. God, I was tired. My eyes were even blurry. I looked around the room for a clock, finally zeroing in on one hanging on the opposite wall. I read the time. My head jerked back. There was no way I'd read that right. I'd always heard fatigue made you see funny things, but this was ridiculous. I squinted my eyes and leaned forward to get a better look. The numbers were the same.

"Holy crap!"

It was nearly eight thirty in the morning, but that wasn't possible. Sure, there weren't any windows or anything in the room to see if the sun was coming up, but there was no way I'd worked for that long.

Gina had shown up on my doorstep at around seven last night. She couldn't have been there for more than an hour before we left. That meant I'd probably arrived at the hotel before ten and started working at... *Oh man.*

I ran a hand down my face and reached for my phone. Gina had told me to call her as soon as the cake was done.

"I can't wait to see it," she'd told me.

Well, she might not be as excited when she saw what I had come up with. While I was proud of the work I'd done, it was a far cry from the original design.

The little blue light at the top of my phone was blinking to tell me I had missed messages and notifications. I unlocked it. There were a few random news alerts. One or two notifications from social media. But what really caught my attention were the texts and missed calls from Derek. I clicked on the first message he'd left. The smile that lit up my face made my cheeks ache after so many hours of frowning in concentration.

Saw your note. You got this, Als!

Then three hours later...

How late do you think you'll be?

That message had come in at almost four in the morning. My stomach dropped. I would feel like the worst roommate in the world if Derek had waited up all night.

I saw that he'd left me a voicemail. I pressed play, and the smile on my face grew even bigger as I listened to his voice.

"Damn, Als, how late are you going to be there? I really hope you're not answering because you're off sleeping. Anyway, don't work too hard. I'll wait up for you. Bye."

Darn. He had waited. Even though the thought of Derek losing sleep over me made me feel like crap, I couldn't help but laugh at the exasperated tone in his voice when he asked how long I would be. I hoped he wasn't serious about waiting up for me. He'd be dead on his feet if he had. The fact he'd even bothered to call warmed my heart. I was a lucky girl for sure.

I deleted the message and snapped a few photos of the cake before calling Gina, fully expecting to leave a voicemail. Most of the brides I'd dealt with over the years made it a point to sleep in as much as possible on their wedding day. I was crafting my message in my head when her excited voice sounded through the phone.

"Ally!"

The sheer volume made me jump. I fumbled with the phone before answering.

"Y-yeah," I said. "It's me. You said you wanted me to call you when I was done with the cake?" Here came the hard part. "Well, it's done, but…"

"I'll be right down."

The line went dead. My stomach swam. She'd hung up before I'd had the chance to warn her.

I'd been able to scrape off the majority of Toni's piping. The little smears of color they left behind were reminiscent of a Monet water scene. That was, of course, if he'd worked in brighter colors and used frosting instead of paint, but that was beside the point.

I'd even gone back and scraped off what I'd done just to make sure it all matched. I redid the details in a creamy white before placing the sculptures I'd managed to save back in their spots. Without the original design, I didn't know if I'd set everything in the exact place, but the big elements that Gina had gushed over were there. I hoped it would be enough to make her happy.

I heard Gina gasp behind me. "Oh my God…"

I flinched. That sound could mean one of only two things—either she loved it, or it was an even bigger disappointment than Toni had delivered.

My muscles screamed at me not to turn around. As long as I didn't do that, I could still pretend everything was fine. The thought that I could just wait for her to say something ran through my head. Maybe it would be better to hear how much she hated it without looking at her. Just hearing Toni had always been better than watching her face go red as she squawked—maybe this would be the same.

I stood with my back to her, waiting. The second hand on the clock ticked by in silence. *This can't be good.* I wiped my sweaty palms on my borrowed apron and readied myself for the onslaught before turning to face the music.

Gina was standing in the doorway, one hand over her mouth and the other resting daintily over her heart. It might have just been a trick of the light, but I could have sworn tears shimmered in her eyes. The cake was so bad that I'd made her cry.

"I..."

What could I say? She had trusted me to save her cake on what was the biggest day of her life, and instead, I was delivering a hazy mess.

"I'm so sor—"

"It's beautiful," Gina whispered.

I blinked. I had to have heard her wrong.

Gina's eyes didn't move from the cake as she floated into the room. Her hands fell away from her mouth to let me see her expression for the first time. Her face glowed so brightly, I wasn't entirely sure I didn't need sunglasses.

"It's amazing." She strolled around the table once, studying it from every angle. "I love it."

"You do?"

Gina nodded her head emphatically. "It's even better than the original. I've never seen another cake like it."

I let out a sigh of relief. My eyes closed, and my shoulders relaxed for the first time all night.

The sudden impact of something hitting me in the chest nearly took me off my feet. I opened my eyes to find Gina hugging me so tight that she may have cracked a rib.

"Thank you so much," she said. "You're amazing."

I gazed back up at my cake. Despite everything, it had turned out beautifully.

Gina released me from her death grip and went to retrieve her bag from where she'd dropped it in the entryway. She started rifling through it, muttering to herself until she found what she was looking for.

"Here." She pulled a fat white envelope from her purse and thrust it toward me. "This is for you."

I stared at her for a moment before taking the envelope. It was heavier than I'd imagined. I pulled back the flap and nearly choked on my tongue when I saw the amount of green stuffed inside. "*Aughph.*"

My brain short-circuited as I looked back and forth from the envelope to Gina's smiling face.

"I-I can't take this." I pushed the envelope back at her like a game of hot potato. "It's too much."

Shoving the envelope back toward me, she wrapped her hands around where mine held it and tilted her head to the side with a knowing smirk. "Of course you can."

While I hadn't checked the amount of all of the bills, I was sure I'd seen a couple of zeros after a one on a few of them.

"Thank you," I croaked.

"Don't mention it. It's the least I could do for you coming down here and working on this all night."

A gentle rapping turned our attention to the doorway to see Chris leaning against the frame.

Gina threw her hands up in the air and shrieked before scurrying to hide behind the cake.

"Go away! You can't see me before the wedding! Go!"

Chris shook his head and chuckled. "I thought that was only if you were in the dress?"

"Get out! Get out! Get out!"

Chris held his hands up in surrender. "All right, all right." He shifted his gaze to me. "Come on, Ally. I called you a cab."

I shouted a final thank you to a still cowering Gina as I followed Chris out into the hall.

"Thank you for doing that," he said as he led me along the corridor.

"Just doing my job."

"No. You did a lot more than that." He stopped walking and spun to face me, his expression pensive. "I don't know a single decorator who would have come down here and tried to redo a cake in the middle of the night, no matter who the bride was. The fact that her family owns this hotel helps, I'm sure, but Gina told me about how you agreed to take a look without even asking about the money. Not many people would do that. You care about what you put your name on, and it shows."

So that was how she did it. Her family owned the hotel? No wonder Robert changed his tune the instant she showed up.

"To be honest with you," Chris went on, "I couldn't care less what the cake looks like, but it's important to Gina. And making her happy is all I care about. So, thank you."

"You're welcome," I whispered.

Chris led me out to the waiting cab and handed the driver a few bills before telling him to take me wherever I asked. When I insisted I could pay for the cab, he just held up his hand and informed me it was the least he could do after all my hard work.

I thanked Chris one last time before stepping into the taxi and giving the driver my address.

I sank back into the seat with a sigh. I dug my thumb into the palm of my hand to ease the cramping from squeezing a piping bag for too long. Maybe I'd squeeze myself into my tiny little apartment tub for a bath when I got home. That would ease the ache in my muscles. I let my head fall back against the headrest and closed my eyes as we drove along the New York City streets. I must have dozed off, because the next thing I knew, the driver was telling me I was home.

Muttering a quick thank you, I stumbled my way up to my apartment. The only thing I wanted was to curl up in bed and sleep until either my bladder or my stomach forced me to get up. I was kicking off my shoes by the door when I looked toward the living room and spotted Derek fast asleep on the couch.

He had a half-empty pizza box beside him. Whatever show he'd been streaming on the TV had long since ended, replaced by the generic landscape backgrounds every screensaver liked to use. My heart warmed at the sight of him. He'd waited up for me like he said he would. Well, he'd tried.

I moved toward the couch and brushed a few strands of hair off his forehead. I couldn't help but notice how innocent he looked when he was sleeping. His face was completely relaxed, his long eyelashes fanning against his high cheekbones making him look almost angelic.

A small groan sounded from Derek's lips as he stirred, his eyes blinking to bring the world into focus, until they landed on me. "Hey," he said, his voice still rough from sleep.

"Hey."

"What time is it?"

I cast a glance at the clock. "Almost nine."

Derek rubbed the sleep from his eyes and moved to sit up before pushing the pizza box out of the way and sliding over so I could sit beside him.

"Are you just now getting home?"

There was an edge of annoyance in his voice that made me hesitate. I knew he wouldn't be happy to learn I'd worked all night without a break, but I didn't want to lie to him about it either.

"Tell me they at least paid you for it."

I looked away sheepishly, and his expression hardened.

"Als, please tell me you didn't do all that work for free."

"I didn't," I whispered. "Gina paid me."

"How much?"

I frowned. I'd never actually stopped to count the money she'd handed me. I held a finger up to tell him to wait while I collected the envelope from my purse. Meandering back to the couch, I thumbed through the envelope. I nearly tripped over myself. It was more than three times what the cake itself had cost.

With a shaking hand, I held the envelope out to Derek. His eyes nearly popped out of his head.

"Holy shit!" He took the envelope from my hand. "Jesus. Are these people drug dealers or something?"

"No." I chuckled. "Her family owns the swanky hotel downtown where they're having the wedding."

Derek peeked inside, shaking his head at the stack of cash before handing the envelope back to me. "That's a lot of money."

"I know." My own disbelief showed in my voice. "This means I don't have to get a job right away. I can keep looking until I find the one I want."

Derek's face glowed. "I'm proud of you, Als."

"Thanks."

He pulled me into a quick hug before not so subtly pushing me toward my room.

"Now. Go. To. Bed."

"Only if you do too. The couch is no place for a good night's sleep."

He lifted an eyebrow at me, and I returned his challenge full force until he gave in, agreeing to go to bed for a few hours after he'd cleaned up a bit.

But my bed kept screaming my name louder and louder. Who was I to tell it no?

I paused in my bedroom doorway. "Thanks for waiting up for me."

"Any time."

I gave him one last look before disappearing into my room and collapsing on my bed for what I hoped would be at least the next twelve hours.

Chapter Ten

A LOUD, SHRILL ringing jolted me out of my sleep. I growled low in the back of my throat before forcing myself into a seated position. Rubbing the sleep from my eyes, I crawled toward the end of the bed to retrieve my phone from the pocket of the pants I'd dropped on the floor on my way to la-la land.

I didn't even bother looking at the caller ID before answering with a gruff "Hello."

"Ally?"

"Gina?"

Why the hell was she calling me? I looked at the clock on my nightstand. It was nearly one o'clock in the afternoon. She should be at her reception right now. Not calling me. The only reason she would have to call me was… My heart dropped out of my chest. The only reason she would have to call me was if there was something wrong with the cake.

"W-what happened?"

"Wait. I can't hear you!" she shouted over the loud music playing in the background. "Just give me a sec." I heard some shuffling and what must have been a door closing, because the pounding bass dropped from a deafening roar to a muted thrum. "Sorry about that."

"It's okay." I tried to keep the panic out of my voice. "How's the wedding?"

"Amazing!"

Gina gushed about the ceremony. Everyone had oohed and awwed over her dress. Chris had even shed a tear or two when he saw her walking down the aisle.

I fiddled with the edge of my comforter while she went on and on about how incredible the ceremony had been.

"And, uh, the reception?"

"It's amazing! Everybody is raving about your cake!"

I threw myself back against the bed and sighed. They liked my cake. *Thank God!*

"That's actually why I was calling you. I've had a lot of people asking me for your card, but I don't have any. Where are you working now?"

"Uh, I'm not."

A gasp of horror sounded on the other end of the line.

"Please tell me you're joking."

I shook my head.

"Ally?"

Right. She couldn't see me. "No. I haven't found anything yet. I've got some interviews lined up though."

I prayed she couldn't hear the lie in my voice. Giovanni's was the only place that had given me an interview, and that had gone over about as well as a maple bacon cupcake at a bar mitzvah.

"Can I just give them your number for now?" she asked. "A couple of them told me they were interested in you doing a cake for them. Is that all right?"

"Sure!"

We talked for a few more minutes before Gina ended the call, but I wasn't paying attention. I was too busy doing a mental happy dance at the thought of her, and others, referring me for work. I would be able to start a business. It was a dream come true. I could…

All of the color drained from my face.

I dropped my phone onto the bed and raced to the kitchen. I stood just behind the couch, staring at the only available workspace I had. Which was to say, none. There was barely any counter space apart from the eat-in island, and that wasn't even a yard.

"Oh hell."

I started ripping through the cabinets. Pots and pans clattered to the floor as I tore open every cabinet and drawer I could find in search of my limited baking supplies.

"Why do I only have four pans?" I shouted as I opened another door. I held them up to get a closer look. "And they're all the same size!"

"Als?"

"Ah!" I screamed.

The pan in my hand clattered to the floor. I whirled to see Derek studying me from his spot on the couch. I placed my hand over my racing heart and tried to slow my breathing.

"What are you doing?" He shifted so that his arm was draped over the back of the couch.

I collapsed against the cabinet with a groan, covering my face with my hands. "I don't know."

Derek was beside me in an instant. "What's wrong?"

I shook my head. How could I explain what was happening inside my mind when I couldn't understand it myself?

"Gina is giving my number to people," I told him. "They want to talk to me about making cakes for them."

"That's great!"

"What am I supposed to do if somebody actually calls me?" I gestured around our cramped apartment kitchen. "I can't do a multilayer cake here. I don't have the equipment."

Derek put his hands on my upper arms to stop my flailing. My word vomit puttered out until I found myself staring into his clear blue eyes, a slight smile dancing along his features.

"What do you need, Ally?"

"Well"—I licked my lips—"I need a mixer, cake stands, rollers, pans…" The knowing smirk that appeared on Derek's face pulled me up short. "Why are you looking at me like that?"

"You said you need a mixer?" He pointed to the corner of the counter near the fridge, where an old secondhand stand mixer sat collecting dust. "I see a mixer right there. Pans?" He picked up one of the small cake pans from the floor. "What else do you call this?"

"They're from Dollar Tree," I grumbled.

Derek waved me off. "They worked just fine when you were in school. They'll work fine now. I'm not sure where you've got it stashed, but I know you have a rolling pin around here somewhere."

I opened my mouth to tell him how ridiculous he was being, but he held up a hand to silence me before I could say a word.

"And I've watched enough of those stupid baking competitions with you to know we can build a stand out of PVC pipe and cardboard if we have to."

He got a chuckle out of me with that one.

"It's not just that." I rolled my eyes at him. "It's the ingredients. Do you have any idea how much flour it takes to make a wedding cake? A lot. We can't store that level of supplies here. Besides, all the cake pans I have are the same size. I'll need at least a dozen different ones to make this thing work."

"Then take some of that massive payday you just got and buy what you need."

"But…"

Once again, Derek stopped me before I could get rolling. "Als"—he placed both of his hands on my shoulders—"I know you're scared, all right? You have a reason to be. Starting over is hard, but you can do this. You just redecorated an entire cake in one night. You can do anything. And I'll be right here with you. You won't have to do this alone."

I stared at him in awe. His sweet lopsided grin made my heart feel a million times lighter.

"How do you do that?" I asked.

He frowned.

"How do you always know what to say to make me feel better?"

"It's a gift." He shrugged. "Honestly, it's because I know you, Als. You're amazing."

We sat there smiling at each other for a moment before I wrapped my arms around him.

"Thank you," I whispered against his chest.

"Anytime."

Chapter Eleven

A SHIVER OF delight ran through me as the warm caramel mocha danced across my tongue. It made the risk of running into Toni worth it.

The café Brooke had chosen for our catch-up lunch was only a block away from the bakery, so running into my former employer was a real possibility. But if Brooke and I wanted to have lunch, it was the only place she could get in and out of fast enough if I ordered ahead for her.

"Hey, sweetheart." Brooke's twangy voice greeted me as she stepped up to the little outdoor table I'd managed to snag.

I sprang to my feet and enveloped her in a hug. Three weeks was too long to go without seeing my friend.

Brooke took the seat opposite me and moaned at the first sip of her dark roast. "You have no idea how bad I needed this."

We fell into conversation, like we always did. I filled her in on my lack of movement on the job front, while she told me about the bakery.

"Is it really that bad?" I asked.

"You don't know the half of it."

The waiter appeared with our food and set the plates in front of us.

"Thank you, darlin'," Brooke drawled before diving into her turkey and Swiss. She was halfway through her sandwich by the time she started in on work. "It's been hell, Ally. We actually ran out of puff pastry the other day."

I stopped with my BLT halfway to my mouth and gawked at her. "Are you serious?"

Brooke nodded.

My jaw went slack. "But that's used in all the most popular treats. There's a reason I always made a ton of it in the morning and before I left for the day."

I couldn't wrap my head around what Brooke was telling me. How many times had Toni lit into me because it looked like we might run out of something? It was like a cardinal sin in her book. The idea that she would let herself run out of something didn't make sense.

"What did she say?" I asked.

Brooke took another sip of her coffee. "That's the weirdest part. When I went in the back to tell her, she was just sitting there staring off into space like she was lost or something."

That didn't sound like Toni.

I drew my eyebrows together. "Was she the only one back there?"

Brooke put down her mug before launching into the tale of woe that had become my former place of employment. Apparently, Toni hadn't been able to find a replacement for me. A few of the regular customers had been in the front when Toni fired me, and word got around that Toni's Tasty Treats was not a good place to be. That left her to do all the work herself for the time being, and she was not doing as well under the pressure as I had.

Did it make me a bad person to admit I kind of enjoyed the idea of her getting a taste of her own medicine?

"That's not all," Brooke said. "The other morning, she actually beat me to the bakery, and when I walked in she was crying. I didn't even know she could do that!"

My eyes bulged in their sockets. In all the years I'd worked for Toni, the only real emotions I'd ever seen from her were frustration and anger. Sure, she'd been nice enough at the start, but she'd just become meaner and more hateful over the last few years. I couldn't imagine the woman smiling at this point, let alone crying.

"That's enough of my drama." Brooke waved her hand in dismissal. "What's new with you? Do you have another interview lined up yet?"

"No. I was kind of hoping I'd get a few referrals from that cake I did, but it's been a few weeks, and nobody's called me."

It was true. Despite Gina's apparent enthusiasm, not a single person had called me to ask about a cake. I was sure I would have heard from at least one of them by now. So I'd written it off as a lost cause. The few places that had been kind enough to grant me an interview had been impressed with the photos I'd shown them of Gina's cake, but none had been willing to hire me because of my "lack of design experience."

"That's their loss." Brooke wiped her mouth with a napkin. "You're gonna find something, and it's going to be amazing."

I gave her a rueful grin and huffed. "Now you sound like Derek."

Brooke's expression brightened. "And how is that gorgeous hunk of man meat doing? You two finally come to your senses yet?"

Her obsession with me and my roommate getting together was something I would never understand. "He's fine. His over-the-top optimism is getting a bit stale though."

Every morning, Derek would say something about how today would be better or I would do great, and it was getting on my nerves. I loved Derek. Everybody needed someone like him in their corner, but the not-so-subtle hints about opening my own place without the smallest glimpse of clientele was getting old.

My face must have shown what my brain was thinking, because Brooke reached across the table and took hold of my hand. I looked up to see her giving me a sympathetic look that let me know that, while she couldn't do anything to help, she'd be there for me regardless.

"It's gonna happen, Ally. Just give it time."

A pathetic attempt at a smile curled the corners of my mouth. "Thanks, Brooke." I gave her hand a little squeeze.

She returned the gesture before glancing at her watch. "I've got to get back. Toni will go insane if I'm late."

"Good luck." I stood and walked around the table to give her a hug. "Same time next week?"

"You know it. See you later, girl."

"See ya."

I waited for Brooke to disappear around the corner before grabbing my things and heading back to the apartment to look for what would no doubt be the next in a long list of rejections.

The apartment was eerily silent when I arrived. There was no TV. No music. Just the low hum of the fan in the corner.

"Hello?" I called.

Nothing.

I frowned. Today was supposed to be Derek's day off. He usually spent those lying on the couch playing video games and watching movies I'd rather not see. I crept toward his room and opened the door gently to keep it from squeaking in case he was asleep. My shoulders dropped when I saw nothing but his neatly made bed.

"What the hell?"

He hadn't done any more shift swaps that I was aware of. The thought that he might have picked up an extra shift to help pay my portion of the bills crossed my mind. I hadn't found a job yet, but we were still doing okay. We hadn't missed a payment on anything that I was aware of. Surely he would have told me if there was an issue. I started to dial his number when I spotted the note on the table.

Als,

I went to play a pickup game with some of the guys down at the Y. There's some lasagna in the fridge. Don't worry. I didn't run out and buy a bunch of stuff. We had a frozen one saved from last time. I'll be home later.

-D

The fact that he'd taken the time to mention he hadn't gone shopping made me giddy. Maybe I'd been a little more freaked out about our finances than I was letting on.

I'd nearly had a conniption fit at the store the week before when I saw the price of a pound of hamburger meat. No, we weren't strapped for cash just yet, but my last check from Toni and the payday from Gina would only hold out for so long.

I felt twitchy when I didn't have at least a thousand dollars in my savings account and a hundred in my checking. Mom had always talked about how hard it was to pay for things after my dad left, and the only thing I could hear when my account balances dropped was her voice in the back of my mind screaming about me not being able to take care of myself. I would have to bite the bullet and take a job at the grocer's bakery if things didn't change soon.

I pulled the pan from the fridge and cut myself a chunk of cheese and pasta goodness. Popping the plate in the microwave, I went to change into a pair of sweatpants and an old NYU hoodie I'd stolen from Derek years ago. I threw my hair up in a messy bun and prepared to eat my dinner in front of the TV while I waited for Derek.

I'd just settled onto the couch to binge an old season of *Nailed It* on Netflix when my phone rang. I jumped, causing my fork of food to tumble onto the front of my shirt.

"Crap."

Wiping myself clean, I set the plate on the coffee table and picked up the phone. I looked at the caller ID and frowned.

It was a local number, but that didn't mean much in New York. There were too many places that did cold calls in this area. I was just about to hit the IGNORE button when the niggling thought it could be a job sprang to mind. I hadn't saved all the bakeries' numbers to my phone yet, so there was a better than zero chance it could be one of them.

I hit the ANSWER button and slowly brought the phone up to my ear. "Hello?"

"Is this Allyson O'Riley?" a woman on the other end of the line asked.

"It's O'Conner, actually." I turned off the television. "Can I help you?"

"My name is Luisa Montoya. I wanted to talk to you about making a cake for my daughter..."

* * *

I STUDIED THE sixteen-inch round pan, turning it over in my hand to get a better look.

"Perfect." I dropped the pan into the cart that Derek pushed behind me.

The meeting with Mrs. Montoya had been one of the most terrifying things I'd ever done. You would think a lunch meeting to discuss a cake for a fifteen-year-old would be easy. Yeah, not when it was the fanciest restaurant you'd ever stepped foot in, and your potential client looked like she'd stepped straight out of the pages of *Vogue*. I was amazed I was able to make it through the meeting without using the wrong fork.

It had taken me exactly ninety seconds after leaving the restaurant to realize I didn't have the pans I needed to make the cake I'd sketched. This cake would require three different sized cake pans. I had one. Cursing myself for not thinking things through, I called Derek to let him know I had to do some shopping before I went home, and he insisted on joining me.

The industrial kitchen store on Broadhurst was a place I'd always wanted to visit. Its rows and rows of pans, mixers, and baking goodies put me in culinary heaven. There were times I found myself just staring at the shelves in awe until Derek bumped me with the cart.

"So, you're really going to run a business out of our kitchen, huh?" Derek asked.

I put a sheet pan I'd been drooling over back on the shelf and turned to find him leaning against the cart, smirking at me.

"Don't give me that look," I scolded, pointing my finger at him for emphasis. "If we were in a sporting goods store, you'd be doing the same thing."

He held his hands up in mock surrender. "I didn't say anything."

"But you were thinking it."

He gave me a shrug, and I lightly punched his arm before resuming my search for the right pan to use for my base layer.

"Seriously though, Als, don't you have to have some sort of special license or something?"

"First of all, one cake does not equal a business."

He nodded.

"Secondly, if I start an actual business, and I'm not saying I am, but if I do, as long as it's small batch baking, I'm fine. I'd only run into issues if I had to start refrigerating things. Then I'd have to start working out of a commercial kitchen."

He frowned at me. "Can you do that?"

I nodded. "Yeah. There are places where you can rent space for a few days to do a project. I'm just not there yet." I dropped a nonstick cake pan into the basket. "I promise you, if we get to the point that we no longer have a kitchen, I'll start renting space, okay?"

"Sounds like you've got this thing all figured out. I'm proud of you,

Als."

I turned to Derek, planning on thanking him, and came up short at the look on his face. He was looking at me with this dreamy expression I didn't remember ever seeing before. It made my insides fizzy.

The corner of his mouth ticked up a fraction of an inch when he saw me looking. I blinked and shook my head.

What the hell was wrong with me?

I wiped my now sweaty palms on my thighs and tried to smile back. "Th-thanks."

Heat bloomed on my cheeks, and I turned away from him to continue my search. There must have been something wrong with the chicken I ate earlier. That's why my stomach felt weird all the sudden. It had nothing to do with the way Derek was looking at me. He was my best friend for Pete's sake. Best friends didn't get all antsy when they looked at each other.

"So," I drawled when the silence started to suffocate me, "you're going to help me deliver the cake, right?"

The items in the cart rattled when Derek came to a sudden halt. I glanced over to see his wide-eyed shock morph into a squinty-eyed look of disapproval. He stood to his full height and lifted one eyebrow. "Come again?"

"Well..."

Derek crossed his arms over his chest.

"She didn't tell me she was going to need it delivered when we talked on the phone. She just dropped it on me at the last second before she left today. I can get an Uber or something to take it there, but I can't get the cake down the stairs by myself."

Derek uncrossed his arms and resumed pushing the cart down the aisle. "I thought Brooke was your all-time favorite cake-carrying buddy."

"Toni won't let her leave to help me. Apparently she's gotten even crazier since I left." I clasped my hands in a prayer pose and gave him my best puppy dog eyes. "Pleeease."

Derek took a deep breath.

I had to fight to keep the grin off my face. "Please, Derek." I laid it on thick with a bat of my eyelashes.

He rubbed his chin with the thumb and forefinger of his right hand. "All right."

I squealed in excitement and threw my hands up in victory. The eyes always worked.

"I'll help on one condition."

I stopped dancing and turned to see him once again staring down at me with the expression he only had when he was getting serious.

"Name it."

"You have to make a batch of those raspberry truffle cupcakes for me to take to the gym next week. It's Jimmy's birthday, and he hasn't stopped bugging me about them since you made a batch for his niece's birthday party a few months ago."

I threw my head back and laughed. I'd been afraid he was going to ask me to clean his bathroom or do his laundry. If his only demand was a batch of cupcakes, I'd make them in a heartbeat.

"Sure. I can do that."

"Great." He motioned toward the front of the store. "Come on. Let's get going. You've got work to do."

As much work as I had to get done, I enjoyed just walking around the store and seeing what it had to offer. I kept imagining what different things would look like in a perfectly stocked bakery with brightly colored walls and a warm, welcoming interior that made people want to sit and soak up the atmosphere. I could see the fire-engine-red stand mixer sitting on a wooden countertop with a mountain of boxed orders beside it. It would be beautiful.

"What are you thinking about?" Derek's voice snapped me back to reality.

"Nothing," I lied.

"Bullshit. I know that look. You were a million miles away. What were you thinking about, Als?"

I looked down at my feet. How did you tell someone you were thinking about what your bakery would look like when you'd told them over and over again that you weren't opening one?

I fiddled with the end of my shirt and looked up through my lashes to see Derek waiting for an answer. He'd stopped moving, and if I wanted to get out of the store without spending every last cent I had, I would have to tell him.

"Just thinking about what my bakery would look like with this stuff in it."

A cocky grin appeared on his face.

"What?"

"So you *are* going to open a place?"

"I didn't say that."

"Sure," he mocked. "Sure. Sure."

"Oh hush."

I started toward the checkout area, but Derek was quick to catch up with me.

"You'll get there someday. I know you will."

I squeezed his side. "Thanks."

"No problem. Now come on. Let's get this crap and get out of here. We've still got to buy the ingredients for the cake."

I groaned. It was going to be a long night.

* * *

ROLLING FONDANT BY hand had to be one of the worst things I had ever done. I'd never thought I would miss Toni's faulty equipment as much as I did in the twenty minutes it took me to work the fondant thin enough to lay over the cake. My shoulders ached from the constant back and forth, and my arms felt like they were made of Jell-O. In that moment, I swore that if I ever had a place of my own, it would have the best automatic roller the world had ever seen, because there was no way in hell I was doing this again.

Carefully lifting the fondant, I placed it on top of the cake and smoothed out the edges until it gave me the perfect base to work with. My back groaned in protest when I stood up straight for the first time in hours. Falling asleep on the couch right after dinner the night before had put a bit of a damper on my decorating plans. Now I had less than twenty-four hours to finish and deliver the cake instead of the two days I'd originally budgeted.

I looked around the kitchen. Every inch of space was covered with something cake related. I had seriously underestimated the number of bowls and spatulas I would need to make this cake a reality. At the bakery, I'd always been able to grab another bowl and keep moving with the understanding I would wash everything up at the end of the day. Now, with a fraction of the space and limited supplies, it was clear that stopping to clean along the way was something I would have to learn. I still needed to mix another batch of frosting, and the two mixing bowls I owned were sitting in the sink, covered in what was left of the batter.

I threw my head back and groaned. I hated cleaning, but it had to be done.

I'd just finished washing up the last of the dishes and was about to start piping the base when I heard a knock at the door.

I glanced at the clock and nearly choked on my tongue when I saw it was almost noon.

Where did the day go?

Another knock echoed through the apartment.

"Coming."

I set my piping bag down and wiped my hands on my apron before making my way to the door. Looking through the peephole, I jerked back in surprise when I saw Mrs. Henderson standing on the other side, holding a plate of sandwiches.

"Well, hello, dear," she greeted me when I opened the door.

"Hi, Mrs. Henderson," I said, albeit with less enthusiasm than she had used. "What are you doing here?"

"Oh, well, I saw Derek on his way out this morning, and he told me you'd be working from home today." She held up the plate in her hand. "So I thought I'd bring up some sandwiches and give you a bit of company while you take a break."

I chuckled. Of course she would think to do something like that.

"I think I can stop long enough for a sandwich or two. Come on in."

I took a step back to let her inside. The old woman smiled at me and made her way over to the island, placing the plate on one of the few clean surfaces left in the kitchen. We each took a seat on a barstool and scarfed down the simple but tasty BLTs she'd brought up.

"That's beautiful." She motioned to the half-finished cake on the opposite side of the counter. "What's it for?"

I swallowed my bite before answering. "A quinceañera. I have to deliver it first thing tomorrow."

"You're doing a wonderful job."

"Thanks, Mrs. Henderson. And thanks for the sandwich. It was delicious."

"Anytime, dear." She slid off the stool and grabbed her now empty plate. "I'd better get going. Pepper gets nervous if I leave him alone for too long."

With a final wave and a promise to give Pepper a scratch behind the ears for me, she was off. I turned my attention back to the cake. As much fun as visiting with her had been, it had set me back almost a whole hour. I still had a lot of work to do to get the cake done and everything cleaned up before starting on dinner.

* * *

"JUST ONE MORE little..." I said to the empty apartment as I brushed on the last of the silver highlights.

I took a step back and couldn't help but survey my handiwork with pride. I'd done good. No. Scratch that. I'd done freaking fantastic. This was a cake worthy of a magazine cover. The gold details and silver highlights made everything look far more sophisticated than anything I'd ever done. Now to put it in the fridge...

A wail of panic leaped out of my throat when I opened the refrigerator door. "Damn it!"

Not only had I forgotten about the shelves, I'd completely spaced on everything sitting on them. Every single shelf was stockpiled with dairy and produce.

My heart pounded rapidly against my ribcage. No way could I let the cake sit on the counter overnight. Delivering a stale cake would ruin any chances I had of ever starting any kind of business, no matter how far in the future that may be.

Looking back and forth between the fridge and the cake, I struggled to come up with an answer. I let out a groan as I grabbed an armful of food and placed it on the counter. Soon I'd cleared out enough space that I could remove the shelves to make room for the cake. Now all I had to do was lift it. *Crap.*

I collapsed back against the cabinets, banging my head against the door in the process. What was I thinking? I couldn't lift this thing by myself. I'd just drop it and have to start all over, and I definitely didn't have time for that.

I thought about calling Brooke, but she was still at work. Mrs.

Henderson would be more than happy to help, but I wasn't entirely sure the seventy-five-year-old woman could lift the three-tier cake without hurting herself or dropping it. My chin dropped to my chest. My only option was to wait for Derek to get home.

No sooner had the thought left my brain than I heard a key in the lock.

I froze, my eyes scanning the destroyed space. I had planned on having everything sorted out and cleaned up before he got home. This was bad. Derek was more of a neat freak about the kitchen than I was.

Derek kept his head down as he came through the door. He still had his earbuds in and wasn't paying attention to anything other than his phone while I stood just waiting for him to notice what I had done to our home.

He glanced up. "Hey, Als." He looked back down before grinding to a halt. His head turned back to me.

The muscles in his face went slack, and his eyes glazed over. "Wow."

My chin dropped to my chest. "I know it's a mess. I promise I'll—"

"Is that the cake?"

I blinked.

Derek sat his things down on the coffee table and came to take a closer look. I watched carefully as he circled the island, taking in the cake from every angle.

"You really outdid yourself with this one, Als. This is amazing."

"Thanks."

He took a step back, and I recognized the instant he spotted the rest of the kitchen.

"What's all this?"

"Food?"

He scowled. "I can see that, 'smartass. Why is it sitting out everywhere?"

"Well…"

"Ally?"

I looked up to see him cocking an eyebrow at me.

I cowered. "I'm sorry. I meant to have everything cleaned up by the time you got back, but I ran into a little problem."

Derek leaned against the island. His other eyebrow lifted up to join its partner.

"I finished the cake, but I couldn't leave it sitting on the counter. It would spoil, and then word would get out that I couldn't deliver on my promises, and nobody would ever order a cake from me again, and then I'd have to…"

"Ally!"

I stopped rambling.

"Breathe."

I followed Derek's lead and took a deep, cleansing breath. *In. Out.* Then again until my brain didn't feel like the Autobahn anymore.

"Now," he continued, "what's the problem?"

"I need to put the cake in the fridge so it will still be good in the morning, but there was a bunch of food and shelves in the way. So I took it all out, but now I'm screwed because I can't lift the stupid thing by myself."

I fiddled with the hem of my shirt, waiting quietly for admonishment. I knew Derek couldn't be happy with the state of things. My poor planning and lack of foresight had turned our kitchen into a war zone. I deserved everything he had to give me. Only thing was, he didn't say anything.

"I thought you said you couldn't do anything that you had to refrigerate at home?"

"I was talking about bigger projects. I didn't think it would be an issue for one single cake. It's not like anyone else has ordered anything from me. I just need to keep it cold for one night."

Derek's eyes moved around the room, studying the various stacks of food and dirty dishes that were no doubt the cause of the slight twitch in his left eye.

"Please don't be mad," I pleaded. "I promise I'll rent some space next time I do anything more than a sheet cake. I didn't think it would be this bad."

My stomach started rolling as the silence went on. A silent Derek usually meant an angry Derek. There were only a handful of times I could recall Derek being mad at me, but each time had resulted in several torturous weeks of us hardly speaking to each other. The thought of dealing with that on top of everything else was too much.

"Whoa." Derek held up his hands like he was trying to stop traffic. "Als, relax. I'm not mad. I promise."

I gawked. "You're not?"

He chuckled. "No. I was just caught off guard. I wasn't expecting to come home to see Hurricane Ally ripping the kitchen apart."

I felt the heat rising in my cheeks. "I guess I didn't really think this through, huh?"

"Probably not." He looked over at the cake. "It really is incredible."

"You know what would really be amazing? You helping me move it into the fridge."

He snorted a laugh. "All right. How do you want to do this thing?"

It felt weird telling Derek how to lift something. He told people how to lift things for a living, but moving a cake was a little different. You had to do it in sync, or all your work could be ruined.

Once we got the cake squared away, we sorted through the food on the counter. Derek grabbed an ice chest from his closet and filled it with ice.

"We'll have to keep putting ice in it for the next few hours," he said, "but it should keep the perishables good until we can put them back in the fridge tomorrow."

I put the milk and cheese in the chest while Derek grabbed the produce and whipped up a quick stir fry for dinner. I started on the dishes while he finished cooking.

"What a day." I collapsed onto the couch after dinner and let my head fall back against the headrest before closing my eyes.

"Yeah."

I peeked my eyes open and rolled my head to the side to see Derek rubbing at the back of his neck and shoulders. Dark circles rimmed his eyes. I was pretty sure the now semi-permanent bags under his eyes were my fault. He'd spent all day working his ass off only to come home and have to help me with my own work. It wasn't fair. He was doing the lion's share right now, and there wasn't a thing I could do about it.

"Come here."

Derek glanced at me from the corner of his eye. I turned my body to face him on the couch and patted the cushion in front of me. He studied me. I patted the cushion again, and he shuffled toward me.

"Now turn around."

He did as I said without any argument. Reaching up, I rubbed the tight muscles along his neck and shoulders. They felt like corded steel. I was almost afraid they would snap if I pushed too hard.

I dragged my thumb along his left trap and felt him melt.

His head fell forward, and a deep groan sounded through the room. "That feels amazing."

I pushed onto my knees for more leverage and dug into the muscles like I was kneading bread dough. Derek's head rolled from side to side as I worked. A long loud moan filled the room. I kept rubbing and digging until I felt his muscles go lax. My hands and fingers ached from the work, but the dopey look on his face was worth it.

Derek took a hold of my hands and pulled me forward until I was hugging him from behind.

"Thank you," he whispered.

"You're welcome." I leaned into him and gave him a squeeze. "Thanks for putting up with me."

He huffed. "You make it sound like a chore."

"It can be." I loosened my arms from around his neck, and he shifted so we were face to face. "I..."

Where did I even begin? There was no way to put into words how grateful I was for everything he'd done for me over the last few months. Between the emotional support and the extra hours he was putting in so I didn't have to worry about finding a job right away, I wasn't sure there were enough words in the English language to express just how grateful I was.

I opened my mouth again to try and express my feelings, but a finger against my lips kept me silent.

Derek shifted closer, leaving just a hair's breadth between us. "You're perfect."

His finger moved from my lips to my jaw, cupping my face in his large hand. He ran his thumb back and forth across my cheek. My heart went into overdrive. It was beating so loud I was positive he could hear it. I looked into his eyes and nearly forgot how to breathe. He was looking at me like I was something precious. Something priceless.

He shifted again, and his breath fanned across my face. A swarm of butterflies formed in my stomach. When I saw his eyes dart down to my lips, I thought I might pass out.

It might have been my imagination, but I thought he leaned in. My body reacted before my brain registered what I was doing. I licked my lips in anticipation and leaned toward him. My heartbeat pounded in my ears like a bass drum. My eyes drifted shut. Tingles danced across my skin. Derek's thumb and forefinger on my chin angled my head up.

At the last second, he tilted my head down and placed a kiss on my forehead.

"Night, Als," he whispered against my skin before releasing me and heading toward his room.

I sat there in stunned silence. I barely managed to squcak out a little "Night, Derek," before his door closed behind him.

What the hell just happened? Best friends didn't kiss each other. Even more, they shouldn't want to. And what was with the way he'd been looking at me? Had he always done that and I'd just never noticed? Was it something new?

I tossed myself back against the couch and sighed. The stress of my first independent bake must have been doing things to me. Rubbing my face with my hands, I decided to sleep it off.

I quickly washed my face and changed into pj's before crawling into bed. I was just about to shut off the light when I noticed the picture on my bedside table. It was the silver-framed photo of Kyle and me at his company's Christmas party the year before. A strange sensation came over me. It wasn't the deep sadness I would have expected. It was more like this vast emptiness, like a void opened up inside my chest. I glanced around the room and noticed all of the other things Kyle had left behind. I'd delayed getting rid of his things in the hopes he would change his mind and ask if we could talk, but that had been months ago. He would have contacted me by now if he was going to.

Throwing back the covers, I grabbed a spare gift bag I'd saved and threw Kyle's things into it. I didn't even stop to think. I just picked up whatever reminded me of him and threw it in.

I must have been more ready to purge Kyle than I'd thought, because an hour later, everything that reminded me of him was ready for the trash. Clothes that had been neatly folded in drawers were now thrown haphazardly around the room. Empty photo frames dotted my table and dresser. It looked like a storm had ripped through my room, but I didn't care.

I opened my bedroom door as quietly as possible and tiptoed across the living room and out into the hall before my movements woke Derek. Once the apartment door was closed behind me, I marched to the garbage chute and tossed everything inside. I held the chute door open until I heard the bags land at the bottom with a satisfying thump.

I felt myself grow taller as an unknown weight lifted from my shoulders. Who would have guessed throwing stuff out would make me feel so much better?

I tiptoed back to my room and crawled into bed. Things were officially starting over as of now, and I, for one, couldn't have been happier.

Chapter Twelve

I WAS STARTING to think that our kitchen would never be clean again, but I wasn't complaining. The near-constant stream of batter and frosting flowing through it was the kind of problem I wanted to have. In the month since delivering Mrs. Montoya's cake, my phone had been ringing off the hook.

That stream of work consisted of mostly small projects. One three-tier cake required renting out a commercial space for a few days, but the majority could be done in my apartment. While having the work was great, it meant our kitchen counters were covered with baking equipment. I did my best to put everything away at the end of the day, but it didn't always work. The fridge situation wasn't much better. Derek managed to buy a secondhand mini fridge from one of his coworkers, but it didn't hold much. We'd resorted to keeping only the bare essentials around and picking up one or two things as we needed them. It wasn't ideal, but it was working.

"Hey, Als," Derek called as he came through the door.

I looked up from the cupcake I was working on to see him returning from one of the extra workouts he'd started doing over the last few weeks.

One of the side effects of us not having as much kitchen to work with while baking was eating out. A lot. Derek loved a greasy burger as much as the next guy, but he wasn't keen on what it was doing to his body.

"Hey." I returned my attention to the cupcake.

Things had been a little tense after our almost kiss. Well, more than a little. The only thing I could focus on any time Derek was near me was his mouth and the way he smelled. I tried to cover it as best I could, but the thought of what his lips would feel like on mine was becoming a real pain in the ass. It wasn't easy to roll out fondant when all you could think about was your roommate's plump lower lip.

"What are you working on now?" he asked, making his way toward the sink for a glass of water.

"Just some cupcakes. Nothing too fancy."

He downed his water and moved to stand beside me. Ugh. Even sweaty and gross, he still managed to smell amazing.

"They sure look fancy to me."

I focused on the daisy cupcake in my hand. He had a point. Most people didn't think of bouquets of flowers when they ordered a dozen cupcakes, and while making them wasn't complicated, it was tedious.

"How many orders do you have now?"

I thought for a minute. "I've got two more lined up after this one."

"That's awesome!" Derek beamed.

I couldn't help but preen at the pride in his voice.

"Brooke said the same thing." A thought shot into my brain at the mention of my former coworker, and I stifled a groan. "Brooke and I had lunch today, and she said she wants us to all go clubbing this weekend."

"Really?" Derek asked in amazement. "She does realize you have two left feet, right?"

I shot him a mocking glare. He just smiled and leaned on the counter beside me while I filled him in on the conversation. Brooke had been so excited when I'd told her I'd had to turn away an order when I couldn't rent out the kitchen to do it that she'd nearly ruptured my eardrums with her squealing.

"She says she wants to celebrate my newfound success." I rolled my eyes and focused on the next cupcake.

Derek looked down at the counter. His eyebrows drew together while he puzzled out whatever was churning in his brain. He was probably trying to find a nice way to say no. Never, in all the years I had known him, had Derek been into the club scene. It just wasn't his thing. His idea of going out was heading to a sports bar with the guys to shoot pool while they watched the game.

"I think it's a great idea."

My head snapped in his direction so fast I wasn't sure I didn't have whiplash.

"Seriously?"

Derek went to fix himself another glass of water. He guzzled it down before setting it in the sink and turning back to face me. "You've been working hard. A night out might do us all some good."

My eyebrows rose up my forehead. "So, you actually want to spend the night at a club with me and Brooke?"

"Yeah. Besides, somebody has to keep an eye on you two. There's no telling what kind of trouble you'd cause if I left you unsupervised. New York might not survive it."

The cheekiest grin in history took over his face. I did my best to send him an angry glare, but the way he wiggled his eyebrows had me laughing too hard to make it convincing. Derek chuckled before making his way to the shower to get cleaned up before dinner, insisting we have something that looked more like a vegetable than a grease trap for once.

"I'll get this cleaned up, and you can chop vegetables to your little heart's content."

He sent me a wink and disappeared behind the bathroom door. I shook my head at his antics and went back to finishing up my order.

* * *

I'D BEEN STANDING in front of my full-length mirror in my underwear for the last ten minutes holding one dress up in front of me and then the other. Half my closet was flung around the room. I'd taken things out and put them back so many times it was ridiculous, but I'd finally narrowed it down to two options. Problem was, I couldn't make up my mind.

I was just about to toss the dresses aside and start over when I heard a knock on my bedroom door.

"Hey, Als, you about ready to...?" Derek had cracked my door open, but he stopped short when he saw me.

It wasn't the first time something like this had happened. You couldn't live with somebody for as long as we had without occasionally seeing too much skin.

The fact I was in my underwear barely registered as I took him in. Derek looked good. Very good. The dark jeans and white button-down with the sleeves rolled to the elbow turned him from my best friend to some sort of cover model. He looked like one of the guys on the front of those fitness magazines. Well, minus the baby oil.

The sound of Derek stammering as he backed out of the room snapped me back to reality.

"S-sorry." He gestured to the door. "I'll just be outside."

"Hold on." I pushed my uncomfortable thoughts about how gorgeous he looked aside and turned to face him. "Which one should I wear? This one?"

I held the dark-green dress in front of me. It wasn't my favorite, but

I had to admit it looked good on me. The long sleeves made it more elegant, and the feeling of the velvety material against my skin was a nice bonus too.

"Or this one?" I switched to a shimmering royal-blue sheath that I'd bought off a clearance rack on a whim a few weeks ago.

The one-shoulder dress didn't have much in the way of embellishments, but the color seemed to change from blue to black and back again depending on how the light hit it. It was a bit shorter than I usually wore, coming only to about mid-thigh, but I'd loved the color so much that I'd bought it anyway.

Derek crossed his arms over his chest, and my eyes zeroed in on his biceps. They looked like they were about to rip his sleeves apart. When did he get so buff? I mean, I knew Derek was fit, but damn.

"Als?"

I startled. "Huh?"

He grinned at me. "The other one?"

"Oh." I looked down, hoping my face didn't show just how embarrassed I was at being caught ogling, and held the other back up.

"Wear the blue one," he said. "It brings out your eyes."

My eyes shot up to meet his.

"Don't take too much longer, okay? We need to head out soon if we're gonna meet Brooke on time."

I nodded. "I'll just be a minute."

Derek returned the gesture before stepping out and closing the door. I tossed the green dress onto the bed and stepped into the one Derek had chosen. Giving myself a once-over in the mirror, I had to admit Derek was right. This one did make my eyes look brighter. There was one problem with it though, and I didn't realize it was an issue until we were waiting in line to get into the club. It was silk, and silk was freaking cold.

A shiver ran through me. Maybe this dress was not the best idea after all. Why hadn't I at least grabbed a jacket on my way out the door?

I groaned and tried shifting my weight to relieve some of the pain in the balls of my feet. These heels were proving to be just as bad of an idea as the dress was. They were fine as long as I didn't have to stay in one place for too long, but standing in line for nearly an hour to get in was not doing me any favors. A recent change in weather had caused my allergies to act up, and a headache was forming behind my left eye. Add that to the fact that I was certain my feet were swelling, and my night was getting off to a bang-up start.

"Don't you know somebody that works here?" Brooke asked.

Derek shrugged.

"Can't you call them and tell them to let us in or something?"

"No." Derek leaned on the supports for the velvet rope keeping us all in line and sighed. "I already told you that they said they were full." He motioned to the security guy standing watch at the front door. "There's a limit to how many people they can let in at a time. Fire code and all that."

Brooke groaned and leaned back against the dividers. She crossed her arms over her chest, the action causing the plunging neckline of her red dress to slide down just enough to show her bra.

"Umm, Brooke."

She looked at me.

"You may want to, uh…" I pointed my finger at her chest and drew a little circle in the air.

She looked down.

"Dang it." She uncrossed her arms and adjusted the dress. "I hate this thing."

"Then why did you wear it?" Derek asked with a laugh.

"Because I make this look good." She gave him an incredulous look and held her arms out to her sides, looking down at herself and back at Derek, challenging him to say otherwise.

We were eventually allowed inside, and the sudden contrast in light and volume made me want to walk right back out. Going from the soft glow of streetlights to neon signs, lasers, and strobe lights hurt. Even after my eyes adjusted, the bass was so loud it rattled my bones.

I took in the space. Most of the strobes and lasers came from the massive dance floor in the center. A few random booths and tables along the edges had their own mini lamps. The bar on the opposite side looked like the only peaceful place in the building. The whole thing was lit with this soothing blue light that was in stark contrast to the rest of the club's rave-like atmosphere. A wave of relief washed over me when Brooke took my arm and dragged me toward the bar instead of the overcrowded dance floor.

"Come on," she said. "It's time to get this party started."

Taking a deep breath, I looked back at Derek with a *wish me luck* expression before following my friend to the bar.

Clubbing wasn't new to Brooke. While she may not have gone out every weekend, she knew the scene well. She used to come into work telling me about her wild adventures and the insane people she'd met. I sent up a silent prayer that tonight wouldn't be anything like the stories I'd heard. The last thing I needed was to be so out of it that I woke up the next morning with gaps in my memory.

"What can I get you?" the bartender asked as Brooke and I slid up to the bar.

It was everything I could do not to roll my eyes at the way Brooke leaned into the bar and shamelessly flirted with him.

"Can I get a couple of redheaded sluts for me and my friend here?" She leaned in even closer.

The bartender cast a quick glance my way. I frowned at him.

He looked back over to Brooke with a smile. "Sure thing."

He sent Brooke a wink and a smirk before wandering off to get our drinks. She turned to me with a victorious smile.

"What did you just get us?" I asked.

"Only the best shot in existence."

My eyes rolled to the back of my head as the bartender returned with our shots. Brooke promptly handed one to me. I eyed the red liquid in the glass suspiciously. It had been a long time since I'd had anything more serious than a beer, and jumping straight in with a shot seemed like a bit much if I didn't want to wake up tomorrow with my underwear on my head.

"To making it on your own." Brooke raised her shot glass into the air.

Taking a deep breath, I threw caution to the wind and raised my glass to meet hers. "To making it on your own."

We tapped our glasses together and threw back the red liquid. I braced myself for the harsh taste and burn I associated with shots, but it never came. A sweet candy flavor tingled its way over my tongue. *It tastes like Twizzlers!*

"Wow! That's good!" I shouted over the music.

"I know, right!" Brooke exclaimed. "They're my favorite."

I tilted the now empty shot glass toward the bartender to ask for another round. The man tipped his chin upward in recognition and made us two more. We knocked those back just as quickly as we had the first. The fact that I barely drank became abundantly clear to me when I could already feel myself warming up before Brooke had finished ordering us another.

The shot was about halfway to my lips when it magically disappeared from my hand.

"Whoa." Derek held the shot glass away from me. "Easy, tiger. I don't want to have to scrape you off the floor later."

I pursed my lips. "Very funny, Derek. Now give me my drink."

I reached for the shot glass, but he easily blocked my hand. I watched in horror as he drank the shot.

"Hey! That was mine!"

It was one thing for him to take a swig of my beer at the house, but you didn't just take a girl's shot from her without asking first.

"Oh God!" He grimaced. "That thing is straight sugar. What is this?"

"A redheaded slut," Brooke said cheerfully. "And what do you think you're doing, taking her shot? This is her party. You should let the girl have fun."

"And I will," he countered. "I just don't want her to regret it in the morning."

I put my hand on his arm to draw his attention back to me and assured him I would be fine. It was sweet the way he worried about me. Really, it was. I just didn't want him to think he had to play watchdog all night and not have any fun of his own.

I ordered myself a Mai Tai and hopped onto a barstool to give my aching feet a much-needed rest.

Derek opened his mouth to argue, but the sound of someone calling his name from across the bar drew his attention.

"Yo, Derek!"

We turned toward the sound to see one of the other bartenders flagging him down while making his way over from the other side of the bar.

"Ryan!" Derek hollered back. "What's up?"

Derek signaled he would be right back before sauntering over to say hello to his friend.

It took me a moment to recognize Ryan without his sweatpants and backward baseball cap. He was one of Derek's workout buddies. He'd been over to the apartment a time or two after he and Derek had played one of their pickup games at the Y.

A hand on my shoulder pulled my attention away from Derek and his friend.

"Girl, look," Brooke said.

I followed the direction of her nod toward one of the tables on the far side of the club. "That man has been eyein' you since we walked through the door."

How could she even tell? It was too dark to see anything. All I could make out were vague shadows and outlines. "Where?"

Brooke downed the rest of her drink. Setting it aside, she stood behind me and pointed to a small booth off to the side of the dance floor with a small group of laughing guys with drinks in front of them. I squinted to get a better look. They were about our age, maybe younger, but I didn't see any of them watching me. I was about to tell Brooke she was seeing things when one of the men gave me a wave. I felt a blush creeping up my neck as I gave him a little wave of my own.

He was cute. At least, I thought he was, from what I could make out in the flashes of light from the dance floor. His black T-shirt showed off his athletic build. I couldn't tell how tall he was, but if the way his legs were stretched out in front of him was any indication, he wasn't short.

He winked at me, and I quickly turned back to the bar before he could see my face turn scarlet. A subtle acknowledgment of each other was one thing. Being caught blatantly checking the guy out was something else altogether.

I picked up my Mai Tai and finished it off in one giant gulp before ordering another.

"Is he still looking?" I asked.

Brooke leaned against the side of the bar and turned her head in his direction. "Yep." She popped the *p* for added emphasis. "Still watching."

I hung my head in my hands. "This is so embarrassing."

"Why?"

"He caught me staring, Brooke!"

She shrugged. "So. He was staring too. The way I see it, you were both staring, so there's no reason for anybody to be embarrassed about anything."

I leaned my head on my fist and sipped my new drink through the little stir straw.

"You should go talk to him."

I shot up in my seat with my eyes as wide as dinner plates. She had to be kidding. There was no way I would go over and chat up some random guy. I shook my head.

"Well, fine then." Brooke's shoulders slumped in defeat. "At least come dance with me. There's no sense in you holding up the bar all night. Come on."

She grabbed my hand and yanked me onto my feet. The combination of sudden movement and the not-so-sure-how-many drinks had me wobbling around like some sort of baby animal, and the tiny balance pegs I called shoes were not helping. I kept my eyes on the floor to make sure my feet could find it.

"Where are you guys going?"

I looked up to see Derek making his way toward us.

"We're gonna go dance," Brooke shouted. "Ally's too chicken to go talk to those guys over there, so I'm dragging her ass to the floor for some fun."

"What guys?"

There was a subtle shift in Derek's tone. He narrowed his eyes and scanned the crowd like he was looking for something, but I couldn't for the life of me figure out what.

I took a step toward the guys Brooke had pointed out earlier and nearly landed on my face.

"Whoa." Derek caught my arm to steady me. "How many drinks have you had, Als?"

At least two Mai Tais and three shots. *Wait. Or was it four?*

I giggled. "I don't know."

Derek's frown deepened. "Maybe you should sit this one out. Come on. Let me get you some water." He led me back to the bar and did some sort of weird hand-wavy thing to someone behind it.

"Derek." I pulled my arm loose. "I'm fiiine."

I didn't spare him another glance before following Brooke onto the dance floor. I heard him calling my name, but I ignored it. It was sweet the way he worried about me, but I deserved a night of fun once in a while. My life had been hell for a while, and now that it was finally turning around, I was determined to have at least one good night to celebrate.

It was hot on the dance floor. The smell of alcohol and sweat was so overpowering it was unreal, but the music thrumming through my body seemed to cut through it all. I let myself get carried away in a sea of people. The strobe lights raced around the room, carrying me away on a cloud of euphoria I hadn't felt in years.

I wasn't much of a dancer—I never had been—but the alcohol running through my system made me not care. I was relaxed and free. To hell with anything else.

The light weight of a hand landing on my hip barely registered until I found myself being spun around. I blinked a few times to stop the room from spinning. Regaining my balance, I looked up to see the guy from the table smiling down at me. He was even better looking up close. He had the kind of naturally bronze skin people paid hundreds of dollars at tanning salons to imitate. His dark hair was slicked back, but I could still see the curl in it. The man was gorgeous!

Table man took my hand and started dancing with me. At least he tried to. My abilities stopped at the Macarena. Add in the heels, and the fact that I managed to stay off my face was impressive. My partner was most definitely the reason for it. He led me through turns and spins that would have made Patrick Swayze proud.

He turned me so my back was facing his front. I let my head fall onto his shoulder as he pulled me closer. This was heaven. Turned out Brooke was right. This was what I needed. A night of unabashed fun with zero worries about tomorrow to just let myself go.

Something slid across my hip and made its way to my ass. It took my brain a moment to realize it was a hand. My eyes flew open. What was I supposed to do? I was dancing with the guy in the middle of a crowded floor. He wouldn't try anything. Not with this many people around.

That was when his hand gave my backside an almost painful squeeze.

"Hey," I shouted over the music, "watch it. We're just dancing."

I tried to step away, but the arm around my waist tightened, forcing me back against him. A ripple of terror ran through me. This was bad.

The guy buried his nose in my hair and started whispering all the things he would do to me once he had me alone.

My heart beat in double time. My eyes darted around the room for any sign of help, but the other dancers were too lost in their own worlds to recognize what was happening in mine.

The hand around my waist tightened again, fingers flexing against my side to the point of pain.

"Let go!" I shouted.

I tried again to wriggle out of his grasp, but his arm was like an iron bar holding me in place. My stomach churned when his hot breath fanned across the back of my neck. Where was Brooke? A tear formed in the corner of my eye. This was it. This was the moment my life as I knew it would end.

"I think she told you to leave her alone."

I took in a shuddering gasp of air. I knew that voice. The arm around my midsection vanished, and I turned to find Derek standing in the middle of the dance floor, glaring down at the man who'd been holding me hostage. He'd crossed his arms over his chest, allowing his muscles to strain against the fabric of his shirt. Derek only had an inch or so on the guy, but he was using every millimeter of it to his advantage. Add that to the murderous glint in his eye, and I was ready to run for the hills. I could only imagine what the guy in front of me was thinking.

"Who are you?" the dancer scoffed. "Her boyfriend or something?"

It was meant to sound cavalier, but there was no denying the tiny tremble in his voice. Not that I blamed him. I'd never seen Derek look this intimidating before.

"Something like that." Derek dropped his arms and took a menacing step forward. "Now beat it."

I held my breath as the two men stared each other down. A few people had stopped to watch the exchange, waiting to see if a fight would break out in the middle of the dance floor. While Derek was imposing, the guy I'd been dancing with didn't look like a pushover. Derek was taller, but this guy was bulkier. He looked like he might have about twenty pounds on Derek, but my money would still have been on my best friend. I'd seen Derek when he was pissed off, and I didn't care how much of a badass you were, Derek Peters was not someone you wanted to tangle with.

The tense moment between them dragged on for what felt like an eternity. My heart thumped so loud in my ears that it drowned out the music. I wanted to run, but my feet refused to take the message.

"Pfft," the man scoffed, taking a step back. He gave me a once-over before turning his attention back to Derek. "She ain't worth it."

My shoulders sagged as I watched him stalk away. My entire body felt like a rubber band that had been stretched to its limit and was finally let go. I took in what felt like my first breath of air in ages. My legs started shaking. I was going to pass out.

"Hey. Hey. Hey. It's all right." Derek's arms closed around me, pulling me against his strong chest. "You okay?"

I nodded.

"See why I didn't want you out here?"

I let myself sink into him, into the safe warm feeling being near him gave me.

"Ah!" I yelped when Derek grabbed me by the waist and spun me around.

I found my footing and looked back at him over my shoulder with a frown as he casually draped his arm around my waist and started swaying with me.

"Derek, what are you…?"

He moved a step closer. "We've got an audience," he said in my ear.

I stared up at him in confusion. He gave a subtle gesture in the direction my former partner had gone. I followed his gaze to see the man leaning against a pole, watching us like a hawk. I froze.

"W-what do we do?" I stammered.

I held back a shudder when I felt Derek's lips against my exposed shoulder.

"Make it convincing," he whispered in my ear.

Thank God for Derek's fast thinking, because my brain had decided to take a holiday.

He guided one of my arms up to drape around his neck and used the other resting lightly on my hip to pull me in close. He must have felt my body tense, because the next thing I knew, he was reminding me that I was supposed to be enjoying myself.

My eyes moved from the man watching us to Derek's face. The way he gazed down at me made all the fear and doubt vanish. My stomach gave a little flip. Plastering a smile on my face, I did my best to ignore my racing heart and just enjoy the dance.

I closed my eyes and let myself get lost in the music. Derek and I moved together like we'd been dancing all our lives. The way my body fit against his was like two pieces of a puzzle joining together.

He caught me off guard with a sudden dip. My initial gasp turned into laughter by the time he brought me back up, but my laugh dissolved into silence when I saw the look in his eyes. Their usually bright-blue hue had turned into a dark midnight that stole my breath away.

The hand that had been holding on to the back of his neck slid down his chest. I could feel his heart beating against my palm, drumming out the rapid rhythm as mine.

The air around us popped and sizzled with electricity. I told myself I was imagining things. The alcohol had gone to my brain. He wasn't looking at me like he wanted me. That was insane.

Derek's eyes moved across my face before settling on my lips, and I couldn't help the tiny whimper I made when his tongue darted to moisten his lips.

That was all it took for what was left of my alcohol-laden brain to override my senses and let my body take the lead. I leaned forward a fraction of an inch. But instead of closing the space between us, Derek let his hands fall away from me and took a step back.

"The, uh"—he cleared his throat—"the guy's gone."

I looked over his shoulder to see our captive audience of one had indeed vanished.

He sighed. "I need a drink."

He was already halfway to the bar by the time his words registered. I hid my face behind one of my hands. I had to get a grip on myself before I did something stupid and ruined the most important relationship in my life.

Deciding a drink sounded like a great idea, I pushed my way toward the bar. I hopped onto the barstool next to Derek, and we proceeded to sit through what was probably the most awkward silence we'd ever shared.

I didn't know what to say. What could I say? *Hey, sorry I almost kissed you back there. I've just been thinking about you a lot lately, and the alcohol took control of me.* Yeah. That was a great idea.

"Hey there."

We both looked up to find a beautiful blond woman standing beside Derek. I gave her a quick appraisal and decided the only thing real about her was her shoes. Her dress accentuated every curve of her impressive figure. Even if she was all plastic, she wore it well.

"Hey," Derek replied.

I tuned them out after that. My desire to watch the guy I'd nearly kissed leave with someone else was zero. No, instead I would get good and snockered and maybe see if Brooke would let me crash on her couch for the evening so I wouldn't run the risk of listening to their sexcapades all night long.

I downed the rest of my drink and put the glass down on the counter.

"Want another one?"

I turned to see Derek still sitting beside me. Alone. "What happened to peroxide Barbie?"

Derek snorted and shook his head before signaling the bartender to bring us another round. "Not my type. Besides, what kind of guy would I be if I left my best friend flying solo all night long?"

I smiled. "Brooke's still here."

"I think she's a bit preoccupied."

Derek gestured toward the dance floor where Brooke was living it up in the middle of a dance circle.

"You've got a point there," I said with a laugh. I thanked the bartender as he sat another drink down in front of me. "Still, it's okay if you want to go. I won't mind."

I didn't look at him while I said it. I couldn't. I was too afraid that I'd look up to see a pitying expression on his face, and that would hurt worse than watching him leave with some blonde bimbo ever could.

The light touch of Derek's hand on top of mine drew my attention back to his face. A small quiver of fear ran through me until I saw his soft, adoring expression.

"There's nowhere else I'd rather be, Als." His voice was just loud enough for the two of us to hear. "I promise."

He held up his glass in salute, and I tapped mine against it while butterflies did ballet in my stomach. I downed the majority of my drink in one go before signaling for another. If he was going to keep sitting next to me looking at me like that for the rest of the night, I would need a lot more drinks.

* * *

I WASN'T DRUNK. Okay, yes. Maybe I'd had a few too many at the club, but I wasn't completely out of it. I was just a giggling hysterical mess, but so was Derek. So it was fine.

"Did you see that guy's face when I told him to back off?" Derek laughed. It took him a couple of tries before he was able to unlock the door. "He was freaking terrified."

I shook my head. I hadn't seen him, but I had seen Derek. "You were pretty scary looking." I stumbled through the door and tried to kick off my shoes without bending over. Just standing up to get out of the car had made my head spin, so I doubted bending over would have been much better.

My first shoe dropped right beside me, but the second one went sailing into the kitchen. I covered my mouth with my hand to stifle my giggle.

I took another step forward and caught my foot in the strap of my first shoe.

Everything moved in slow motion. I could see the floor rising up to meet me, but I couldn't stop falling. I slammed my eyes shut and waited for the impact. Instead, I felt my arm being yanked in the opposite direction before I collided with something solid.

My eyes cracked open. Instead of the scuffed wood floor, I was staring at a wall of white fabric. My gaze trailed upward to Derek's crystal-blue eyes.

He didn't look away. Didn't move. He just stood there, hand on my elbow, looking down at me with a dreamy expression that made my heart forget how to pump blood.

We stood there staring at each other for what felt like hours. Neither of us said a word. We just kept drinking the other in. Derek's eyes flitted toward my lips.

I took a shuffling step closer. His eyes locked with mine, and I was a goner. My hands came up to the back of his neck, drawing him down into a kiss that had my head spinning from more than just the alcohol. It was like I was floating. Everything else faded away until the only thing left was what had to be the most earth-shattering kiss in the history of the universe.

Derek's hand moved to my waist, his fingers flexing against my side. It was like a switch being thrown. All I could think about was touching every inch of him. I fumbled with his shirt buttons. I'd only gotten through a couple when I felt his hands gripping the backs of my thighs and lifting me up to wrap my legs around his waist. I linked my arms around his neck, deepening the kiss as he carried me toward his bedroom.

Chapter Thirteen

COULD SOMEONE PLEASE tell the Jamaican steel drum band giving a free concert in my skull to shut the hell up?

I felt like I was dying. Between the pounding in my head and the alcohol-soaked cotton taste in my mouth, my morning was not off to a killer start. I tried to open my eyes, but the dim light coming in from underneath the door tried to split my skull open. I closed my eyes again and tried to roll away from the light, but something solid and warm stopped me. That was when I noticed the arm draped around my waist.

My eyes flew open. I didn't remember inviting anyone back to the apartment last night. Come to think of it, I didn't remember much of anything. I racked my brain to come up with an explanation.

The hand around my waist slid along my hip. My *naked* hip. I closed my eyes and said a silent prayer before peeking under the blanket to confirm my suspicion. Birthday suit city.

"Crap."

The body behind me shifted, letting me know for a fact he was just as naked as I was.

I looked toward the bedside table to see what time it was. My clock wasn't there. That was weird. My brain must be fuzzier than I thought. I closed my eyes and took a deep breath before opening them again. Not only was my clock still not there, I wasn't even looking at my table.

I whimpered.

My eyes darted around the room for any clue to where I was. There weren't any windows, so I couldn't even tell if I was still in the city. My heart raced. I was screwed. Not only had I slept with some stranger, I'd let him drag me off to God knows where.

I glanced around the room for my clothes. If I could just find my dress, then maybe I could sneak out and find my way back home.

I'd just started to lift the arm around my waist when I noticed an all-too-familiar autographed Tom Brady jersey in a frame on the far wall. My breathing stopped. I looked around the room to find other familiar things. A pair of worn-out sneakers by the door. A polo shirt with a gym logo hanging on the closet door. A photo of a family I knew all too well sitting on top of the beat-up old dresser.

I slammed my eyes shut. Images from the night before rolled over me. Derek kissing me. Us giggling like idiots when he nearly crushed me as we fell onto the bed. I covered my face with my hands and shook my head. Maybe it would work like the Etch-A-Sketch my grandmother kept around for me to play with. If I shook my head hard enough, I could erase the last eight hours.

"Morning," Derek said in a gruff, early morning tone.

I took in a sharp breath, my body going rigid. "M-morning."

Rolling onto my back, I took in the sight of Derek's sleep-tousled hair and early morning stubble. He looked good. I mean, really good. Nobody who had been out drinking the night before had any right to look that good.

I groaned. Not only had I had a drunken one-night stand with my best friend, now I was ogling him as well. What was wrong with me?

Derek let out his own groan of protest. "How's your head?" he asked me, his voice ten decibels too loud for my current state.

"Hurts."

He nodded. "We need coffee and pancakes."

The mention of food made my stomach remember that the majority of what it held was little more than poison. I shut my eyes and tried to hold back the bile making its way up my throat. "I'm not sure I can eat."

Derek squeezed his eyes shut tight. "I know, but we've got to eat something. Why don't you go get in the shower, and I'll make us some breakfast, okay?"

I nodded, regretting the decision when my head swam. I pulled the blanket up to my chin and tried to make myself as little as possible so Derek wouldn't see me. I knew I was being ridiculous considering what we'd done the night before, but the tiny shield it gave me made me feel better about the situation. That was, of course, until the sheet slid away from Derek's body to give me a perfect view of his naked ass. He bent over to grab a pair of shorts off the floor, and I had to bite my lip to stifle a moan.

Oh God. What was I thinking?

I turned my head in the opposite direction and waited until I heard the door closing behind him.

"Hell." I groaned.

Sleeping with my best friend and ogling his naked ass. The craziness running through my brain was too much to deal with during a hangover.

Pushing myself into a seated position, I ran a hand down my face and tried to sort through the chaos in my head. I threw on one of Derek's shirts that I found on the floor. At least it would cover my butt when I darted to my room.

Once safely hidden behind my own bedroom door, I pieced together the night before while making my way to the shower.

I clearly remembered Derek carrying me to his room, but I couldn't remember how we got home. It was funny how some details were fuzzy, while others were so vivid that I could practically feel Derek's hand gliding along my skin, and the way he...

"No, Ally. Don't go there."

I forced the memory aside. The last thing I needed was to be thinking about how good my best friend was in bed while I tried to wash the scent of him off my skin, even if it had been the best sex I'd ever had.

Damn it! Why can't I stop thinking about him?

I shut the water off and stepped out of the shower. I took my time patting myself dry and putting on clothes. The thought of facing Derek felt like going to the executioner's block. He'd been my best friend for as long as I could remember. He was the only one who'd stood by me when I dropped out of college to go to culinary school. The thought that this little misadventure might have somehow ruined the most important relationship in my life hurt worse than dipping my hand in boiling sugar.

The smell of butter and sugar greeted me when I worked up the courage to leave my room. I padded to the kitchen and took my seat at the bar just as Derek was placing the last of the pancakes onto a plate. Butter and syrup waited in front of me, along with the perfect cup of coffee. He placed a stack of pancakes on the bar top.

"Eat up." He sat next to me and started devouring his own plate.

I tried to enjoy my breakfast, but the only thing I could focus on was the awkward tension filling the room. I knew we had to address the elephant in the bed sheets if we stood any chance of keeping our friendship, but if this silence was any indication, talking about it was not something either of us was looking forward to.

"So..." I swirled a chunk of pancake in the syrup on my plate, "about last night..."

"Yeah…" Derek took a long sip of coffee before setting his mug back on the counter. "It was pretty wild, huh?"

"Yeah."

I kept my eyes trained on my plate. This was the most uncomfortable situation I'd ever been in. I should just come out and say it. *We slept together.* There. Done. But every time I tried to speak, my lips clamped even tighter.

"Well…" Derek's voice broke me out of my trance. "I'm gonna go get in the shower. I'm supposed to meet some of the guys for a pickup game. We might go get pizza after. You have any plans?"

Sitting in the same spot and worrying that we'd ruined our friendship sounded like a reasonable option.

"No. Not really."

He nodded. It wasn't until he took his dishes to the sink that I realized he wasn't going to say anything about last night. In fact, he was acting like it'd never happened.

"Just take it easy today. Okay, Als?" He placed a hand on my shoulder as he passed, and I looked up into the same warm, caring eyes I always saw waiting for me. "You've earned it."

The warmth in his expression made me think that maybe we hadn't ruined things after all.

"Okay."

Derek started to bend toward me, and I thought he was going to kiss me. My heart pounded. Maybe I'd been reading everything wrong. Maybe he didn't say anything because he didn't think we needed to talk. Maybe he wanted this. Wanted me.

He moved his hand to the back of my head and placed a chaste kiss on my forehead. It was the kind of kiss a brother gave his little sister. Not something you would expect from the person you just spent the night with.

I sat there like a dazed idiot as Derek got ready to leave. He gave me a quick wave as he headed out the door. I rested my head on the counter with a sigh.

"Good talk, Ally. Good talk."

* * *

BROOKE PICKED UP the steaming mug of coffee. Taking a sip, she closed her eyes and moaned in pleasure before sinking back into the couch.

"No offense, Brooke," I told her, "but you look like shit."

She'd called me about an hour ago saying that her hot water tank was busted, so I'd offered to let her come use my shower. She'd shown up looking like she'd just crawled out of someone else's grave. She was still wearing her club dress. Her hair was a giant rat's nest, and the black smears of last night's mascara paraded over her face.

"Gee thanks." She took another sip of coffee and groaned. "I never should have had that fifth shot of tequila after you guys left."

I snorted in agreement.

"How's your head doing?"

"Better," I told her. "Derek got up and made pancakes this morning."

"Carbs and caffeine." Brooke raised her mug in a toast.

"Carbs and caffeine." We clinked our mugs together, Brooke wincing at the harsh sound.

We downed the rest of our cups before she shuffled toward my bathroom. I turned on the TV and found an old sitcom while I waited for her, hoping some mindless entertainment would keep my mind off Derek.

Maybe I was reading too much into things. There was no reason for me to think that what happened was anything other than a drunken roll in the sheets. He'd never shown any interest in me before, so there was no reason he should start now.

Brooke emerged from the bathroom an hour later in a pair of sweats I loaned her and a towel wrapped around her head. "So, how'd you and Derek end up making out last night?"

"What?" I nearly spit my coffee across the room.

Her choice of words had to be a coincidence. She couldn't have known about what happened. I didn't have any hickeys or stubble burn. I'd checked.

"After you left, what did you guys do?"

"Uh..."

I tried to come up with something other than the truth, but all I could think about was the way Derek's skin had felt against mine. My temperature rose just thinking about it.

"Oh. My. God." Brooke clearly noticed the blush on my cheeks. "Girl, you better start talking right now. Did you meet somebody? Derek caught him sneaking out this morning, didn't he? Oh, I bet that was a hoot."

"No. No." I held up a hand to stop her raving. "I didn't bring anyone home."

"Then what? Nobody's face gets that red for no reason. So spill it. What did you two get up to last night?"

Did I wanted to tell Brooke? She would make it out to be this big deal when I didn't know what it was myself. Derek had acted like nothing had happened this morning. I'd hoped that it was something more, but that was clearly just my imagination.

"Ally..." For somebody who never wanted kids, she sure had a good mom voice.

I put my face in my hands. "Ve swft tgeder."

"What?"

I let my hands fall limply into my lap. "We slept together."

There was a moment of silence where I wondered if she'd had a stroke. Her mouth hung open, and her eyes bulging out of their sockets made her look like one of those crazy insects on *Animal Planet*.

"You *what!*" The volume of her voice made us both flinch.

Now, this was the reaction I expected. She couldn't have looked more shocked if I'd told her we went streaking through Central Park with an escaped tiger chasing us.

My face was on fire. I looked at my lap and fidgeted with the hem of my shirt. "I...I, uh, I kinda slept with Derek."

Another moment of silence. When I looked at her, the grin spreading across her face was so wide, I was surprised her face hadn't split.

"Oh my God!" She launched herself at me, knocking us both back on the couch while she wrapped me in a giant bear hug. "Tell me everything."

She pulled away. "How was it? Was it good? I bet it was good. There is no way a man can do what he does for a living and not know how to work his body. How many times did he get you off?"

"Brooke!" I looked away in hopes that my blush wouldn't become permanent.

"What? Did you not like it?"

I pushed off the couch and made my way toward the kitchen to get another cup of coffee. "I don't really wanna talk about it."

"Oh no you don't." She was off the couch and stalking toward me in an instant. "There's no way you get to drop a bombshell like that and just walk off, Allyson Marie. So you best start talking."

She put her hands on her hips and leveled me with a stare that could melt polar ice caps. My shoulders slumped in defeat. I told her everything. I started with the guy harassing me and went all the way through to Derek and me falling into bed after he'd kept me from smashing my face on the floor.

"Wow," Brooke said after a brief pause. "Th-that's..."

"Insane," I offered.

"Freaking awesome!"

I jumped at the increase in volume. "Wait, what?"

Brooke rolled her eyes. "This is good, Ally. I've always thought he was better for you than that asshole, Kyle. Now that you've finally gotten over yourselves and admitted how much you like each other, maybe..." She came up short when she saw the confused look on my face. "What?"

"We're not together, Brooke." I dumped what was left of my coffee in the sink and rinsed my mug.

"What do you mean you're not together? You had sex, didn't you?"

"Well yes, but..."

"Then what's the problem?"

How was I supposed to answer that question when I didn't even understand it myself?

I took a deep breath and recounted everything that had transpired at breakfast and how Derek and Ally, two best friends who shared an apartment, just so happened to have drunken sex one night. That was all.

"You mean to tell me that neither of you brought it up?"

I shook my head.

"Why the hell not?"

"Because I don't want to risk losing my best friend!"

I jumped when the apartment door opened. I'd been so focused on my conversation with Brooke and the swirling thoughts in my head that I hadn't even heard the key in the lock.

Derek walked into the apartment looking at the whole world like nothing could bother him. A fine sheen of sweat was visible on his skin, but he looked as relaxed and at peace as I'd ever seen him.

"Oh hey, Brooke." He dropped his keys on the coffee table. "How's it going?"

If Derek noticed the awkward tension, he didn't show it. He smiled and carried on like he had that morning. Everything was normal. No need to draw attention to anything unusual.

Brooke threw me a sideways glance before turning her attention back to Derek.

"Just nursing a hangover," she said.

Derek chuckled. "Yeah. Crazy night, huh?"

My jaw clenched as I tried to keep myself in check.

"I'm gonna go get cleaned up. See ya in a bit."

I deflated against the counter. How much longer would I have to do this? Pretending nothing had happened was becoming worse than the nonstop daydreaming I'd been doing.

"Girl..." Brooke shook her head. "You're in trouble."

I let my chin fall to my chest. "Don't I know it."

* * *

JUST EXACTLY HOW long could two people go without addressing the fact that they'd slept together? I didn't know, but Derek and I were apparently trying to go for the record. Tension crept into every interaction we had. We weren't talking as much. Instead of looking me in the eye when he did say something, he looked over my shoulder or the top of my head.

Part of me wished I could go back in time and erase our night in bed. Not only did it feel like my best friend was slipping away from me, but he was taking up even more time in my thoughts than he had before. I could hardly look at him without some flash of memory or brief daydream interrupting my train of thought.

I'd nearly choked on my coffee one morning when Derek came walking out of his bedroom in nothing but a pair of boxer briefs with the sexiest case of bed head I had ever seen. I mean, it wasn't like I hadn't seen him like that before. He walked out of his bedroom in just his underwear all the time in the morning. But now I couldn't just wave it off with a simple "good morning" and go about my day, because I knew what he looked like without them. I knew what it felt like to kiss him and feel that glorious skin against mine. How was a girl supposed to concentrate on anything else with that playing on IMAX in her brain?

"Hey," Derek muttered as he shuffled toward the steaming pot of coffee I'd just finished making.

"Hey."

The all-too-familiar tension settled over us again. Our usual morning conversation had devolved into a lingering silence that I didn't know how to break, and it was driving me insane.

"Okay. This is ridiculous," Derek said after what felt like an eternity.

"Huh?"

Derek sat his mug on the counter and faced me, raising an eyebrow in question.

I gulped.

You'd think I'd be happy one of us had finally started the discussion, but I wasn't. A pit formed in the bottom of my stomach. This was it. The moment when my worst fear was realized, and Derek decided he couldn't be my friend anymore because we'd been drunk and naked.

"How long are we going to pretend nothing happened?" he asked.

I shrugged. "Until we're dead?"

Derek shook his head and gave a little chuckle. It was a horrible joke, but it had eased tensions a bit.

"Do you regret it?" he asked. "Sleeping with me?"

Was he seriously asking me that? I looked over to gauge his reaction and was surprised by how defeated he looked. He had his head down, and a crease had formed between his eyebrows. He was afraid I would say yes. Was he insane? I mean, he was an Adonis. With his broad shoulders and defined muscles, he was every girl's dream. I looked like the Pillsbury Doughboy standing next to him.

155

"No," I said, my voice strong and confident. "Do you?"

My stomach rolled. For a moment, I wished we could go back to pretending nothing had happened. No matter his answer, our relationship was never going to be the same after this conversation.

"No," he said, his voice just above a whisper. "No, I don't."

That dreamy look was back on his face. It made me feel drunk all over again, but I liked it. I liked it a lot.

"So…" He shuffled closer.

My throat felt tight. I took a shuddering breath.

He reached for my hand. "Do you think—?"

Someone knocking on our door put a sudden halt to our conversation. We didn't move. Maybe whoever it was would just go away if we acted like we weren't here. They knocked again, and I seriously wondered if opening the door and screaming at them to go away would be acceptable.

"Son of a…" Derek trailed off.

I couldn't quite make out the rest of what he was saying, but I was pretty sure there was an impressive string of expletives involved.

Derek wrenched the door open and froze. I tilted my head to the side to peek around him and saw Mrs. Henderson standing there with a tray of cookies in her hands.

"Oh my." Her eyes went as wide as the plate in her hand as she gave Derek a once-over.

He followed her gaze and immediately ducked behind the door.

"I-I'm sorry, Mrs. Henderson," Derek stammered, his cheeks bright red. "We weren't expecting anyone."

The old woman smiled. "That's quite alright." She fanned herself dramatically with her hand. "Well, that's more excitement than I've had in ages. I just wanted to see if you two wanted some cookies, but I can always come back later if I'm interrupting something…"

She looked knowingly between the two of us, a smirk on her lips.

Trust the little old woman to have the dirtiest mind of the three of us.

"Actually, Mrs. Henderson," I called from my spot in the kitchen, "could you come back in—"

She stepped into the apartment like she hadn't heard me.

Derek went to shut the door behind her, and she gave him another once-over. "Are you allowed to eat sugar, dear?"

Derek frowned. "Yeah. Why do you ask?"

She shrugged. "I just didn't think people like you ate this sort of thing, is all."

I couldn't stop myself from laughing at the look on Derek's face. He went from mildly confused to beet red in about three seconds. He muttered something about putting on some clothes and disappeared into his room. Mrs. Henderson watched him go with a smile on her face.

"Such a nice young man." She walked toward me.

"Yeah. He is."

I offered her a seat and a cup of coffee before taking a cookie off the plate. An appreciative moan left my mouth when that first taste of brown sugar and chocolate hit my tongue. Nobody made chocolate chip cookies better than Mrs. Henderson.

"I didn't know they made them like that," she said.

I frowned. "What?"

"That boy." She gestured to the door. "He's quite the looker. You should hurry up and say something about that little crush you have on him before he gets away."

I coughed and nearly choked on my cookie. "E-excuse me?"

"It's all right, dear. I notice these things. He likes you too. I've seen the way he looks at you. Very sweet."

I stared at my neighbor slack jawed. I couldn't believe she'd just said that.

Derek chose that moment to emerge from his room.

"So"—he picked up a cookie and took a large bite—"what did I miss?"

"Nothing much," Mrs. Henderson offered. "Just girl talk."

She smiled knowingly and patted my hand, and I nearly collapsed against the island. How hot did my blush have to be for me to start melting through the floor?

* * *

MY LATEST CLIENT, Patricia, radiated pure joy when I handed her the plain white box full of cupcakes.

"These are absolutely perfect!" she exclaimed. "Thank you so much."

"You're welcome." I opened the door and gestured toward the hallway.

Having people come to the apartment to pick up their orders still creeped me out, but after a cake nearly toppled over in the back of an Uber a few weeks ago, I'd decided that deliveries were not an option. Yes, it meant I couldn't take a catnap before cleaning up the kitchen, but it was a sacrifice I was willing to make to keep the bills paid.

"When is your store opening?" she asked.

I paused. You'd think I'd have come up with a good answer by now with the number of times I'd been asked that over the last few weeks, but my answer was always the same. I fumbled around for a minute before finally saying I didn't have a date yet. The fact that I wasn't actually working on it never came up.

Most of my projects were quick and simple ones I could do in a few hours. I only rented out a kitchen to do large cakes about once a month. Everything else was small enough I could do it from home.

"Well," Patricia said, "once you do, will you let me know? I'd love to come to the grand opening. I know a lot of people who'll be beating down the door to get ahold of one of these if they taste half as good as they look."

"Thank you." I beamed at her.

"Oh, you're welcome. Bye now."

"Bye."

She gave me one last wave before turning and heading out the door. I shut it softly behind her and looked down at the check in my hand. Not bad for a half a day's work. I took a quick glance at the clock—only 3:30. That gave me more than enough time to run the check to the bank and stop by the store to get something to make a home-cooked meal with. By that, I meant grilled cheese sandwiches and a can of tomato soup, but at least it wasn't takeout.

Hopefully, Derek and I could finish the conversation we'd started last week before Mrs. Henderson interrupted us. Every time one of us tried to start the conversation, something else would happen. A phone would ring. There'd be a commotion in the hall. Something. It was enough to make me want to scream.

I grabbed my purse and set out on my little adventure. I couldn't wait to see the look on Derek's face when he saw that I'd actually cooked something not made of flour and sugar.

I was so absorbed in my own thoughts that I didn't notice the person standing on the other side of my door until I plowed into them. They dropped their handbag, items scattering all over the floor.

"I'm so sorry." I stooped to help the woman gather her things. "I wasn't paying attention. I'm sorry. I..."

I was passing her her wallet when she finally looked at me. My eyes bulged in their sockets. "Toni? What are you doing here?"

She looked exhausted. Her normally silky black hair was frizzy and wild. The bags under her eyes had bags. She was a mess.

"I need to talk to you," she told me.

Talk? The last time I'd talked to this woman, she'd kicked me out the door. What possible reason could she have for wanting to talk to me now?

I shook my head. "I'm sorry, Toni, but I'm on my way out. Maybe you can call me later, and we can talk about whatever it is then, okay?"

I tried to usher her toward the stairs, but it was no use. Talking to a brick wall would have been a better use of my time.

Toni pushed past me and into the apartment the instant I turned to lock the door. I stood there with my mouth hanging open. In all the years I'd known her, I never would have expected her to force her way into my home. I was tempted to call the cops.

"By all means, make yourself at home," I grumbled as I walked back into the apartment and shut the door.

I didn't offer her a seat. I barely stepped back into the apartment myself. The sooner I could get her back out the door the better.

"I want you to come back to the bakery," she said

I blinked. There was no way she'd just said that.

"Excuse me?"

"I want you to come back to work for me."

"No."

Toni looked shocked. It was like me denying her had never crossed her mind. "Well," she began after regaining her composure, "where are you working now?"

"Here."

She gave me an incredulous look. "Here?"

I nodded.

She turned around to take a look at the kitchen. I could see her giving it the same critical eye she gave my workspace at the bakery. Only this time, I didn't have to wait for her inevitable insult.

"Look, Toni, I'm sorry, but I really do need to go somewhere, so if you don't mind…" I gestured toward the door, but she didn't move.

"Come back to work for me," she said again. "I'll pay you more than before."

"No." I'd had enough. I started making my way to the door. Maybe opening it would be enough for her to realize that I was serious about wanting her gone.

"Please?"

I stopped with my hand on the knob and turned. She had to be joking. There was no way this woman could actually think I would want to go back to working for her after everything she'd put me through. But the pleading look on her face said otherwise.

"You treated me like shit, Toni." I no longer cared if I kept the anger out of my voice. "You told me my work was crap and called me lazy when I couldn't keep up after everyone else quit. You belittled me every single day for years. The only reason I kept coming back was because I didn't have anywhere else to go. But you know what? I'm doing just fine right where I am. People like my work and are willing to pay me for it. So as long as I can keep paying my bills, no way in hell will I ever go back to work for you."

It wasn't until I stopped ranting that I realized how loud I'd gotten. My chest was heaving, and I was pretty sure my face was the color of an overripe tomato, but I didn't care. It felt good. No—it felt great! I'd been carrying that weight around with me for so long I hadn't even realized it was there. Now that I'd let it all out, I felt a thousand times better.

That was when I noticed the look on Toni's face. Her eyes were glassy. I knew I'd been harsh, but it was nothing compared to what she used to throw at me every day.

"Please." Her eyes were wide and desperate. "I'll let you do as many custom orders as you want. I just can't do it on my own. I need your help."

This had to be a dream. There was no way Toni was actually saying this. She'd made it clear on more than one occasion that she would rather spit on my grave than work alongside me.

"I can't spend enough time at the bakery to keep up. I..." A sob caught in her throat. "My husband is dying."

I stood there stunned as a tear ran down Toni's face. Then another. She reached into her handbag and pulled out a packet of tissues.

"Cancer," she said. "He was diagnosed three years ago. We've been to every doctor and specialist in the country, but none of them can help us. He stopped responding to treatments a few months ago, and I'm not sure how much time he has left."

Three years? A lightbulb went on in my brain. That had been about the time everything had gone to hell at the bakery. Toni had started getting short with everybody.

"That's why you were always gone," I said.

She nodded. "That's why I need you to come back. I can't be there and take care of him. I don't know how much time he has left, and I want to be there for him."

I'd only met Toni's husband once or twice, but he'd seemed like a nice man. Maybe I could go back just long enough to get them through this, then go back to doing my own thing. I started to open my mouth, then stopped. I thought about all the stress and strain the last few years had caused *me*. How many near breakdowns had Derek had to get me through? I didn't want to go back to that. I couldn't. No matter how bad I felt for Toni and her husband, I couldn't put myself through that again. I had to take care of myself.

"I'm sorry, Toni," I said. "Really, I am. I wish you guys all the best, but I can't go back to work for you."

Toni didn't say anything. She didn't even move. She just stood there, eyes watering and lip trembling, before squaring her shoulders and pulling herself together. She nodded and walked to the door.

I followed her, one question still tingling at the corner of my mind.

"Why'd you change my design?" I asked her.

She slowly turned her head towards me. Before she even opened her mouth, I could see the defeat on her face. "I ran out of time." She gave me a watery attempt at a smile. "Good luck with your bakery. You're a good artist. You'll do well."

My eyes widened before I was able to pick my jaw up off the floor and open the door for her. "Thank you, Toni. I hope you figure it all out."

I waited until she was out of view before closing the door. I fell against it with a thud. My brain couldn't seem to process what had just happened. Toni had told me I was good. Toni! The woman who'd made my life hell and treated me like a second-class citizen thought I would do well with my own bakery.

A smile slid across my face. If Toni thought I could handle it, then maybe I could. I couldn't stop the giggle that bubbled out of my throat.

All thoughts of dinner were abandoned as I raced to my room for my computer and a notebook.

* * *

"OKAY," I SAID to my empty apartment. "A standard cake uses two to three cups of flour per layer. So, a fifty-pound bag of flour would make roughly…"

I was so lost in my own little world that I didn't hear Derek's greeting. It wasn't until the couch bounced with the force of him collapsing onto it that I realized he was there.

My laptop dipped toward the floor. A jolt of panic shot through me. I waited for the inevitable crash, but Derek's hand darted out to save my precious piece of equipment. I sagged in relief. I hadn't saved everything to the cloud yet. If my computer hit the floor, that'd be it. All my work would be gone.

"Thank you."

"No problem."

I gave him an appreciative smile before turning my attention back to my computer. "Crap."

Derek's thumb must have smashed the zero button when he caught it, because there were a thousand zeros littered across my beautifully crafted spreadsheet.

"I'm sorry, Als." He slid closer. "I didn't mean to mess you up."

I closed my eyes and took a deep breath. "It's okay. Nothing the delete button can't cure."

"What are you working on?"

An impish grin formed on my face. "Just a business proposal for a small bakery."

My eyes shifted from my computer screen to Derek's face so I could revel in his expression, but my smile vanished when I didn't see any shock. Instead of that pleasant look of surprise, Derek was frowning. I'd expected him to be excited. He'd been trying to convince me to open my own place for years. Now I was going to do it, and he didn't seem happy.

"Are you serious?" The frown didn't leave his face. "You're finally going to do it? You're gonna open your own place?"

I nodded.

There was a pause. Derek's frown shifted into a smile so bright it rivaled the sun. He gave an excited laugh as he threw his arms around me. I grabbed my computer and did my best to hug him back before he returned to his seated position.

"What made you change your mind?"

"Toni."

After keeping him from bolting off the couch once I'd told him she'd shown up at our door, Derek listened carefully while I told him what she'd said. I didn't give him all the details about Toni's husband, but I put enough in there so he would understand when I said I didn't hold anything against her.

"As she was leaving, she told me I'd do well with a bakery. I know it's kind of crazy, but something about hearing that from her made it seem like an actual possibility." I tilted the laptop toward him. "Think you can help me?"

Derek set my laptop on the coffee table. Taking both my hands in his, he looked so deeply into my eyes that I got the impression he might be able to see the chaos inside my brain when he touched me.

"Of course I'll help you. I'd do anything for you."

I reminded myself that Derek had been saying things like that to me for years, but this time it felt different. Maybe it was just my imagination, but there seemed to be something more behind his words this time.

Derek leaned toward me. My eyes darted to his lips and back up again, but he didn't seem to notice. He just pulled me against his chest in a tight hug.

"I'm proud of you, Als," he murmured into my hair. "I'm really proud of you."

"Thank you."

Hearing Derek say he was proud of me should have made me happy. I mean, he was the most important person in the world to me. So why was I disappointed that all he did was hug me?

Chapter Fourteen

ADMITTING THAT SOMETHING looked good on me was never easy, but I had to say, the skirt and blouse I'd picked out for my meeting with the loan officer looked pretty damn good. Now all I needed was to feel as put together as I looked.

Derek and I had been working on my proposal around the clock for the last few weeks. While I knew the baking side of things, his experience in helping manage the gym gave me insight into the hidden aspects of running a business.

Running a business. Just the thought had my stomach churning. I knew that was basically what I'd been doing, but this, this was different. This involved rental space and employees. That was a lot more complicated than me and a hand mixer.

"Hey, Als!" Derek called.

"Yeah?"

I gave myself one last look in the mirror before walking into the living room. Derek was just coming out of his room, and the sight of him took my breath away. His dark-gray suit looked like it'd been made for him, the way the jacket hugged his broad shoulders before tapering down to his narrow waist. It was all I could do to keep from drooling.

"Have you seen my tie?"

His voice snapped me back to reality. "What?"

"My blue tie. I can't find it. Have you seen it?"

"Isn't it in your room?" I marched to the tie rack hanging on the back of his closet. Well, it wasn't really a tie rack. More like an old hanger he used to store the few ties he had, but it worked. "Where did you see it last?"

He ran a hand down his face. "If I knew, I wouldn't be asking you to help me find it, would I?"

I lifted my hands in surrender before searching the rest of the room. Derek didn't have a reason to wear a tie that often, so there was no telling where it could have gone.

I squatted to look under the bed and instantly regretted it.

Movies made it look as if crouching in a pencil skirt and heels was easy. That must be an editing trick, because I only bent about halfway to the floor before losing my balance and landing flat on my back.

"Ow!"

Derek snickered behind me. I gave him my best hateful glare, but it only made him laugh harder.

"Sorry, Als," he spat out between bouts of laughter. "You should have seen the look on your face." A look of mock horror covered his face before dissolving back into laughter.

"Stupid skirt," I muttered, trying and failing to get back on my feet. "Help me up."

A rueful smile stayed on Derek's face. I took his hand, and together we worked to get me back on my feet. I was just pulling my feet under me when his eyes slid to the side. He squinted and bent to reach under the table.

"What are you...?" Then I spotted it. There, just under the edge of the table, was the tie we'd spent the last ten minutes looking for.

"Thanks, Als. Who knew you being such a klutz would come in so handy?"

"Shut up." I tried to sound mad, but we both knew I couldn't stay mad at him if I tried.

The way he smiled at me made me feel like I was melting. My mind wandered back to my last conversation with Brooke. The girl had done everything in her power to make me admit that my feelings for Derek were more than friendly, but I wouldn't give in. There was no point. I wasn't about to risk our friendship over something as silly as a crush.

"Ally?"

"Hmm?"

"Think you can help me with this?" Derek held up one side of the tie that was now draped around his neck.

I snorted. Derek never had been any good with a tie. Not even YouTube had been able to help.

"It's a good thing at least one of us knows what we're doing," I teased. "Otherwise, you'd be in a world of—" I finished tightening the knot and looked up. Big mistake. "—hurt."

I gulped. He was so close. Just one little movement, and he'd be kissing me. His tongue darted out to moisten his lips, and I practically swooned. All I could think about was what his lips would feel like. Sure, I'd kissed him before, something we still hadn't really talked about, but I'd been drunk. We both had been. Sloppy drunken kisses when you were barely aware of your surroundings couldn't compare to the real thing, could they?

"What would I do without you?" he whispered, putting his hand on my waist and urging me closer.

My heart tried to beat its way out of my chest. This couldn't be happening. Not now.

The blare of the alarm on my phone sounded in the other room. I put my hand on his chest and took a step back.

"W-we'd better go," I stuttered. "We don't want to be late."

If I didn't know any better, I would have said that Derek looked disappointed when I backed away. Why else would he be frowning? But it was my future that was about to be decided. Not his.

I brushed the thought aside and went to grab the rest of my things. I could worry about the look on Derek's face later. Right now, I needed to focus on getting my bakery. The rest could wait until all this was all over.

* * *

WHY WAS EVERYTHING in a loan office designed to make you uncomfortable? It was like they were trying to make me change my mind before the meeting even started. The plush office chair I was sitting in looked great, but after five minutes, my butt hurt. Even the golden nameplate on the desk that said *Mr. Bailey* was intimidating. I hated it.

I drummed my fingers on the armrest and looked at the clock again. What was the point of scheduling an appointment if the other person didn't have the decency to show up on time?

"Relax," Derek whispered, putting his hand on top of mine.

"Sorry. I'm just so nervous."

Derek gave me a reassuring pat on the arm. "You'll do great. The proposal is solid. You've got this."

"But what if...?"

"Good morning." The office door opened. Derek and I turned to see an older man with horn-rimmed glasses standing in the doorway. "I'm Greg Bailey." He offered his hand to Derek and then me. "I understand you're needing a small business loan?"

"Yes, sir," I said in a voice that sounded about as confident as a child explaining astrophysics.

He motioned for us to take our seats before walking around to the other side of the desk. He settled in his chair and folded his hands neatly on top of the desk. He looked directly at Derek. "What kind of business do you intend to open?"

That was my cue. Leaning over the side of the chair, I pulled a large manila folder out of my bag and handed it to Mr. Bailey. He didn't take it at first. Instead, he kept looking from me to Derek and back again. I was ready to start shaking the thing in his face when he finally reached out and took it.

Opening it to the first page, I watched with bated breath as he read over the documents.

The only sound in the room was the turning of pages and the rhythmic ticking of the clock. He never looked up. Hell, he may not have even blinked. He just kept reading. *Why doesn't he say something?*

I wasn't even aware my leg was bouncing up and down until Derek put his hand on my knee to stop it.

"Do you really think you can create this kind of sales revenue in only three months?" Mr. Bailey asked.

"I do." Derek and I had run the numbers a thousand times. If I was sure of anything in that document, it was the math. "I've already built up a small client base. They'll account for about fifty percent of that. The rest will come from foot traffic."

He raised an eyebrow at me. "Do you already have a location in mind?"

"Yes, sir."

I told him about the old deli on Eighth Street that had closed down a year ago. The owner's family hadn't wanted to keep the place going after he retired, so they closed up shop and put the building on the market. Derek and I had contacted the realtor a few weeks ago to go take a look. It would require some renovations, but the location was perfect.

"It's close to the college," Derek offered.

Mr. Bailey studied him over the rim of his glasses.

"Most of the kids will have slept in or be too lazy to fix anything. They'll see the shop as the perfect place to grab breakfast or a snack on the way to and from campus. I guess you could say this bakery will help them with their education, since they'll be able to focus on their lectures instead of how hungry they are."

I smiled over at Derek. He looked at me out of the corner of his eye and gave a little wink. He was laying it on a little thick with the education bit, but I didn't mind. Anything that would help me get this loan was all right in my book.

"And what will your part be in all of this?" Mr. Bailey asked.

Derek waved him off. "No part. Just here for moral support."

A moment of tense silence filled the room. My stomach felt like it was turning to stone. It would sink into my shoes any second.

"Well"—Mr. Bailey removed his glasses and cleaned them with a cloth he'd retrieved from his breast pocket—"I think we might be able to help you out."

My nerves morphed into bubbles of pure joy. It was everything I could do to keep from bouncing in my seat and smiling like an idiot for the rest of the meeting. I was barely able to focus on the terms of the loan I was so excited. The single thought that kept running through my head was that this was actually happening.

I held myself together just long enough to make it onto the sidewalk outside of the bank before letting loose a squeal of excitement. "We did it!"

"No. You did it, Als."

I threw my arms around Derek's neck. He lifted me off my feet, twirling me around in a circle. This was the moment I'd been waiting for all my life. I felt like laughing and crying all at once. My dream was finally coming true!

Derek set my feet back on the ground. I took a half step back and looked up at him.

I shook my head in denial. "It was us. I never could have done it without you."

"Yes, you could. You can do anything you set your mind to, Als."

His fingers grazed along my cheek as he tucked a strand of hair behind my ear. My mouth went dry when I thought I caught him looking at my lips. I started to move forward, but he took a step back.

Derek clapped his hands and rubbed them together. "We need to celebrate."

The sudden brush-off stung more than I thought it would. All of this wishful thinking was only making things worse, so I decided to do what I always did when I wanted to forget about the way I was feeling. Work.

"Or I could call that realtor and put in an offer on the building," I suggested, keeping my eyes focused on his chest. Getting caught in Derek's eyes the way I had earlier was too easy. Getting swept up in them every time he was around me was becoming a serious issue. "It doesn't do much good to get the loan if I don't have a building."

A chuckle rumbled in Derek's chest. I gave in and looked up to see him shaking his head at me. "All right, little miss killjoy. We'll go put in an offer. Then I'm taking you out to celebrate. Deal?" He held a hand out to me.

"Deal." I gave his hand a firm shake.

Derek draped his arm around my shoulders as we walked. "I'm proud of you, Als."

I didn't say anything. I just leaned my head against him and kept walking on in silence. Better to stay silent and keep the relationship we had than to push things too far and ruin it all.

* * *

WHY COULDN'T MY life be as simple as baking? Just once, I wanted something to go my way. Just once!

"So, still no word yet, huh?" Brooke asked.

We'd opted to do a Skype call over her lunch this week, since I had a last-minute order to finish. I'd put my laptop on the counter so I could see and talk to her while I worked.

I dropped my whisk into the bowl and set it on the counter. "No."

The realtor had been optimistic when I called him about putting in an offer. From what he understood, not many people had toured at the property, so buying my bakery would be simple, right? Wrong. Two other businesses put in offers the same day, landing me right smack dab in the middle of a bidding war that I had not been ready to fight.

"I don't know how much more I can offer," I told her. "I've already scrapped most of my decoration ideas, and all of the equipment is going to have to be secondhand. I don't know what else I can cut and still make it a working bakery."

"It can't be that bad."

I frowned at the screen.

"Really? You can come up with some—"

The sound of my phone ringing stopped her mid-sentence. I reached for the device. My eyes widened when I saw the name.

"Hold that thought," I told Brooke. I took a deep breath to slow down my racing heart before answering the call from my realtor. "Tyson? Please tell me you have good news for me."

"I do."

My teeth sank into my lower lip. "And?"

"One of the bidders dropped out."

I could feel a glimmer of hope for the first time since this whole thing began. "And the other one?"

There was a heavy sigh on the other end of the line.

"They raised their offer by another five grand."

A cold shiver made its way through my body. Five grand was seriously going to cut into the renovation budget. I was going to have to go to the ReStore for countertops if I wasn't careful. Even that might not save it.

I hadn't realized that I'd zoned out until Tyson started asking if I was still there.

"Yeah. I'm here." My voice sounded small and pathetic in my own ears.

"Do you want to counter their offer?"

No. I just wasn't sure I had another choice. I'd fallen in love with that space when I saw it. I was so convinced that nothing else would match up that I hadn't even looked at any more properties.

"Can I, uh, can I think about it and call you back?" I rubbed my face tiredly.

"If you want to, but I've got to tell you, Allyson, they really like this offer. If I don't get back to them in the next hour, I can't promise the building will still be on the market."

"I understand."

A dejected sigh left my mouth as I hung up the phone.

"That doesn't sound good."

I jumped at the sudden voice coming from the empty room. *Right, Brooke.*

"Yeah. Hey, can I call you back later? One of the other buyers just upped their offer, and I need to do some serious reworking to see if I can meet it."

"Sure. Sure. Just let me know how it goes, okay?"

"Will do."

Sitting the last of my baking aside, I went to grab my computer and took a seat on the couch. I pulled up my renovation budget and examined each item. I might be able to use the existing deli case for the display. I mean, it was already refrigerated. There just wouldn't be the nice, curved glass I'd pictured. That could save a few thousand. But would it be enough?

"Hey, Als."

I looked up to see Derek still dressed in his trainer's uniform. I think I muttered some sort of greeting in reply, but I was too busy staring at all the numbers and dollar signs to pay attention.

The couch cushions shifted when he sat next to me, the weight of his hand on my knee drawing my attention away from the screen. "What's wrong?"

I filled him in on the latest news from Tyson.

"I don't know what else to do." I sank into the cushions and let my head fall to my chest. "I can't make any more concessions or the building won't work. I don't even know if I can find another space, and the bank's already given me the money. I have to start paying on it soon. If I don't get this building, I…"

"Hey. Hey. Hey. Ally, look at me. Breathe."

I took a shuddering breath to try and calm myself back down.

"Good. Now, show me what you've got."

I turned the screen to face him. Derek listened intently while I talked about the things I'd already decided on and what it was going to take to make the place workable. He asked a few questions here and there, but for the most part, he let me talk through everything on my own. I finished my spiel and leaned back to let my head fall against the back of the couch.

"I don't know what else I can do."

There was a beat of silence.

"What about closing costs?" Derek offered.

I lifted my head to stare at him. "What?"

"You said yourself that you can't make the offer any higher. So how about offering to cover the closing costs instead? They can roll it into your monthly payments. I know it's not ideal, but at least it leaves you more to work with on the remodel than if you tried to raise the offer."

Closing costs could be a big deal. If I could take them off the current owner's plate, that just might be enough to get my bakery.

I grabbed my phone and dialed Tyson's number.

He answered on the second ring. "What do you have for me?"

"How about instead of upping the offer, we cover the closing costs?"

There was silence on the other end of the line. I pulled the phone away from my ear to make sure I hadn't lost him.

"Tyson?" I brought the phone back to my ear.

"That could work. I'll give them the counter and get back to you."

The call ended. I put the phone down on the table and turned to Derek.

"Now we wait."

Half an hour later there was still no word. Derek had to reach over to stop my leg from bouncing so many times that he eventually forced me to sit sideways and pulled my legs into his lap so I would stop shaking the couch. He tried distracting me with a rerun *Friends*, but it didn't work.

The single thought that kept running through my head was that the only reason I hadn't heard from Tyson yet was because they had rejected the offer and he didn't know how to tell me. He would have called me otherwise. My toe started tapping at the air.

The shrill ringing of my cellphone pierced the silence. I jumped, nearly kneeing Derek in the face as I scrambled for the phone. One look at the name on the screen and my chest tightened.

This was it. The call I'd been waiting for. But I couldn't bring myself to answer. My entire future was riding on this one phone call, and I couldn't muster up the courage to swipe the screen.

"Who is it?" Derek asked.

He pried the phone loose from my shaking fingers. Glancing at the screen, his eyebrows rose before answering it for me. "Tyson? Hey man, it's Derek. Ally's right here. I've got you on speaker."

If I'd been wearing a heart monitor, it would have been screaming for a crash cart. I started feeling lightheaded and nauseous as my anxiety rose to new levels of insanity. I was never going to survive this call.

"Ally? Can you hear me?" Tyson called.

"Yeah." I swallowed. "I hear you."

"They accepted your offer."

I blinked. I must have heard that wrong. I looked to Derek for confirmation, and he just beamed at me. I was going to pass out. I looked back down at the phone. "What?"

"Congratulations, Allyson. You just bought yourself a building."

The sounds of the street outside our window faded away. It was like I was in a trance. Nothing else seemed to exist. I sat there staring down at the phone, trying to wrap my head around the fact that I was getting my bakery.

Derek shook my knee, and I blinked myself out of my trance. "Thanks, Tyson. I can't tell you how much this means to me."

I could hear the smile in his voice. "You're welcome, Ally. I'll be in touch in a few days."

I ended the call and placed my phone back down on the table. Part of me wanted to pinch myself to make sure I wasn't dreaming. The other part wanted to run around the apartment screaming. Lucky for me, my brain was too startled to let me do either.

"You did it, Als." Derek placed his hand on my shoulder. "You got your bakery."

"I did it," I said in amazement. It felt like I was floating. It was all so surreal. A smile took over my face as reality began to sink in. "I actually did it."

I launched myself across the couch and tackled Derek in a tight hug. The surprise attack threw us off balance, resulting in me lying on top of him while he laughed at my antics.

"Thank you," I whispered.

"For what?"

I pulled away just far enough to look him in the eye. "For believing in me."

He ran a soothing hand along my back before pushing a strand of hair out of my face.

"I'll always believe in you, Als," he told me. "You're the most amazing woman I've ever met."

The sincerity in his sparkling blue eyes took my breath away. My mouth fell open slightly. I tried to find the words, but they seemed to be lost somewhere in my brain. Maybe it was the clean woodsy scent of his cologne, or the way his thumb was gliding across my cheek. All I knew was that I was being pulled to him like gravity.

My eyes cast a quick glance down at his lips before going back up to his eyes to see a spark of recognition. I'm not sure which of us moved first. I didn't even care. I just wanted to feel his soft warm lips molded against mine.

The universe melted away. I could still taste the faintest hint of a sports drink he'd had at work. A sudden wave of boldness swept over me and I moved to deepen the kiss. Derek pulled away.

My eyes flew open. Derek stared back at me with wide, terrified eyes. I could see the gears in his head going into overdrive. He gently pushed me away and moved to the opposite side of the couch.

I melted into the far corner, slowly drawing my knees up to my chest. What the hell was I thinking? Keeping Derek in my life as my friend was more important than the crazy crush I'd suddenly developed. How many times had I said that? Now I was throwing it all away because I couldn't keep myself from being so damned impulsive.

"Als." He licked his lips. "I...about that night..."

I didn't know if I could listen to this. He was going to tell me he regretted it. Our night together was a mistake, and so was letting me kiss him. Our entire friendship was about to go out the window, and it was all my fault.

"It's fine." I held up a hand to stop him. Maybe if he didn't say it, we could just keep on pretending. "I get it. That was a bad idea. So was that night. We were drunk. It didn't mean anythi—"

"It meant everything."

My eyes snapped to his face. I studied his expression for any hint he was lying. The muscles along the outside edge of his left eye always twitched when he lied, but they were still. He was as steady and unwavering as I'd ever seen him. His gaze was so intense that he was almost looking through me.

I gasped. "What?"

He moved closer. "I've dreamed about kissing you every day for years. The only reason I never said anything was because you were dating that douche bag, and then after, I..." He looked away. "I know we were drunk. If you don't feel—"

I pressed a finger against his lips. I opened my mouth to speak and had to close it again when the words wouldn't come out. Taking a deep breath, I spoke just over a whisper. "It meant something to me too."

The frown line between Derek's eyebrows faded away. Crinkling formed at the corners of his eyes as the most radiant smile I'd ever seen engulfed his face. His shoulders relaxed before shaking with a chuckle as he reached up to cup my face in his hands and draw me toward him.

His kiss was better than a triple fudge brownie and Mrs. Henderson's cookies all rolled into one. I wrapped my arms around his neck and pulled him closer.

Chapter Fifteen

CONTENT. THAT WAS the best way I could describe waking up in Derek's arms. The feeling of his warm, solid body behind me paired with his arm holding me close had me wanting to ignore the growing daylight creeping in from under his door. I shifted to get more comfortable, and the arm around my waist tightened. I was powerless to stop the smile that broke out across my face as I thought about the night before.

Derek had practically turned me into the gooey center of a molten chocolate cake.

"Morning," he grumbled, his voice heavy with sleep.

"Hmm." I snuggled back into his embrace.

Derek placed a kiss on my exposed shoulder before loosening his grip just enough for me to roll onto my back and gaze up at him.

I placed a hand on the side of his face, running my thumb across his stubbly cheek before guiding his lips down to mine for a good-morning kiss.

He slid his hand up my torso to my shoulders, pulling me closer as he deepened the kiss. This was definitely the kind of wake-up call I could get used to. In fact, if I didn't watch it, kissing Derek was likely to turn into my new favorite activity.

I ran my fingers through his hair, tugging gently at the longer strands on top of his head. Derek's answering moan sent a shiver down my spine. A repeat of the previous night's performance seemed inevitable. Unfortunately, that was also the moment Derek's stomach let loose a growl so powerful that even I could feel the vibrations.

Derek dropped his head on my shoulder and sighed. "Guess that means we ought to make breakfast, huh?"

I giggled. "I guess so."

Derek pushed himself up onto his elbows to look at me. The way he looked at me at that moment could have melted glass. Placing a final kiss on my lips, he slid out of bed. I groaned in frustration when he stood and pulled on a pair of boxer shorts before heading out of the room.

Stretching, I rolled to the side of the bed and picked up Derek's discarded shirt from the night before. When I slipped it over my head, the hem fell just far enough to keep me covered as long as I didn't try to bend over.

It didn't take long for us to realize that neither of us felt like cooking. We settled on frozen waffles and some leftover fruit from the cake I'd made the day before.

I took a bite of one of the strawberries and let the sweet juices dance across my tongue, moaning at the flavor.

"I thought I was the only one who could make you sound like that," Derek teased.

I nearly choked on my strawberry. He threw his head back and laughed. I stuck my tongue out at him before giving his shoulder a playful shove and going back to my food.

It was amazing the difference one night could make. The nervous hum I'd felt any time we were together had been replaced with a peaceful calm. The lack of tension in Derek's neck and shoulders told me he felt it too. His muscles had been so tense I was surprised he hadn't pulled something. Now he looked relaxed, happy. It was one of the most beautiful sights I'd seen in a long time.

"What?" His eyes never left his plate.

"Hmm?"

He swallowed a bite of waffle and turned to look at me. "You're staring at me with that dopey grin on your face you usually reserve for kitchen stuff. Why?"

I shrugged. "Just happy."

"Good." He moved to stand behind me, turning my stool until we were facing each other. He stepped between my legs and caged me in against the countertop with his arms. "I like seeing my Ally happy."

"*Your* Ally, huh?"

He nodded. "Yeah." He tilted my chin up for a brief kiss. "You okay with that?"

"More than okay."

His smile widened. I loved that smile. It was like bottled sunshine and Christmas lights all rolled into one.

"So," he said before leaning back in for another kiss. "What's on the agenda for today?"

I placed my arms around his neck. "I've got a couple dozen sugar cookies to make." I gave him another kiss. "Then I think I'm going to start working on finding a contractor to renovate the bakery."

Derek nodded. "Probably should get on that, huh?"

I nodded.

"What about the staff? Do you know what you'll need yet?" He placed one last kiss on my lips before grabbing our abandoned plates and heading for the sink.

I turned my stool back around. "Not really. I'm going to need someone up front when we open. The rest I can wait and see, depending on the type of buzz we get. Why?" I hopped down from my seat and sauntered toward him. "You want to strap on a little apron and help me out in the back?"

Derek snorted. "No thanks." Finishing the last of the dishes, he pulled the stopper from the sink and dried his hands before placing them on my hips to draw me close. "I'll stick to the sidelines on this one. Besides, I may have my own place to run soon."

That's right. The gym.

In all of my excitement about the bakery, I'd forgotten about the gym's owner possibly opening a second location for Derek.

"When are you going to hear back on that? It's been what, two months?" I asked.

"No idea. We're supposed to go over everything soon, but he hasn't scheduled a meeting yet. Rumor has it they're still working on a location."

I nodded. I might not know anything about gyms, but if trying to start this bakery had taught me anything, it was that location was everything.

I hoped Derek would have an answer soon. He tried to play it off like it was no big deal, but I could tell how badly he wanted this. It was something he'd dreamed about for years. Now that all of my dreams seemed to be coming true, I wanted him to have his too.

* * *

"THANKS AGAIN FOR coming." I held my hand out to Steve, the general contractor I'd hired to renovate my building. It had taken me nearly a month to find him, but thank God I had.

"Pleasure is all mine." He shook my hand. "We'll see you on Monday."

"Monday it is." I gave him one final wave before locking up behind him, giving the door an affectionate pat. I couldn't stop smiling as I turned to survey what was about to become my bakery. There were times when it still didn't feel real.

There was enough workable material left by the previous owner to allow me to spruce up parts of it instead of completely redoing them. The floors would have to be redone, but the counters just needed new tops. A couple of booths could be used for cake tastings. It would all be fine.

An unexpected knock on the glass door made me shriek. I turned to see Brooke standing on the other side, holding up a to-go cup of coffee from my favorite café. God bless her.

"Hey!" The hand that had flown up to cover my heart slowly fell to my side. I opened the door and greeted her with a hug before happily taking the steaming cup from her hand. "Welcome to my humble little bakery."

"Thanks," Brooke said, her voice flat.

I blinked. That didn't sound like the Brooke I knew. She'd been so excited to see the bakery when I talked to her about it yesterday that she'd practically begged me to bring her down here in the middle of the night. Now she looked like she'd rather be anywhere else in the world.

"So, when do you think you'll open?" She was clearly faking her enthusiasm.

"A couple of months probably."

Brooke nodded. She was trying not to look at me. If she thought it would keep me from noticing how red and puffy her eyes were, she was wrong.

"Brooke? What's wrong?"

More tears began building in her eyes. "I'm out of a job," she whispered, lifting her arms in a slight shrug. "Toni is closing the bakery."

I gawked at her. There had to be some kind of mistake. Toni would never close the bakery. She loved it too much.

"What?"

Brooke took a seat in one of the abandoned booths and started rifling through her purse. She pulled out a sheet of paper and handed it to me. I sat down across from her and shifted from studying her face to studying the sheet. She nodded in confirmation before I unfolded the paper.

After 35 years in business, Toni's Tasty Treats will be closing its doors effective Friday, March 18th. Final paychecks will be mailed the following week. Any employees who wish to obtain a letter of reference may request one prior to closure. Thank you for your service.

I read the notice again. This couldn't be right. I flipped the notice over and looked at the back like it would reveal some hidden secret about what was really going on. I read the note again, scrutinizing every word. Toni's flowery signature at the bottom was one of a kind. It looked real enough. I shook my head. My bakery wasn't even open yet, and it already felt like my baby. I couldn't imagine writing anything like this. I looked at the date and frowned.

"This is for two weeks from now."

Brooke nodded. "I knew things had slowed down since you left. I just didn't think…" Brooke trailed off, resting her head on her hand.

Things had slowed down since I left? But Toni had made it sound like they were swamped. That was why she showed up at my apartment. Right?

I handed the letter back to her. "Brooke, what do you mean things slowed down after I left?"

"Once word spread that you were working on your own, a few of our regulars sent their orders to you."

Now that she mentioned it, I was doing a lot of regular orders from home that I used to do at Toni's, but it was only a small fraction of the business. They had to be getting more work than that.

"Is it really that bad?"

Brooke shrugged. "I didn't think so, but I guess it doesn't really matter. I'm job hunting anyway." She gave an emotionless laugh. "Know anyone willing to hire a high school dropout with a GED and a give-'em-hell attitude?" Her flippant tone made it clear that she was joking, but as her words sank in, I smiled.

"Actually"—I drew out the word—"I'm going to need someone up front. It'll be a while before we open, so I was waiting to hire anyone, but the job is yours if you want it."

The look on Brooke's face went from distraught to sheer astonishment. "Are you serious?" She leaned across the table and reached for my hand. "You want me to work for you?"

I nodded. "It's perfect timing. We already know we work well together. I trust you, and there's no way I will ever treat any of my employees the way Toni treated us. I'll never ask you to do anything that I'm not wi—"

Brooke squealed and jumped to her feet before I could even finish. She raced around the table and threw her arms around me with so much force that she nearly sent us both tumbling back into the booth.

"Thank you." She laughed as she pulled away. "I guess we won't have to go to lunch anymore just to see each other."

"Nope." I was opening my mouth to say something else when Queen sounded from somewhere inside my purse. The smile on my face grew wider. Signaling Brooke to hold her thought, I dug my phone out.

"Hey."

"Hey, babe."

Brooke must have been able to hear Derek from the saucy look and shoulder shimmy she gave me. I rolled my eyes at her and turned my body in the opposite direction to give myself the illusion of privacy.

"How was the meeting with the contractor?"

"Great. I think we found a way for me to get pretty much everything I wanted out of this place."

Genuine pride shone in his voice. "That's awesome! I'm so proud of you."

"Thanks."

"Tell that boy I said hi," Brooke shouted behind me. She sounded more excited than I was that Derek and I were giving romance a try.

Derek chuckled.

"Did you get all that?" I asked.

"Yeah." His tone shifted to something more serious. "Hey, I'm really sorry, but I'm gonna have to skip lunch with you guys. My boss called, and he said he wants to talk to me about the new location. This could be it, Als. This could be the offer."

Any disappointment at hearing he was missing our lunch date vanished.

"I hope so," I told him. "Tell me about it when you get home?"

"Will do. I gotta go. Bye, Als."

"Bye."

I ended the call and turned to see a rather satisfied grin on Brooke's face.

"Oh," I scoffed, waving a hand at her. "Will you stop."

She feigned innocence. "What? I didn't say anything."

"Yeah, but you were thinking awfully loud." I put my phone back in my purse. "Looks like it's going to be just you and me today. Derek's boss called him in for a meeting about the new gym, so he won't be able to get across town in time to meet us."

"That good?"

I threw my bag over my shoulder. "I hope so. Come on. I'm starving."

* * *

THE RICH, VELVETY voice of "Ol' Blue Eyes" floated through the Bluetooth speaker on the counter. I hummed and swayed along with the music, letting myself get lost in my own little world.

I threw a dash of edible glitter on top of my creation before standing back to examine it. The cake almost looked too good to eat. Almost. I grabbed a plain white pastry box from its hiding place on top of the fridge and packed up the cake.

The sound of the door opening and closing followed by a pair of keys landing in the bowl faintly registered while I looked down at the bakery box and dreamed. Soon the plain white boxes would be replaced with green and pink ones bearing my company logo. I ran a hand affectionately over the box before storing it in the fridge.

A pair of strong arms wrapped around me from behind just as I closed the door. They pulled me into a now-familiar embrace that I looked forward to at the end of each day.

"Hey." I sighed, leaning my head back against Derek's shoulder. "How was your meeting?"

Derek spun me in his arms and put one of my hands on his shoulder before taking ahold of the other.

I frowned. "What are you doing?"

"Dance with me." He moved us gently to the music.

I snorted. "But I need to clean the kitchen."

I tried to wiggle my way out of his arms, but Derek just pulled me closer.

"We'll do it later. Let's just finish the song."

I quirked an eyebrow at him. "What's going on?"

"Can't I just want to dance with my girl?"

He gave me one of those sweet little-boy smiles that I always fell for and pulled me a step closer. I rested my head on his shoulder. Closing my eyes, I let the rest of the world melt away. I couldn't remember ever being this happy before. It was like a dream, and I was in no hurry to wake from it.

Chapter Sixteen

MY EYES CLOSED for what felt like the millionth time since I'd plopped onto the sofa. I should have known I'd be a goner as soon as Derek pulled me into his side. It didn't matter what he found to watch. The instant my head hit his shoulder, I was ready for a nap.

"So," Derek began, running his fingers up and down my arm, "they finally came up with a possible location for the new gym."

My eyes flew open. The exhaustion from a moment before turned into pure adrenaline. I sat up and turned so I was facing him. "And?"

The long, slow breath he let out was not comforting. He only did that when he was about to say something he knew I wouldn't like. Were we going to have to move? I mean, we didn't exactly live in Central Park West or anything, but I loved our apartment.

"It looks like there's a good chance they'll build it in Las Vegas."

"What?"

Derek kept his eyes trained on the coffee table as he nodded. "Nothing has been decided for sure yet. But my boss found a building that he can..."

I didn't hear the rest. The only thing I could focus on was one word. Vegas.

I couldn't move to Vegas. I was opening a bakery. No way I could pick up and move across the country if Derek's boss sent him there.

"Als." His calm tone broke me out of my mental marathon. My eyes shifted from the blank space they'd been staring at to the knowing smile on his face. "Nothing is decided for sure yet, okay? He's flying out to take a look at the location later this week and see what all needs to be done. Then he'll make his decision from there."

I blanched. "How are we gonna make this work? I mean, I can't go with you if you move to Vegas. I have to stay here for the bakery. What if you move and everything just falls apart? I…"

"Hey. Hey. Hey." Derek took my face in his hands and forced me to look at him. He led me through a calming breath before continuing. "It's gonna be okay. Besides, nothing is decided yet. He may still build the gym here. He's just exploring his options." The hand Derek ran along my arm wasn't nearly as comforting as it should have been. "Either way, we'll find a way to make it work."

"You promise?"

His face softened. "I promise."

He pulled me close and placed a soft kiss on my lips. I let my body melt into him. He placed a final kiss on my forehead as he pulled away, tucking my head under his chin and wrapping his arms around me.

"It'll be okay, Als. I promise. Whatever happens, we'll find a way to make it work."

I nodded, clutching his shirt in my fist just a little bit tighter.

* * *

I CRINGED AT the clinking sound coming from the box as I hoisted it a little higher on my hip. The old deli booths had given me an idea for the bakery decor. My rustic tables and wooden stools idea was out of the budget now, so I'd decided to use the booths to create a classic

'50s vibe. A quick search on Craigslist and the Facebook marketplace gave me a box full of goodies I could use for decoration.

I shifted the box a little higher and squeezed my way through the door. I dropped the box onto the folding table I'd been using for a desk with a thud before flopping into the metal chair behind it.

"All right." There was a rustle of heavy plastic behind me.

I turned to see my contractor stepping through the temporary barrier that protected the rest of the bakery from the work being done in the kitchen.

"Appliances will be in tomorrow," he said. "We'll get those put in and then start on the floors."

I beamed. "Thank you so much, Steve. You guys are amazing!"

He gave a half smile and looked down at his shoes. "Thank you, Miss O'Connor. We'll see you tomorrow."

I thanked him again for all his hard work before bidding him farewell and turning my attention back to the box of decorations. It was a little early to do too much—I needed to paint before I could do anything—but I could at least get an idea for where I wanted to put everything.

I pulled the items out of the box one at a time, carefully considering each one. There were some old records that were too scratched up to play but would still look good on the wall. I'd even found an old black-and-white image someone made of James Dean and Marilyn Monroe sitting around a bar with a few other Hollywood icons. My favorite, by far, had to be the off-color print of a '67 Mustang that had been rigged with little lightbulbs in the headlights. Cheesy, I knew, but I couldn't resist. Now I just had to figure out where to put it.

A spot over one of the booths caught my eye. I pulled a few thumbtacks out of the bottom of the box and made my way over to the booth. There was no way the little plastic tacks could hold the picture indefinitely, but at least I would get a feel for it. Putting the tacks in my mouth, I climbed up onto the table.

Once the picture was in place, I hopped down. Crooked. I climbed back up on the table and adjusted the photo. Now the other side was too high.

"Oh, come on." I threw my arms up in the air and let them fall to my side with a smack.

Moving back into place, I prepared to adjust the photo for what I hoped would be the final time when the bell over the door sounded. I jumped. The table underneath me rocked. What happened next was like something out of an old cartoon. I windmilled my arms in a desperate attempt to keep my balance, but it was no use.

A startled scream flew from my lips as my body suddenly became weightless. Was it possible to break your neck falling off a table? I closed my eyes and waited for the pain of impact with the hard floor, only to find myself landing on something softer and a lot more vocal than concrete.

"Umf."

My eyes flew open. The soft, non-floor thing I'd landed on was a person.

"Oh my God!" I scrambled to my feet and turned to see a man in a slate-gray suit sprawled face first across my floor. I held out a hand to help him up, but he waved me off. He rose to his feet and dusted off his slacks. "I am so sorry. Are you…?" I stopped dead in my tracks when I saw his face. "Kyle?"

He stopped cleaning himself off and looked up at me. "Hi, Ally."

I was flabbergasted. Of all the people I might have expected to see standing in my unfinished bakery, my ex didn't even rank in the top hundred. "What are you doing here?"

Kyle finished dusting off his suit and grinned at me. "Saving you, apparently."

Funny.

"No, I mean, why are you in my bakery?"

Kyle shook his head and straightened his perfectly tailored jacket. "You always wanted your own place. Good for you."

It was like looking at a ghost. I was bombarded with memories of all the wonderful times we'd shared. The corner of my mouth tried to turn up into a smile, but I shut it down. "What do you want, Kyle?"

"Isn't it obvious?" He smiled. "I want to order a cake."

"We're not open yet."

He chuckled. "I can see that."

Crossing my arms over my chest, I used every ounce of restraint I had not to roll my eyes at him before turning my back to him. I tried to make it look like I was busy sorting decorations. Maybe if I ignored him, he would just go away.

"One of my clients gave me this."

I turned to see Kyle reaching for the inside pocket of his jacket. He fished around for a moment before producing a business card and holding it out to me. I gave it a quick glance, but I didn't need to read it to know what it was. The pink and green stripes stretched across the surface were enough to tell me it was mine.

I'd had a couple of boxes of business cards made up for the bakery a few weeks ago to give to my regular clients. There weren't many in circulation. Just a few here and there to start getting the name out there. I guess it was working if people were showing up to order things before we were even open.

He gestured at me with the card. I put the record I'd been pretending to examine back in the box and turned to take the card from him. "He said it was for the person who made his daughter's birthday cake. His wife hasn't been able to stop raving about her and keeps ordering treats every week for her book club. It wasn't until he gave me the card that I realized it was you."

I nodded. That would have to be Jeanie. She was a sweet lady.

Always ordered a dozen cupcakes or frosted cookies decorated to fit the theme of whatever they were reading that week.

I put the card on the counter and went back to trying to make everything fit into the box. Having Kyle this close to me again was unsettling. In a city the size of New York, you'd think it would be easy enough to avoid your ex. Apparently not.

"What kind of cake do you want?" I did my best to keep my voice flat and dull.

"Oh, come on, Ally." He took my hand and turned me to face him.

I didn't exactly yank my arm out of his grasp, but it wasn't a gentle tug either.

"Really?" He flashed me one of those movie-star smiles that had always made me weak in the knees. "You don't have to be like that."

I feigned an innocent expression, making my eyes big and round. "Like what?"

His smile faltered, but it didn't go away. "Look, I know things didn't end well between us, but that doesn't mean we have to hate each other, does it?"

"I don't hate you." I sighed, running my fingers across my forehead to try and ward off a headache. "At least, not anymore."

"Not anymore?"

I waved off his question. I didn't want to talk about our past relationship. I just wanted to do my job and go home. "You said you needed a cake. What is it for?"

He took a step closer. I sucked in a breath and could smell his aftershave. It was the same scent that had clung to my sheets for weeks after he left me. Every time I tried to sleep, the scent would invade my nostrils and bring a flood of memories with it. I'd had to wash the things twice to get rid of it.

"The cake?" I crossed my arms over my body like a shield.

He let out a heavy breath. "It's for an investor luncheon at the office.

My boss is hoping we can convince enough people to invest so we can expand the business. He wants the whole thing to be this over-the-top, extravagant display of prominence, and if what Rhodey tells me is true, you're the one to do that."

Releasing the death grip on my right biceps, I let out a controlled breath and reached for my bag. I retrieved a pen and a notebook out of the bottom.

"How many people?" I tried to keep my voice even.

Kyle shrugged. "Nothing too big. Forty or fifty."

"Is there a theme?"

"Give me your money?" he quipped.

I looked at him over the edge of the notepad. He was grinning and shaking his shoulders in silent laughter, as if he'd just told a funny joke. I frowned. He was in serious trouble if he thought that joke was funny.

He looked up at me and sobered when he saw I wasn't laughing. "Uh…" He cleared his throat. "No. Not really."

I nodded. "How about you give me a couple of days to see what I can come up with, and I'll get back to you?"

The dazzling smile returned. "Sounds good. I'll see you then." I went to sit the notebook on the counter, and Kyle put his hand on top of mine.

My eyes shot up to meet his.

"It's good to see you again, Ally."

The twinkle in his eye caught me off guard. It was the same look he'd given me a thousand times when we were together, the one that had been missing when we'd had lunch. It was the kind of look that could make a girl forget herself if she wasn't careful.

"I'll see you later."

He ran his thumb across the back of my hand before giving me another dazzling smile and heading out.

I turned my back toward the door the instant he walked through it. I forced the muscles in my neck and shoulders to relax. Having Kyle touch me like that again had felt like an invasion. It was a simple touch. Nothing intimate. But it was still so familiar. I suppressed a shiver at the memory of it. This job would be anything but simple.

The bell over the door sounded, and my back stiffened. My eyes clamped shut, and I begged whoever was listening to not let it be him again. Carefully peeking over my shoulder, my muscles relaxed when I saw Brooke with her own box of decorations in tow. She had the most gobsmacked expression on her face. Her mouth hung open, eyes wide, as she looked from me to the street and back again.

"Oh my God," she drawled. "I must be losing my mind, because I could have sworn that I just saw Kyle walk out this door." She leaned back and craned her neck to get a better look down the street.

I rubbed at my forehead absentmindedly before tucking a strand of hair behind my ear. "Yeah. That was him."

Brooke's head whipped around.

"Excuse me?" She sounded almost as scandalized as I felt.

"He dropped by to order a cake."

Brooke's eyes narrowed. "And just why in the world would he do that?"

"Ugh." My body sagged as I let out a massive groan.

Brooke set her box next to mine and listened in patient silence while I explained, the frown on her face deepening the longer I went.

"You don't really believe that sack of bull, do you?" she asked when I had finally finished.

I frowned. "Excuse me?"

She placed a hand on my shoulder. "Ally, I love you, but if you honestly believe that the only reason that boy came here was to order a cake, then you are not nearly as bright as I thought you were."

I rolled my eyes. Leave it to Brooke to turn this into a thing when I just wanted to forget it and move on.

"You told him to get lost, right?"

I purposefully kept my gaze on the box.

"Ally, you didn't?" she asked, scandalized.

"Well, it's not like I can turn away business, now, can I?" I turned to face her. "Until this place is up and running, I can't pick and choose my customers."

It wasn't like I wanted to work with Kyle. God, if I'd had it my way, I never would have seen that asshole again. It had taken me months to pull myself back together after what he did. Having to spend time with him again in any capacity was not exactly on my bucket list. Hell, it didn't get consideration.

"What are you going to tell Derek?" Brooke asked.

I froze. I hadn't thought about that. As much *fun* as interacting with my ex had been, Derek would enjoy it about as much as a sugar-free sundae.

I schooled my features into something I hoped looked like indifference. "What do you mean?"

Brooke scoffed. "Seriously? Your current boyfriend helped you pick up the pieces of your life when the man you thought you were going to marry dumped you, and now, when said man suddenly shows back up, you aren't going to say a single word to Derek about him?"

Why did she have to make it sound like a conspiracy theory? What was I supposed to tell him? He only ever put up with Kyle for my sake. Derek was always the one to celebrate with me when Kyle forgot my birthday. He'd even stepped in to be my date for a gala event Kyle was supposed to take me to when he backed out at the last minute. I was pretty sure Derek was ready to kill Kyle on sight after the breakup. Telling him my ex had hired me to bake a cake didn't sound like such a great idea.

"I don't know."

Brooke put a hand on her hip and thrust it to the side. "Well, you better figure it out. That boy deserves to know the truth."

Something about the way she said *the truth* sounded like an accusation. "The truth?"

She nodded. "There is no way you can honestly believe that Kyle waltzed in here all sweet and charming, caressing your hand and acting like nothing ever happened, just to order a cake. You mark my words. He's up to something."

I replayed Kyle's visit in my head. The way he'd smiled and held my hand. The bucket of charm. It was the same routine that had made me interested in him when we first met. A boulder landed in my stomach at the thought that Brooke might be right.

* * *

THE FIRST THING I noticed when I walked through the door was the silence. The TV wasn't on. There was no call of greeting. Nothing.

I sat the bag of takeout on the counter and made my way to Derek's room. "Derek, I'm home."

Still nothing. For the past few weeks, he'd been beating me home almost every day. The few times I'd beaten him, he met me at the door before I could even finish getting my key in the lock.

My first thought was that he was in the bathroom, but the door was cracked open, so that couldn't be it. My phone vibrated in my pocket. I pulled It out to see a text from Derek.

Running late. Be home soon.

I breathed a sigh of relief. One of these days I was going to stop worrying about him disappearing on me. I reminded myself that he wasn't Kyle. He wouldn't run out on me like that.

Kyle. I tossed the bags onto the counter. What was I going to tell Derek about him? Yes, it was only a cake, but I couldn't shake the niggling thought Brooke had put in the back of my mind about Kyle's trying to weasel his way back into my life. Sure, it was possible, but I didn't put too much faith in it. He was the one that ended it. If he wanted to be with me so badly, he wouldn't have walked away in the first place.

Shaking away the thought, I unpacked the white boxes of takeout I'd picked up on the way home. I'd just pulled the last one out of the bag when I heard Derek's key in the door.

"Hey," I greeted. "You're just in time."

Derek put his keys in the bowl and tossed his coat on the back of the couch. I tilted my head back in anticipation of a kiss, but instead of kissing my lips, he gave me a quick peck on the cheek before grabbing a carton of lo mein and heading to the couch.

Warning bells blasted inside my head. Derek had never greeted me with anything less than a kiss on the lips since we started dating. A kiss on the cheek or the top of the head was only something he did when I was upset. He hadn't even said hello.

"What's wrong?" I asked.

Derek turned on the TV and shoved a forkful of food into his mouth without answering.

Okay. Now he was ignoring me. Not good.

Abandoning the food on the counter, I paced to the couch and sat beside him. The tension in his jaw made the vein on the side of his neck stick out like piped frosting. I put my hand on his thigh and started rubbing soothing circles with my thumb.

"Derek?"

"They got the building," he said, his tone flat and hollow as he kept his eyes trained on the game in front of him.

"What building?"

Derek's shoulders slumped. He tapped his fork against the side of the container and kept his eyes down as he spoke. "The building in

Vegas. They bought it. They're going to renovate it and put the new gym out there."

My hand stilled. It felt like I'd swallowed a frosting rose before chewing it. I didn't even know what to say.

Derek never looked at me. He kept his eyes trained on the floor, looking more through it than at it.

"Do they still want you to run it?" I licked my lips. I could feel the tightness in my chest growing. He didn't have to answer. I could already read it on his face.

He nodded.

I collapsed back against the cushions. This couldn't be happening. Everything was finally starting to turn around, and now this.

"I don't have to take the job."

Everything froze. I had to be hearing him wrong. This was his dream. He couldn't turn it down. Not after working so hard. "What do you mean?"

Derek placed the container on the coffee table before turning to me and taking both of my hands. His eyes met mine for the first time since he'd come through the door. I could see the uncertainty and guilt swirling behind his eyes. If I was upset, he was devastated.

He took a deep breath, letting his shoulders rise and fall before speaking. "I can tell them I don't want the job."

"But you—"

He held up a hand to stop me. "This wasn't supposed to be out of town. I mean, I know they told me they were looking at Vegas, but I didn't think it would really happen. The owner likes keeping a close eye on things, so I never thought... Now that it's out west, I..." He paused to gather himself.

I'd never seen Derek this conflicted before. He looked like somebody had put him in a blender and set it on high. His usually tousled hair looked like he'd been tearing at the ends with his fingers. The worry lines across his forehead cut deep grooves into his skin. This decision was tearing him apart.

"This affects both of us," he said. "If it was just across town, I wouldn't worry about it, but it's not. We're talking about me moving across the country. I'm willing to do whatever it takes to make this thing work long distance, but if you don't want me to go, I'll tell them to find somebody else to run the gym."

I was flabbergasted. Never in a million years had I imagined somebody would be willing to do something like this for me. My teeth sank into my lower lip as I looked down at our clasped hands. There was a nervous rattle inside my chest. Derek was offering me his future on a silver platter, and I didn't know if I could accept it.

A hand cupped my cheek, bringing my gaze up to his face. The vulnerability in his clear blue eyes took my breath away. He was serious. All I had to do was say the word, and he would walk away from a job he had been dreaming about for ages...just to make me happy.

I opened my mouth to say something, but I couldn't find the words. How do you respond to somebody that is willing to give up that much for you? What can you possibly say that compares to that?

"I love you, Ally."

My lip trembled. What had I done to deserve this man?

"I love you too."

The smile that engulfed Derek's face was almost blinding. His hand moved to the back of my neck, drawing me to him. The kiss was brief, but it held every bit of promise I could have wished for. I blinked my eyes open to see him grinning like an idiot before giving me another swift kiss.

"Go get your food." He nodded toward the kitchen. "You don't want it to get cold."

"But what about...?"

He shook his head. "It's okay. I don't have to give them an answer for another month. We'll just take tonight for ourselves and start figuring it all out tomorrow. Okay?"

I smiled back at him and headed to the kitchen to get my takeout. I felt like I was floating. Things weren't settled yet, not by a long shot, but I had a feeling it was all going to work out in the long run.

Something caught my attention out of the corner of my eye. I turned my head to see my phone resting on the counter, the blue message light on my phone blinking away. Unlocking the phone, I pulled up the notification. My hand barely managed to hold onto the phone as I read the message.

Kyle: It was good seeing you again.

Chapter Seventeen

BROOKE STOOD IN the middle of the bakery and looked around in awe. "This place looks great!"

I finished painting along the baseboard and stood to stretch my aching muscles. Brooke and I had been giving the front of the shop a facelift with a fresh coat of paint while we waited for the kitchen to be done.

I took a quick look around the room. "Yeah, it does."

The paint breathed new life into the place. It already looked brighter and more airy than the day before.

"Thanks for all of your help today, Brooke. I really appreciate it."

Brooke waved a dismissive hand in my direction. "No problem, Boss."

I rolled my eyes at her. "Don't call me that."

I set my paint brush back in the bucket and carried it to the drop cloth-covered counter.

Brooke laughed. "Whatever. Anything else we need to get done today?"

I shook my head. "No. We have to wait for the paint to dry before we can put anything on the walls, and we can't do anything back there"—I gestured toward the kitchen—"until they're done putting everything in. I say we call it a day. We can work on flyers and stuff tomorrow."

The grand opening wasn't for another month, but I wanted to get some word of mouth going. It wouldn't do me any good to open a place if nobody knew to walk through the door, and word of mouth was all the budget could handle.

"Sounds good." Brooke took off her paint-splashed overshirt and tossed it aside. "Want to go grab some lunch or something?"

"I can't." I put away the rest of our supplies. "I have a lunch meeting with Kyle today."

Brooke gave me a raised eyebrow look straight out of a telenovela. "Excuse me? I must be hearing things. Did you just say you were having lunch with Kyle? As in ex-boyfriend Kyle?"

"No." I groaned. "We are having a lunch *meeting* so we can go over the design for the cake he's ordering. There's a big difference."

"If it's all business, why aren't you just meeting here?"

I gestured to the disaster area around us. Paint cans, drop cloths, and a fine layer of dust did not make this an ideal place for a business meeting.

"I see your point."

I nodded and gathered my things.

"Just be careful, Ally. I don't trust him."

"I'll be on guard. I promise." I looked at the time on my phone. "I'd better get going if I'm gonna make it on time. Will you lock up for me on your way out?"

"Sure thing, *Boss.*"

Brooke dragged out the last word and flashed me a cheeky grin. I snorted a laugh and shook my head at her before grabbing my handbag and heading for the door.

Since sprinting across town and arriving out of breath would look unprofessional, I hailed a cab. Every block we passed ratcheted my anxiety that much higher. My heart was practically lodged in my throat by the time we pulled up outside the bistro. I'd been avoiding this place. Now I had to go back in.

The bell over the door chimed, and I was greeted by the familiar smell of roasted meats and mayonnaise-laden pasta salad.

"Ally!" Sal called from behind the counter. "It's been too long. I'll get your old usual fixed up."

"Thanks." I smiled at him before scanning the room for Kyle.

It didn't take me long to spot him. His perfectly tailored suit and shiny shoes stood out like a sore thumb in a place like this. He waved me over, but I couldn't get my feet to move.

Of all the places he could have chosen to sit, he had to pick *that* booth. The window seat with a view of the street. The same view I'd stared at for so long after he dumped me that I was late getting back to work. *Oh hell.*

"Hey, Ally." He rose just long enough for me to take my seat.

I forced a smile. Sliding into the booth was like being transported back in time. I could feel that same nervous bubble of anticipation for what was about to come. Only this time, I wouldn't let him embarrass me.

I shook myself out of the thoughts and wasted zero time pulling out my sketchbook. This was a work meeting. I wanted to get my work done and get out of there.

"So…" I laid the book out in front of him. "Here are a few ideas I came up with that I thought might—"

My well-prepared speech stopped dead when Kyle laid his palm out flat on my sketchbook. I jerked my head back. What the hell was he doing? I shot him a questioning look, but he just smiled with the same cool, confident manner he always had.

"So that's it?" he asked. "No 'hello, nice to see you'? Just 'here you go. Pick a cake'?"

I frowned. "This is a work lunch, right?"

He nodded.

"And you have a limited amount of time you can spend away from the office?"

He nodded again.

"Then we need to make the best use of our time."

The sickeningly sweet smile I gave him was about as real as margarine, but I couldn't help it. Being around him made my skin crawl. All I wanted to do was take care of this cake and go back to pretending he didn't exist.

I redirected the conversation back to the designs, but Kyle reached across the table and took my hand. It took every ounce of strength I had not to rip it out of his grasp. I looked up to see him giving me one of those sexy half smiles all male celebrities seemed to have. My insides softened against my wishes, making me want to kick myself for being such an idiot.

"All right then." Kyle let go of me to lean back in his seat. "Show me what you've got."

I blinked. I knew he was talking to me, but the words didn't register with my brain.

Sal bringing over my food shook me from my trance.

"Thanks."

I glanced back across the table to see Kyle smirking at me. That bastard knew exactly what he had done! Well, two could play at this game. If he could dazzle me with a smile, I could dazzle him with cake.

Pushing the designs back toward him, I detailed the various design elements. There was no mistaking the pride in my voice. These designs were good, and I knew it.

A moment of silence fell over us when I finished describing my visions. Looking up, I could see the little half smile making its way onto Kyle's face again.

"They're wonderful." He looked me right in the eye.

Something about that predatory smile had my hackles rising. I moved as far away from him as I could without scooting out of the booth. "Thank you. Which one do you like best?"

It was his turn to balk. I had to fight to keep the smirk off my face. Our years together might have taught Kyle how to read me, but that meant I could read him too. Kyle was never really paying attention when he had that look on his face. There was no way he'd heard a word I'd said.

He held my gaze for a moment before looking down at the pages in front of him. "I like the one with the smaller cakes orbiting it. Using the colors from our logo is a nice touch." And just like that, he was all business.

He effortlessly turned to the design that featured smaller cupcakes circling a larger three-layer cake. I guess he *had* been paying attention.

"The concept is different," he said, studying the design more closely. "It catches the eye and integrates a lot of different aspects of the company. I just have one small issue."

"What's that?"

"Can we just do smaller cakes instead of cupcakes?"

"I can do that." I nodded. "Still need it next Tuesday?"

"Yes."

I grabbed a pen from my bag and started making notes in the margins of the design. "What flavors do you want?"

"Vanilla with buttercream will be fine."

Boring it is then.

I finished up my note and turned towards the counter. "Sal, I'm really sorry, but I've got to run. Is there any way I can get a to-go box for mine?"

"Sure thing, Ally."

I crammed my sketchpad into my bag. While the meeting had gone well, I didn't want to spend more time with Kyle than was absolutely necessary. The fact that he kept smiling at me like we were on some kind of date didn't help much either.

"Where are you going?" he asked.

"I'm leaving. You wanted to meet to order a cake. You've ordered a cake." I graciously took the to-go box from Sal and packed up my food. Throwing the strap of my bag over my shoulder, I gave him one last polite smile as I stood. "I'll have it ready for you to pick up at the bakery."

"Ally, wait." I hadn't made it more than a step before he took hold of my wrist.

I looked down at where his hand held mine in confusion before raising my eyes to meet his.

"Will you sit back down? Please? I need to talk to you about something."

My instincts told me to grab my things and run, but something about the way he looked at me had my feet glued to the floor. He kept licking his lips, a nervous habit of his that made him seem more human.

The confident, cocky businessman was gone, replaced with the unsure charmer I'd met so many years ago. It was for that guy's sake that I sank back onto my seat.

"I miss you, Ally," he said simply.

I blinked at him. He couldn't be serious. What possible reason could he have for missing me?

"Say something, Ally," he pleaded.

"I, uh…" I tried to shake away the cobwebs in my brain, but it didn't work. "I don't know what to say."

"Say you'll have dinner with me next Friday night."

Now, that got my attention. There had been a time when I would have crawled naked over broken glass to hear him say that. I'd cried myself to sleep for weeks dreaming about this moment, but now, as

I studied his face, I didn't feel a thing. I expected my palms to start sweating and my heart to race, but it never happened. Those warm brown eyes that used to draw me in like a tractor beam may as well have been made of glass.

"Thanks for the offer, but…"

"Please, Ally." He leaned forward in his seat. "Just this once."

I held firm. "No. I'm sorry, Kyle. I can't." I stood, gathering my things as I went. "I'll have the cake ready by next Tuesday."

And with that, I turned and headed for the door.

* * *

PLACING THE LAST cake in the box, I smiled down at my creation with pride. One large cake with the company logo and three smaller ones highlighting the different services the firm offered. There was no way this wasn't going to be a hit.

"This looks amazing, Ally," Brooke said.

I placed the last box in the storage fridge, beside the others. "Thanks. I'm glad they were able to get the kitchen ready in time for me to make this here. I got worried when I couldn't rent my usual space. It's too big of a project for me to do at home."

"Not to mention you would have had to explain to Derek why you were making a cake with the logo for Kyle's company on it." Her eyebrows rose.

I let out huff. Not telling Derek about the cake order was turning into a point of contention between Brooke and me, especially after I told her what Kyle had said as I was leaving. Brooke had been right about his reasons for coming to the bakery, but I wasn't going to let his motivations dictate the way I ran my business. The man wanted a cake. I'd give him a cake. After that, I never had to see him again.

"Whatever." I walked past Brooke and her *you're in trouble* expression to push through the saloon-style doors that separated the decorating floor from the store front. "We need to finalize our marketing strategy. I want to make sure there's a good buzz going before we open. What do you think about…"

The bell over the front door sounded. I looked over, expecting to see Kyle, and nearly tripped over myself when I saw Derek smiling at me from the doorway.

A sliver of panic made its way up my spine. Of all the times for him to randomly show up, he had to pick this one.

"Hey!" My voice sounded about as confident as an eight-year-old giving her first violin recital. "I thought you were working today."

If Derek noticed the quiver in my voice, he didn't show it. He made his way over to me, giving me a swift peck on the lips before answering.

"Yeah"—he looked down—"my boss gave me the rest of the day off." He ran his hand down my arm until he was holding my hand. "Think you can take a break from all of your hard work for a bit so we can talk?"

Talk? That sounded ominous.

"Well," Brooke declared a bit louder than was absolutely necessary, "I think I'll go ahead and go to lunch and give you two some privacy. Want me to bring you anything?"

I shook my head, but I didn't look at her. My eyes were too busy studying Derek. His smile was forced, and the way he kept running his thumb back and forth across my knuckles did little to soothe the unease settling in my stomach.

Derek gave Brooke a little wave as she walked out the door before turning his attention to me.

I cut to the chase. "What's wrong?"

His shoulders slumped. He reached for my other hand and took the tiniest step forward. He brought our joined hands up between us.

"We need to—"

The bell over the door cut him off midsentence. A growl of irritation formed in my throat. Why couldn't Brooke have just come back later for whatever it was she forgot? I looked over Derek's shoulder, ready to tell her to come back later, when my eyes landed on the last person I wanted to see right now.

"Kyle?"

This wasn't good. This was the exact opposite of good. This was a freaking disaster.

"I'm here for the cake," Kyle said, not even acknowledging Derek's presence in the room. He just kept his eyes on me and smiled for all he was worth.

The grip on my hand tightened. I looked up at Derek to see the muscles twitching in his clenched jaw. This was bad. I needed to get Kyle out of here fast so I could talk down my boyfriend.

"I'll go get it." Pulling one of my hands from Derek's iron grip, I placed it on his biceps and gave it a quick squeeze. "It's just in the back."

I could feel both of their eyes boring into my back like lasers as I walked to the fridge. The second the doors closed behind me, I slid to the side and pressed my back up against the wall.

I screwed my eyes shut, balling my hands into fists as I cursed the universe for putting me in this position. Kyle and Derek were never supposed to see each other. I was just supposed to hand off a cake and go on with my life like it had never happened.

Crap!

I ran my hands down my face. I had to keep it together and focus on the task at hand. The sooner I gave Kyle his cake, the sooner he would be gone. Then Derek and I could talk this out like reasonable human beings, and everything would be just fine.

I pulled the pink-and-green-striped boxes out of the fridge and couldn't help but smile down at the bakery logo stretched across the top.

"You're a professional," I whispered to myself. "You can do this."

I picked up the first two boxes and made my way back to the front.

The doors made a gentle *thwapping* sound behind me as I stepped through them. I froze.

The tension in the room was so thick I thought I was going to need a chainsaw to cut it. While Derek looked like his spine was doing an impersonation of an ironing board, Kyle leaned against the counter like he owned the place. He didn't look at Derek. Didn't act like he knew he was there. That in and of itself probably pissed my boyfriend off more than him being in my bakery in the first place.

"Here's the first half," I declared, hoping to ease some of the tension. "I'll go get the rest."

I hurried to grab the other cakes and sat them on the counter.

Kyle gestured to one of the boxes. "May I?"

"Of course."

A few beads of sweat broke out across my forehead from the feel of Derek's eyes boring into me. I looked over at him and gulped. The perfect combination of anger and betrayal shaped his features. He tried to meet my eyes, but I looked away. Seeing the hurt I knew had to be there would only make me feel worse.

"These are great, Ally," Kyle said, drawing my attention back to him.

I took his card to the register and rang up his order.

"Help me get these to the car?"

I handed him his receipt and saw Derek's jaw clench out of the corner of my eye. I needed to get Kyle out of there before Derek decided to rip him, or me, a new one.

"Okay." I grabbed the smaller stack of boxes and followed him to the Mustang parked at the curb. We loaded everything into the backseat. Once it was secure, I turned to head back inside. Derek was waiting for me with what I could only assume would be scathing questions. I just hoped I could soothe him before things got too out of hand.

"You did an amazing job," Kyle said, causing me to turn. "Why don't you let me take you to dinner as a thank you?"

I looked at him in astonishment before schooling my features into a polite smile. "I don't think so."

I tried to turn away again, but this time he reached for my hand to pull me back. My head spun in his direction. What on earth? Was he trying to get his ass beat? Derek wasn't necessarily a violent guy, but if the look he was throwing Kyle through the window was any indication, he was about five seconds from turning into the Hulk and smashing him into the pavement puny god-style.

"Come on, Ally. It'll be fun."

I jerked my hand out of his grasp. "Goodbye, Kyle," I said, the finality in my voice unmistakable.

Kyle studied me for a second before nodding in resignation. "Okay. I'll see you later. Thanks again."

He walked around to the driver's side and climbed in. I waited for him to drive off before heading back inside. The bell over the door gave a little ding, and I fell back against the glass. Who would have thought handing over a cake could be so exhausting?

"You want to tell me what that was about?"

The edge in Derek's voice cut through the air like a knife. He stood there, arms crossed, looking for the whole world like a man ready to explode.

Taking a deep breath, I pushed away from the door. "He ordered a cake for an event his office is having."

"And you didn't think to tell me?"

"I didn't want to make a big deal out of it."

I knew it was a mistake the moment the words were out of my mouth. Still, I couldn't seem to keep the rest of them from following. I told him about Kyle's surprise visit to the bakery and the subsequent lunch to finalize the design.

Derek's expression darkened. He held up a hand to stop my ramblings and leveled me with a cold stare. "You went to lunch with the guy, and you never said a word?"

I wanted to kick myself. Why couldn't I have just left that little detail out?

I held my arms out to the side and let them fall against my body with a smack. "I guess I didn't really think about it."

It was a boldfaced lie, and we both knew it. I hadn't said anything because I didn't want to make him mad. Clearly that had backfired.

"Didn't think..." Derek ran a hand down his face and turned away from me. "Jesus, Als." He took two steps before turning back to face me. "Did he try anything?"

"Not really."

Fire ignited in Derek's eyes. "What did he...?" He looked between me and the door, the gears in his head grinding together. It was like watching a countdown. Only instead of champagne and fireworks, it was the fuse on a bomb. I saw the second it hit zero. Derek's hands balled into fists as he moved toward the door.

"Whoa." I took hold of his arm to stop him before he hunted Kyle down and did something he would regret. "It's okay. He asked me to dinner, and I shot him down. Just like I did today."

Derek didn't say anything. He just watched me, his eyes scanning my face for some piece of information. It was only a minute, but it felt like an eternity before he closed his eyes and took a deep breath to ease the tension from his body.

I slid my hand along his arm and brought it to rest on his shoulder. "I've got to go," he said, his voice hollow.

"Derek, I..."

He didn't even look at me before walking out the door.

I watched him go, my hand still hanging in the air where it had been resting on his shoulder. God help me. What had I done?

Chapter Eighteen

"ALLY?"

"Huh?"

I hadn't realized I'd been staring off into space until Brooke called my name.

She snorted. "You didn't hear a word I just said, did you?"

I blinked. "Of course I did. You were…" I racked my brain and came up with nothing. "Okay. No. Sorry."

Brooke just shook her head. "It's okay. Would you rather we finish this tomorrow?"

As much as I hated to admit it, Brooke's suggestion was probably for the best. I hadn't been able to focus on a single thing since Derek stormed out of the bakery. My mind kept drifting back to the look of betrayal on his face when I told him about my meeting with Kyle. He'd been furious, and I honestly couldn't say that I blamed him.

"Okay." I shut my notebook. "Same time tomorrow. We've only got a few weeks left until we open, and I want to make sure it's a success."

Brooke and I closed up shop and headed our separate ways.

The walk back to the apartment felt like some kind of death march. I kept trying to come up with something to say, some sort of explanation that would magically make everything better, but there wasn't one. All I could do was walk Derek through my train of thought and hope he understood where I was coming from enough to forgive me.

I ran through what I was going to say as I walked. Each block I passed added to the trembling sensation in my chest. Then I walked through the door and saw Derek sitting on the couch. The words I'd been practicing for the last half hour flew right out of my brain.

He didn't look at me. He just sat there, eyes facing front, as an eerie silence cloaked our apartment.

My feet felt like lumps of lead as I padded to my seat beside him on the couch. I tried to recall what I'd wanted to say, but it didn't seem to matter. I placed my hand gently on his forearm in a silent plea for acknowledgment.

He didn't move. He kept his eyes straight ahead. When he did finally look down at where my hand rested on his arm, he stayed silent. I desperately wanted him to say something. Anything. Having him scream at me would have been better than this.

My heart pounded in my ears. I tried to open my mouth to speak, but my breath caught in my throat. He had every right to be upset, and I knew it.

"I'm sorry," I managed to whisper.

Derek's eyes shifted towards me without moving his head.

"I'm not mad. At least, not anymore." He placed his hand on top of mine. "I just can't understand why you didn't tell me. I mean, the man is an asshole who left you sitting by yourself in a restaurant. I saw what that did to you, and the thought that you would let him do that again, it just…"

"Wait. You think I want to get back together with Kyle?"

"Do you?"

My jaw fell open in shock. How could he ever think that? "Derek, that's never going to happen."

I scooted closer to him and wrapped my arms around his shoulders. My nails scratched along the short hairs on the back of his neck. Derek closed his eyes and released a breath, the tension in his shoulders slowly fading.

"Why would I want him when I have you?"

His eyes opened. They weren't as vacant as they had been a moment before, but they still lacked the usual spark.

Reaching up, he took my wrists and carefully unwrapped my arms from around his neck.

The grim expression on his face made bile rise at the back of my throat. The only time Derek distanced himself from me was when he was going to tell me something I wouldn't like.

"I talked to my boss today." He glanced down at our joined hands. "He pressed me for an answer about Vegas until I gave him one."

The atmosphere in the room shifted. The air grew heavy as I watched Derek search for the words. He didn't need them. I already knew what he was going to say.

"You told him you'd take it."

Derek nodded.

"That's what you came to the bakery to tell me."

"Yes." His pain-filled eyes looked up at me.

Derek and I had had more than one conversation about the offer. I wanted him to take advantage of the opportunity just as badly as he did, but I wanted to be selfish too. I didn't want him to leave me. A life without Derek in it was not something I could imagine. He had been a daily part of my life since we were kids. Losing him would be like losing an arm. I didn't think I could function without him, but as I looked into his tearful, pleading eyes, I knew I couldn't be the thing that held him back.

"When are you leaving?" I whispered.

Derek's grip on my hands tightened. "The end of next week."

"What!" I jerked out of his grasp and sprang up from the couch. "But that's not enough time. We have to figure out how we're going to make this work. And what about the bakery? You promised you'd be there for the opening. You can't do that if you're in Vegas. I can't do this without you. We haven't..."

My breath came in short gasps. Everything had been perfect between us when I woke that morning. Now my entire universe was crumbling around me.

Derek was on his feet in an instant, pulling me into his arms.

"It's okay," he soothed. "It's okay, Als. Just breathe with me. I've got you."

I focused on the rise and fall of Derek's chest, trying to breathe with him. In. Out. In. Out. My breathing slowed, and Derek loosened his grip on me just enough to look at my face.

A tear ran silently down my cheek. "How are we going to make this work? We don't have enough time."

"We'll figure it out."

"But what if we can't? What if we get too busy, and we can't go see each other? What if we don't have enough time?"

He smoothed the hair back from my face, placing a gentle kiss against my lips. "We'll make time."

"But what if we can't?" I cried. "What if the distance is too much? What happens then?"

For the first time since he told me he was leaving, I saw defeat in Derek's eyes.

"I don't know," he admitted.

We stared at each other as his words sank in. I could already feel the distance between us growing, and he hadn't even left yet.

"I don't want you to leave." The confession was little more than a breath of air, but I knew he'd heard me. "I know I said I would support whatever you decided, and I do. I just don't want you to go out there and decide there's more to life than some stupid baker with a tiny little shop and leave me."

He pulled me in close, lifting my chin with his finger until I was looking him in the eye. "That's not going to happen. You're it for me, Als. No matter where I go or what I do, you are always going to be it for me. I love you."

"I love you too." My voice cracked on the final syllable.

My heart plummeted. You were supposed to be giddy with excitement when someone said they loved you. Instead, all I felt was grief. I'd finally found my other half, and I was losing him.

I looked up at him with wide, fearful eyes to see the same uncertainty staring back at me. Pressing up onto my tiptoes, I kissed him soundly on the lips. Derek might be leaving, but I'd be damned if that meant I was letting him go.

Chapter Nineteen

FEW THINGS IN life made me as happy as a well-stocked store room. It had taken Brooke and me nearly three hours this morning to unload the delivery truck and sort it all out, but the sense of pride I felt when I looked around the room made it all worth it. Even if I did have to finish checking off the inventory list by myself while Brooke went to get us lunch.

The bell over the front door chimed just as my stomach rumbled.

"Thank God!" Hanging the clipboard on its peg near the door, I shut off the light and strode to the front. "My stomach is about to start eating itself. What did you…?"

My shoes squeaked against the freshly laid linoleum. It was like I'd hit an invisible wall.

Kyle was once again standing in my bakery, his most debonair smile on full display. My throat felt like it was trying to close off my air supply. The only reason he would possibly have to be here was if there'd been an issue with the cake. But would he be smiling like that if there'd been an issue?

"Hi." He took his hands out of his pockets and sauntered toward the counter.

"H-hello." My legs finally started working, and I moved to stand behind the counter. He didn't look upset, but if he was going to turn into an irate customer, it was best to keep a barrier between us. "What are you doing here?"

His smile widened. "I just wanted to stop by and tell you what a hit your cake was. Everybody loved it. My boss won't stop raving about it. In fact, he and a few of the VPs are hosting a dinner meeting at Daniel tomorrow night, and they wanted me to see if you would be willing to come along to talk about possibly doing a few more events for us."

I almost swallowed my tongue. Hell, I may have lost brain function for a minute.

Kyle's bosses wanted to meet with me about doing more work for them? Holy crap! Maybe there would be a contract. Oh! That would be perfect to put in the press release I was planning to draft for next week's papers. Having something like that to flaunt right off the bat could help boost sales.

Fighting not to jump up and down like a crazy person, I kept my professional mask in place with a polite smile. "Okay. Sounds great."

"Wonderful." Kyle rapped his knuckles on the counter. "Be ready by seven. I'll have a car come pick you up."

I nodded, waiting for him to disappear around the corner before throwing my head back in a scream of joy. I threw my hands up in the air and shimmied back and forth to a nonexistent beat.

This was amazing. My first solo corporate gig, and already they wanted to meet with me about working for them again. This bakery was going to be brilliant!

I pulled out my phone to text Derek the exciting news when it hit me. The smile melted from my face. This meant I would be working with Kyle again. I tossed the phone onto the counter and folded my arms on it before dropping my head on top of them. All the joy from a moment ago was replaced with sickening dread.

Derek and I had already had one fight because I'd agreed to work for Kyle. Well, that wasn't entirely true. The fight had been more about me not telling him I was working with Kyle. Maybe if I told him and stressed the fact that it was Kyle's bosses that wanted me, not Kyle himself, maybe it wouldn't be such an issue. The dinner meeting was with them, not Kyle, so there was absolutely nothing for us to worry about.

* * *

TENSION ROLLED OFF Derek in waves as he watched me get ready from the doorway.

"I don't understand why you have to go to dinner with him." He crossed his arms over his chest and leaned against the frame.

He'd been less than thrilled about the dinner meeting. To his credit, he was trying to be supportive, but there'd been a strain on our relationship the past few days that hadn't been there before. I'd expected to spend his last few days in New York going at it like rabbits since we didn't know when we would see each other again. Instead, everything felt like it was about to explode.

"I'm not going to dinner with Kyle." I suppressed a groan. "I'm going to a business dinner with his bosses, and he's just going to be there."

"I still don't see why you have to go. Can't you send Brooke?"

I shook my head. "No. They want to meet with me, not my store manager." I struggled with the zipper on my dress for a moment before turning around and gesturing to Derek for help.

He pushed away from the doorframe and zipped up my dress.

I smoothed out the fabric along my torso. "People get together and talk things out over a meal so that everyone's more comfortable. It's just part of business."

Derek placed a kiss on the spot where my neck and shoulder met as he ran his hands down my arms. "I don't like it."

I turned, but he wouldn't meet my eyes. He reached for my hand and brought it up to his lips for a gentle kiss.

"I don't trust him, Als." Derek took a shuffling step in my direction and brought his other hand up to cup my cheek. "Promise me you'll keep your phone on you. And if he tries anything—I mean anything—you'll call me. I swear to God, if he tries to pull anything, I'll…"

I pressed a finger to his lips. "I promise." Rising onto my tiptoes, I placed a chaste kiss on his lips and watched the tension in his shoulders ease ever so slightly.

The sound of my phone chirping from the nightstand caught my attention. I gave Derek a reassuring smile, then retrieved my phone. It was a text from Kyle.

I'm here.

I was a bit surprised that we would be riding together, but I shook it off and looked up at Derek. "My ride's here."

He just nodded and walked out into the living room.

I sighed. Why couldn't being a business owner be simple? You come in. You order. You're gone. Why did there have to be so much networking involved, especially with people that made you and everyone else around you miserable?

My phone chimed again.

You coming?

Stifling a groan, I grabbed my purse and made my way toward the door. I passed Derek sitting on the couch, absentmindedly flipping through the channels, and stopped to place a kiss on his cheek.

He never even looked up.

Pausing at the door to cast one last glance his way, I promised him I would be home soon.

My heart hurt as I made my way down the stairs. Hopefully, the dinner would be quick and simple so I could get home and enjoy the little time Derek and I had left.

Stepping out onto the street, I scanned the area for the classic town car Kyle's company had always used to take us to events. Instead, I almost tripped over a crack in the sidewalk when my eyes landed on Kyle's cherry-red Mustang parked at the curb.

He leaned against the side of the car, hands in his pockets, the smile on his face designed to make every woman in the vicinity swoon.

I contemplated turning around and heading back upstairs. "Where's the car?"

Kyle laughed as he pushed away from the vehicle. "What does this look like?" He opened the passenger door and gestured for me to step inside. "Come on. We don't want to be late."

"What about the company car?"

"We're taking mine tonight. Come on. We don't want to get stuck in traffic."

Swallowing my unease, I crawled inside. I shrank against the door, my hands in my lap and my eyes straight forward. My skin crawled. I closed my eyes and reminded myself it was for the bakery. I could put up with Kyle for one night if it meant good things for my bakery.

* * *

LIGHT ORCHESTRAL MUSIC floated through the air as the maître d' escorted us to our table. Our small, two-person table.

I frowned. "Um, we are…"

Kyle cut me off. "This is perfect. Thank you." He pulled my chair out for me, his eyes pleading for me to sit down.

I narrowed my eyes before slowly lowering myself into the chair as the maître d' informed us that our waiter would be along shortly.

"Kyle," I said, my hackles rising, "why are we at a table for two?"

To his credit, Kyle tried to look sheepish, but I knew him better than that. He never did anything without a reason.

"You said your bosses wanted to meet with me?"

"Okay." Kyle held up his hands in surrender. "I may have lied a little bit."

My mouth hardened into a thin line.

"They do want to meet with you about an exclusive contract to do all their events for the foreseeable future. They just aren't going to be here tonight to discuss it."

I could feel my face growing flush with anger. Squashing down my rising temper, I leveled Kyle with a cold stare. "Then why the hell did you tell me they would be?"

He looked away. "Because I knew you would just keep saying no otherwise."

Damn right I would have! I shook my head at my own stupidity. Derek had told me not to trust Kyle, and he'd been right.

"I'm leaving now."

I grabbed my purse and started to stand.

"No, wait!" Kyle darted to his feet and reached out to grab my hand.

I whipped around to face him. "I'm leaving, Kyle," I said, my voice as cold and flat as an unused baking sheet.

I marched to the door without looking back. The nerve of him. Who in their right mind took their ex to dinner and disguised it as a business meeting expecting it to go well? What did it say about me that I fell for it?

Reaching into my purse, I pulled out my phone. I waited until I was outside to make my call. No need for everyone to hear me eating crow.

"Als?" the voice on the other end of the line said.

"Derek, can you come get me?"

"Dinner not going well?"

I'm sure he was trying to sound supportive, but the little lift in his voice at the end had a distinct *told you so* quality to it.

"Will you please just come and get me? I promise I'll tell you everything when you get here."

"Okay. What's the address?"

I quickly gave Derek the address for the restaurant and ended the call. Thank goodness it was a nice night out. It was going to take him at least half an hour to get here, and the last thing I wanted was to wait inside the restaurant with everyone staring at me.

"Ally!"

I closed my eyes at the sound of Kyle calling out behind me. I was wrong. *This* was the last thing I wanted.

"What do you want, Kyle?" I asked without turning around.

"I want you to give me another chance."

My eyes bulged out of their sockets. I whipped around to face him.

He trotted down the short flight of stairs leading to the restaurant and came to a stop in front of me. "I hate the way things ended between us, and I want to make it right. I never should have left you, and I'm sorry."

I had to be hearing things. There was no way Kyle just said what I thought he said. Not after humiliating me in public and not contacting me for months afterward. He had to be out of his mind.

"Please, Ally."

"You're joking, right?"

He frowned at me like he didn't understand the question.

"Kyle, you're the one that chose to leave me! Remember? You dropped me like a hot pan with no good reason, and now, months later, you suddenly decide you want another chance? It doesn't work that way."

He took a step toward me, arms outreached. "Ally, I..."

I took a step back. "Nothing you say is going to change my mind."

"But we were so good together."

"*Were* is the key word, Kyle. Were. Besides, I'm with Derek now."

Kyle blinked. I don't think he could have looked any more shocked if I'd slapped him with a cannoli.

"I love him," I said, "and even if I didn't, I still wouldn't go back to you. It took me being away from you for me to realize I wasn't happy, and I deserve to be happy."

"You can't honestly think Derek makes you happy?"

"Yes!" I hadn't realized that we'd been steadily getting louder until an old couple passing us on the street stopped to stare at us. Heat filled my cheeks. I looked down at the sidewalk to hide it, but there was no hiding my crimson face once I got going.

"Yes," I repeated, my voice much softer than before. "Derek makes me happy. He makes me feel special. He treats me like I'm the only person who matters, and he supports me and my decisions even if he doesn't agree with them. He told me he didn't want me having dinner with you tonight, but he supported me because I told him it was for my business. He believes in me, and that's a hell of a lot more than I can say for all my years with you."

The muscles along Kyle's jaw twitched. He dropped his chin toward his chest. "You love him, don't you?"

"Yeah," I said, a beaming smile spreading across my face. "I do."

I thought I saw his jaw clench for the briefest of moments before he lifted his eyes to mine. There was a strange look in them, like he was fluctuating between pissed off and heartbroken. The battle raged on for a second before settling on the latter.

"Then I hope he makes you happy," he said, a barely detectable tremor in his voice.

"Thank you."

I faintly registered the sound of a car pulling up behind me.

"Maybe someday we can work our way into being friends?" Kyle asked, the faintest light of hope in his eyes.

I didn't have the heart to tell him no. Despite everything he'd done, I couldn't find it in me to hurt him even more than my little confession already had.

He waved me forward. "Come here."

I stepped forward and accepted one final hug from Kyle. Placing a peck on his cheek, I wished him well before turning toward Derek's car waiting at the curb. There was a newfound lightness in my step. Closure was one hell of a mood lifter.

I opened the door and climbed into Derek's old Cavalier.

"Thanks for picking me up," I said as I settled myself into the passenger seat.

"Have a good time?"

The harshness in his voice made me blink at him. "What do you think?"

Derek hummed in response before pulling away from the curb and pointing us toward home.

I studied his face, illuminated briefly by the streetlights before descending back into darkness.

"Are you okay?" I asked tentatively.

"Fine."

"Are you sure? The strangle hold you have on the wheel says otherwise."

He released his death grip on the wheel, extending and flexing his fingers to let blood flow through them again. His chest rose and fell with the type of long slow breath he always guided me through when I was upset. Something was on his mind. Something I had a feeling I was not going to like.

"Anything happen I should know about?" he asked.

I filled him in on everything that had happened from the time Kyle picked me up to the moment I stepped into the Cavalier.

"You should have listened to me, Als. I told you he was up to something, and you just brushed me off."

I placed a hand on his forearm as he drove. "I know. I'm sorry. I promise I'll listen to you more in the future."

"Good."

The corner of his mouth curled up ever so slightly. I heaved a sigh of relief. We were okay.

"You know," I said as we pulled to a stop near our building, "what I can't understand is why he never contacted me. If he really missed me and wanted to get back together, why didn't he call or show up at the apartment or something? It's not like he didn't know how to find me."

Derek stiffened in the driver's seat and stayed that way all the way up to the apartment. Unlocking the door, he put his keys down and immediately headed for his room.

"I'm going to bed. See you tomorrow, Als."

I gawked after him in silence. What did I say to cause his mood to shift like that? Something was definitely bothering him. I just didn't know what.

Chapter Twenty

SLEEP WAS NOT on the menu that night. I stretched out my arm toward Derek's side of the bed only to find cold sheets where he should have been. Opening my eyes, I glanced around the room in confusion until I heard him puttering around the kitchen.

Something was off about him. It had been ever since he picked me up at the restaurant the night before. If his weird behavior in the car hadn't given it away, the way he'd shut me out when we got home had.

A low grumble of hunger worked its way through my stomach. Throwing the blankets off with a huff, I dragged myself out of bed and shuffled toward the door.

Derek was sitting at the counter eating breakfast. The hinges on the door announced my presence with their usual squeak, but he never moved. He usually turned to greet me with a smile, but this time he kept his back to me like he hadn't heard a thing.

I summoned up all the courage I could muster, effectively gaining about as much as a field mouse, and made my way toward him.

"Hey," I said just above a whisper as I stepped up beside him.

Derek shoved another forkful of scrambled eggs into his mouth. "Hey."

I opened my mouth to say something but couldn't find a way to ask him about last night without sounding like some crazy person. Shaking my head, I went to fix myself a much-needed cup of coffee.

My hand was just reaching into the cabinet for a mug when I heard Derek's voice. "I already made you one."

I looked toward the coffeepot to see a still-steaming mug waiting for me. My heart gave a little flutter. Maybe he wasn't as mad as I thought.

"Thanks."

I wrapped my hands around the warm mug and raised it to my lips. The first sip was like a little piece of heaven. Just the right amount of sugar and creamer, as always.

I turned my attention back to Derek to see that he still wasn't looking at me. Instead, he'd stopped eating and was pushing the food around his plate with his fork.

"I'm sorry," I whispered.

Derek looked up at me, his eyebrows raised in surprise.

"You were right. I shouldn't have gone to that dinner. I'm sorry."

Derek's fork clinked against the plate as he set it down and brought his hand up to rub along his stubbled jaw.

I watched him warily. It was moments like this that made me wish I could read his mind. He didn't look mad, but there was some unnamed emotion simmered just below the surface.

His shoulders rose and fell with his breath. "Kyle's been coming to the gym at least once a week to ask about you."

My body went slack. I just managed to regain my grip on my mug before it went smashing to the ground.

"What?"

Derek pushed his plate away, but he still didn't look at me.

"It started about a month after the two of you broke up," he said hesitantly. "He came by to ask me how you were. I told him it was none of his business, but he wouldn't let it go."

"Why wouldn't he just come see me?"

Derek gave a dry laugh. "He said Brooke would have just thrown him out of the bakery, and he knew I would kick his ass if he showed up at the apartment. He figured if he talked to me at the gym, I couldn't punch him without getting fired."

I couldn't argue with that.

"He showed up often enough that one of the other trainers told him he was going to have to buy a membership and hire me as a trainer if he wanted to keep talking to me. So he did. I started training him once a week, and every week he would find a way to bring you into the conversation."

An odd numbing sensation spread throughout my body. I tried to make sense of everything, but my brain couldn't seem to understand what Derek was telling me. I sat my mug down on the counter and went to sit on the stool next to him.

"Why didn't you tell me?"

He still wouldn't look at me. "He hurt you, Als, and I'll be damned before I let the bastard do it again."

"Don't you think it's a little hypocritical for you to get upset that I didn't tell you Kyle came to the bakery when you never mentioned anything about the gym?"

The look in Derek's eyes when he finally looked at me was gut wrenching. I could see the near frantic desperation in them. "I know. I'm sorry."

I scoffed and rolled my eyes toward the ceiling. "God, we're idiots," I blurted. "Both of us were trying to keep the other from getting hurt, and we ended up doing it ourselves anyway."

Derek took a sip of coffee. "Yeah."

"I'm sorry I didn't tell you about Kyle ordering a cake," I told him. "I didn't think much of it at the time. It was only supposed to be the once and I'd never have to see him again. But you knew he would keep coming back to the gym and never said a word to me."

I worried my lip between my teeth. Part of me wanted to tear into Derek for the hypocritical way he'd reacted to me working with Kyle. What were a few interactions when compared to constant contact? Then I looked at him. I could see the way holding all of this in had been slowly eating away at him. He kept biting the inside of his cheek hard enough to make his jaw quiver. It didn't matter what his reasons were. He regretted it. So did I.

"Let's call it a wash," I offered. "We both screwed up by not saying anything. Let's agree that we'll be open about contact from our crazy exes in the future and try to move on. Okay?"

"Okay." A small smile tugged at the corner of his mouth.

I sighed in relief. We could finally put this mess behind us and move on.

I snorted. "I can't believe he showed up like that. The asshole never tries to contact me, but harassing you at work is apparently okay?"

"He did."

Derek's eyes once again found the half-eaten breakfast on his plate. A subtle tremor made its way through his body. I watched his Adam's apple bob up and down as he swallowed before turning his gaze toward me. There was something close to fear in those crystal-blue eyes of his. Something that had my heart pausing between beats for his response.

"He did try to contact you. I saw his name pop up on your phone a few times before he started showing up at the gym."

I frowned. "I never got any messages."

"That's because I erased them."

My face scrunched in confusion. "You what?"

Derek took a long shuddering breath. "I saw his name pop up on your phone when you were out of the room and rejected the call. He left a voicemail, but I deleted it. Same with the text messages."

A twinge of anger crept up my spine.

"What!" I moved to the far side of the kitchen to give myself some space.

"I'm sorry, Als."

"Why would you do that?" I demanded, turning to face him. "Not telling me about the gym I get, but this... Why on earth would you go through my phone like that? Don't you trust me to make my own decisions?"

"Of course I do. It's just, I saw how badly that asshole hurt you, and I didn't want him to keep jerking you around just so he could do it again."

"So you decided I just shouldn't have a choice?"

I slammed my eyes closed and rubbed at my temples. It felt like the subway was running through my skull. There was a roar in my ears, and the more I thought about what Derek was telling me, the louder it got. I didn't even realize he was standing in front of me until he placed his hand on my arm, jolting me back to reality.

My muscles went rigid. I turned my head to look at him. His eyes pleaded with me to hear him out, but I couldn't think straight. All I could think about was how little he trusted me.

"Don't touch me."

His jaw went slack. A crease formed between his brows as he studied me.

"I need a minute."

With that, I marched to my room. The door rattled inside its frame when I slammed it. I leaned my back against it with a quiet thump. My body shook.

What was happening? Derek and I never fought. Not like this. I ran my fingers through my hair. I needed to escape.

Throwing on some sweatpants and an old ratty shirt, I grabbed my earbuds and headed for the door. Relief washed over me when I didn't see Derek in the living room. I couldn't handle another confrontation right now. Not without yelling at him anyway.

* * *

WALKING THE STREETS for a few hours gave me time to think. While Derek keeping secrets about Kyle's gym visits pissed me off, I couldn't fault him for it. Especially not when I'd been keeping the cake order from him. Still, that didn't excuse him deleting my messages like that. It was a complete invasion of privacy. Just thinking about it made my jaw clench. We were going to have to sit down and have a nice long talk about everything now that I'd had a chance to cool off.

"Derek," I called as I walked through the apartment door.

I looked over to my right to see him emerging from his room, a duffel bag flung over his shoulder. "What's going on?"

Derek set the bag down with a thump. Rubbing the back of his neck, he looked up at me mournfully through his long lashes. "I'm going to go stay with Jackson for a few days."

"Why?"

"You were right," he said. "I should have told you about Kyle coming to the gym. I knew what he was doing, and I should have told you. I never should have touched your phone. It was a dick move, and I'm sorry."

I was across the room and had my arms around his waist in the blink of an eye. "I'm sorry too," I whispered into his chest.

Derek's strong hands took hold of my upper arms and pushed me away. A dull ache formed inside my chest as I looked up at him in question.

"Ally." He sighed. "I think it's probably best if we just go ahead and cut our losses."

The ache exploded into a searing pain that tore away at my insides.

"W-what do you mean?"

A tear formed in the corner of Derek's left eye. "Come on. We're already lying to each other. How can we possibly make this work from opposite ends of the country when we can't even be honest with each other when we live in the same apartment? It's better to do this now instead of trying to hold on for a few more days until I leave." He took a step back and reached for his duffel bag. "I'll be back later for the rest of my stuff. Don't worry about packing anything. I'll take care of it."

He tucked a strand of hair behind my ear with a sorrowful smile before moving past me toward the door.

I opened my mouth to take a breath, but I couldn't get air into my lungs. A boulder had lodged itself in my throat. I swallowed against it and was finally able to take in a gasp of air.

"Derek, wait," I cried.

He was already standing with the door half open. My vision swam with unshed tears, but I could just make out the little droplets making their way down his face.

I stood there with my arm stretched out toward him, but he didn't move away from the door.

"Goodbye, Als," he whispered.

The sound of the door shutting behind him was like a shotgun blast straight to the heart. My knees wobbled. I barely made it to the couch before my legs refused to hold me up anymore.

A single tear made its way down my face. I kept my eyes on the door, willing him to turn around and come back.

Chapter Twenty-One

~ ∞ ~

"YOU READY FOR this?"

I turned away from the bakery window to see Brooke beaming at me.

"I guess we'll find out." We shared a laugh before I gestured to the dozen or so people gathered outside. "Looks like your idea worked."

She grinned. "I told you handing out cookies with those flyers would bring people in. Give them a taste of what they can look forward to."

"This is so exciting!" my new assistant, Max, squealed as she bounced on her toes in excitement.

She was a culinary student at the nearby college who would be working for me part time in the mornings while she finished school.

"Are you ready, Miss O'Connor?" Councilwoman Stone asked. "It's time to cut the ribbon."

A nest of hornets erupted in my stomach. Plastering a smile onto my face, I gave her a quick nod before turning the lock on the door.

Our small band stepped out into the crisp morning air. Councilwoman Stone addressed the crowd, but I didn't pay attention to what she was saying. I spotted a few of my "kitchen clients" in the crowd and gave them a small wave, but the one face I most wanted to see wasn't there.

"Miss O'Connor."

My eyes snapped back to the councilwoman.

"If you would do the honors." She held out the oversized pair of scissors and motioned for me to step behind the large red ribbon stretched out in front of the bakery.

"Go on," Brooke urged in a stage whisper.

I stepped forward and thanked Councilwoman Stone before taking the scissors from her. My hands shook as I closed them around the large handles.

Councilwoman Stone's voice boomed above the crowd. "I declare this bakery officially open!"

I held my breath as I plunged the handles together and the blades sliced through the ribbon. The crowd clapped. I handed the scissors back and moved aside to let the crowd funnel into the bakery. I nodded and smiled, but I'm sure people could tell I was faking. Despite my excitement, the hollowness inside my chest wouldn't go away. I finally had everything I ever wanted, but it meant nothing without him.

* * *

I LET OUT a long sigh and turned the lock on the door.

"What a day!" Brooke exclaimed as she shuttered the windows.

I nodded in agreement. There wasn't a muscle in my body that wasn't sore. Don't get me wrong. Having a bustling grand opening was amazing. I just hadn't thought it would be this tiring.

"Let's just hope it stays this way." Pushing away from the door, I fished my phone out of my pocket to check my messages. A blank screen stared back at me.

"Still no word?"

I looked over to see Brooke putting the cash box in the safe and shook my head.

She put a comforting hand on my shoulder. "I'm sure you'll hear from him soon."

I tried to return her reassuring smile, but all I could muster was a half-hearted lift at the corners. The last time I'd heard from Derek was when he left to stay with Jackson. I'd been checking my phone all day, convinced that he would at least send me a good-luck text. All of our years of friendship at least warranted that, right?

Walking out the back door, Brooke and I said our final goodbyes for the night before heading our separate ways. I only made it about three blocks before hailing a cab. It was an added expense I wasn't sure I could afford now that I was down a roommate, but my twitching thighs still had to make it up the stairs.

I closed my eyes and let my head fall back against the seat. A chirping sound echoed in the otherwise silent cab, and my eyes flew open. I frantically dug through my purse. My hand closed around the little pink rectangle and yanked it out of the bag. My pulse accelerated as I unlocked the screen. A smile formed on my face when I saw the message notification and tapped it.

My leg started bouncing as I waited for the message to open. It wasn't until the name flashed across the top of the screen that I realized I'd been holding my breath. Letting it out in a sigh, I read the message from one of my regulars congratulating me on my grand opening.

Dagger. Plunge. Twist.

The cab pulled up to a stop in front of my building. I thanked the cabby before dragging myself from the seat with a groan I'd expect to hear from a person twice my age.

I zombie-shuffled into the building. My bed was calling to me like a mythical siren, and I was all too ready to let myself be dashed against the rocks for the night.

"Hello, Ally, dear," a familiar voice called.

I paused with my foot on the first step and turned to see Mrs. Henderson standing near the bank of mailboxes with a smile on her kind face.

"Hey, Mrs. Henderson."

She grinned up at me before looking back down at the stack of mail she was pulling from her mailbox.

"Where's Pepper?"

"Oh, he's sleeping," she said. "I figured I could check my mail alone just this once. How was your opening? I'm so sorry I missed it."

I backed away from the stairs and went to stand in front of her. "Good. Exhausting. We had people in and out all day."

The grandmotherly smile on her face was infectious. "I'm so proud of you. I bet that man of yours is too."

My smile faltered. It wasn't her fault. Derek and I hadn't exactly advertised our split in the tenant newsletter, and with all the work prepping for the bakery, I'd barely had time to eat or sleep, let alone fill everyone in on my ever-complicated relationship status.

"Have a good evening, Mrs. Henderson."

"You too, dear."

I collected my own mail and headed back toward the stairs.

I flipped through the usual stack of bills and junk mail. Moving another useless credit card offer to the back of the stack, a glossy four-by-six postcard caught my eye. There was a photo of the world-famous Las Vegas sign with the strip in the background. My heart started beating double-time. There was only one person who would send me a postcard from Vegas.

I sprinted up the rest of the stairs. My hands shook furiously as I struggled to unlock the door. After the third miss, I stopped, closed my eyes, and took a deep breath before refocusing on the lock.

The key slid in. The tumblers clicked into place, allowing the door to swing open. I tossed my things onto the side table and turned my attention back to the postcard.

My mouth felt like a jar of cotton balls. What if the card wasn't actually for me? I hadn't checked the back to see if my name was on it. Mail was put in the wrong box in my building all the time.

"Just read it, Ally," I scolded myself.

Flipping over the card, I let my eyes wander over the writing on the back. It took me less than a second to recognize the familiar script.

Congrats on your opening. I hope it went well. - D

I flipped the card back and forth a few times. There was nothing else written anywhere on the card. I drew my lower lip between my teeth and dropped the card onto the table with the rest of the mail. Reaching for my phone, I pull up Derek's number, then stopped.

He didn't want to talk to me. He would have called if he did, not sent a generic card he could easily have picked up anywhere in town.

I walked unseeingly to the couch and collapsed, my head tilted back against the cushions. A familiar twinge worked its way through my heart. I closed my eyes and could see the look of disgust on Derek's face just as clearly as the last time I saw him. Letting myself fall to the side, I curled up in a ball on the couch and let the pain of what should have been the best day of my life take over.

* * *

I LOOKED AT the numbers again.

"Are you sure these numbers are right?" I lifted an eyebrow.

"Are you doubting my math skills," Brooke sassed with a grin. She placed her mug on the coffee table and turned sideways on the couch so she was facing me completely. "I double-checked them twice."

"Wow."

I looked back down at the bakery's financial statement for the first month. Profits were way above what I'd projected. I knew we'd been doing a lot of business. That was the whole reason Brooke and I sat together at my place to look over the numbers on the day we were closed. We couldn't find time anywhere else.

"Thank God for word of mouth," Brooke declared.

Foot traffic had increased since NYU was back in session. Max had even started coming after classes a few days a week to take over restocks so I could focus on orders, and I had her working some of those too.

"Think we're ready to hire someone full time?" Brooke drawled.

I looked from the ledger to Brooke and back again. I shrugged. "It's hard to say. The numbers are good, but I don't want to get ahead of myself."

I sat the laptop on the coffee table and rose to my feet. I tilted my coffee mug toward Brooke in a silent question.

"Sure."

I refilled both of our mugs. Placing the steaming mug in front of her, I noticed her studying something sitting on the table. I followed her gaze to the postcard Derek had sent me the day of the opening. Staring at it had become a nightly ritual. I'd tried to throw it away once, but I didn't have it in me. I'd broken out into a cold sweat and hyperventilated to the point that I had to sit on the kitchen floor until I pulled myself together. Tossing out that card would be the end of it. As long as I had it, I had hope.

"Still no word?" she asked.

I shook my head. "Not yet."

"You know," she said conspiratorially, "if you hired somebody full time, you could probably sneak away to see him for a few days."

My head jerked back. "Do I have to remind you how much work we have to do at the bakery? Even with an extra person, there's no way I could just leave. I have to take care of the business."

She scoffed. "That's what I'm here for. I can watch the place for a few days while you go get your man back."

"It's not going to happen, Brooke."

She set her mug down with a clank and turned to face me. "How many times a day do I see you staring at your phone, hoping it will ring?" she asked. "Or what about the number of times I've seen you race to open a text message just to be disappointed when it's not from him? Hmm?"

I looked away.

"Face it, Ally. You need to talk to him, and your whole moping-about thing isn't going to get better until you do." She snatched the card off the table and waved it at me. "You have his address. Just take a few days and fly out to see him for a weekend. Maybe then you two will stop acting like three-year-olds and actually talk."

"No," I said emphatically.

"Why not?"

"Because ambush isn't exactly my style, okay?"

I pushed up off the couch and marched back into the kitchen. I was going to need something stronger than coffee if we were having this conversation.

"Then call him when you're getting on the plane," Brooke said.

"No."

"Yes."

My hand had already closed around a wine glass before I thought better of it. Drinking before noon was never a good sign.

"Okay. Fine." I pulled a water glass from the shelf and filled it before turning back to Brooke. "Let's say I do decide to go see Derek. Who's going to take care of everything at the bakery? Max is only there in the mornings. She can't do pastries and manage the cake orders in five hours a day."

"I can make pastries," Brooke offered.

I gave her a knowing smirk. "You're willing to get up at four a.m.

every day to go to work."

Her face scrunched up in disgust. "Good point."

I saluted her with my glass.

"That's just another reason to hire somebody," she said.

I shook my head and took a drink.

"I appreciate the fact that you want to give newbies like Max a shot, but you need somebody with some experience back there with you. We've only been open a month, and you're already working through lunch five days out of the six we're open. Forget Derek for a minute, and think about yourself. You need help, Ally."

I pursed my lips. The woman had a point. Between the regulars and the new business coming in off the street, I was already drowning in work. I'd actually had to turn down an order this week because of it, and that wasn't good for business.

"All right," I conceded. "I'll put out some feelers, but I'm not promising to hire anyone right now, and I'm definitely not doing it just so I can go see Derek."

Brooke waved her hand dismissively. "Fine. Fine. As long as you take lunches this week, we'll call it even."

"You drive a hard bargain, Miss Dalton, but I'll take it."

I stuck my hand out, ready to shake on it. Brooke took my hand and shook it with authority. The straight no-nonsense business faces only lasted for about .01 seconds before we both dissolved into laughter.

* * *

KEEPING A PROFESSIONALLY pleasant smile on my face during an interview was one of the hardest things I'd done as a bakery owner. Finding Max to help part time had been easy. Her portfolio of work from school had been outstanding, and her class schedule made her the perfect fit for the morning shift. Finding another full-time decorator, on the other hand—now, that was a challenge.

"Thank you for coming in, Sasha." I stood and extended my hand toward the woman in front of me. "I'll be in touch."

Brooke caught my eye as I led Sasha to the door. She raised her eyebrows in question. I shook my head before plastering a smile back on my face and waving goodbye to the latest in a line of not-quite-right bakers.

"So?"

I locked the bakery door and pulled the shades before flopping into an empty booth.

"Not enough experience to do the kind of orders we've had coming in." I groaned, tilting my head back to look at the ceiling. "Ugh. This sucks."

Brooke walked around the counter and sat across from me. "You'll find someone. Just give it time."

I hummed in agreement. My eyes drifted toward a newspaper someone had left in the corner of the booth. I dragged the paper toward me and let my eyes absentmindedly wander over the black ink. There were at least a dozen more résumés on my desk that I needed to look through, but I just couldn't bring myself to do it at the moment.

Flipping the page, my eyes drifted to the obituaries, as if I would find someone there. Shaking my head at my own stupidity, I started to close the paper, when a name jumped out at me. *Mohamed Alfied.* Where did I know that name from?

I read over the tiny article, my eyes growing wider the farther I went. *Survived by his wife, Toni, and their son...*

My heart clenched at the mention of my former boss. *First the bakery and now this. She must be so devastated.*

A lightbulb clicked on in my head. I looked from Brooke to the paper and back again, a half-crazed smile spreading across my lips.

"What is it?" Brooke asked, her eyebrows knitting together.

I slid the paper toward her and pointed to the obit.

Brooke looked down at the paper. "A dead guy?" she asked. "Really, Ally? I don't think people are going to want to eat something baked by a zombie. I know people love *The Walking Dead* and all but..."

"No." I chuckled. "Read it."

I watched with bated breath as Brooke's mouth fell open.

"Holy shit!" She sputtered for a moment before pulling herself together. "Um, Ally, I know the woman made your life a living hell, but isn't being happy about her husband dying a bit much?"

The smile slid off my face. It hadn't occurred to me how it would look for me to be grinning like an idiot at the news of his demise.

"No. No." I waved her off. "That's not it. It's Toni."

She shook her head at me.

"I could hire Toni."

Her back went ramrod straight. "Please tell me you're joking."

"Nope. She has all the things I'm looking for. She may have been a nightmare to work for, but the woman knows her stuff. And she knows what it takes to make a business run. She's perfect."

Brooke pursed her lips. "I think you're forgetting one little thing."

I cocked my head to the side.

"She's a monster."

I huffed a laugh and smiled. "Point, but look at what she had to have been dealing with. I'm willing to cut her a little slack for that. Anyone would have been a bitch with that kind of stress. Besides, she won't be the one in charge this time. I will. If she tries to pull any of that stuff again, she's gone."

If you'd told me a year ago that I would be defending Toni, I would have told you to give me some of whatever it was you were on. It's funny how one little conversation can change your entire perception of a person.

Brooke pushed the paper toward me. "So, are you going to call her?"

* * *

HAVING TONI SITTING across from me at my desk was surreal. Here I was sitting in the power seat, and Toni was the one that looked like she wanted to sink through the floor.

"I'm sorry to hear about your husband," I sputtered, hoping my expression was more pained than nauseated.

Maybe Brooke was right. Maybe this was a bad idea. Here I was sitting in the power seat, and Toni still had me shaking.

"Thank you." She looked down at her clasped hands resting in her lap.

She looked like she'd lost weight since the last time I'd seen her, and the undeniable bags and dark circles under her eyes made her look like she'd aged ten years overnight. I couldn't even imagine what she must have been going through. If anything like that ever happened to Derek, I... No. I was not going there.

I cleared my throat, and Toni looked up at me.

"I, uh, I guess you were surprised to hear from me."

"I was," Toni confirmed. "You said you wanted me to join your team?"

"That's right. You'd be helping me with the everyday stuff as well as taking special orders when they come in."

"And why would I do that?" Toni asked. "So you can take the credit for my work?"

"Of course not. Whoever does a special order here gets the credit and a commission. I've put together a basic scale for pricing a cake so that everything will be fair."

I reached into my desk and pulled out the laminated sheet. I held it out to her. Toni gave me the eye for a moment before taking the offered paper from my hand.

She read over the page carefully before flipping it over and doing the same to the back, then looked up at me over the edge of the paper, her eyebrows raised slightly.

"This is a rather comprehensive list."

I beamed. "Thank you."

She handed the paper back to me. I put it away and looked up to see her studying me carefully.

"Why me? You don't like me, so why would you want to work with me again?"

That was the question I'd been asking myself repeatedly since the idea first crossed my mind.

Taking a deep breath, I looked her straight in the eye. "Because you're good at what you do," I told her. "Despite our differences, I know the kind of work you can do, and that's the kind of work I want coming out of my bakery. To get that level of quality, I need the best people working for me. That's you. I just need to know that you will stick to whatever design the customer chooses. You run out of time, ask for help. Don't make changes without clearing them first. You do that and treat people with respect, I don't see any reason why we can't work together."

My heart was beating so hard that I was sure Toni could see the outline of it through my shirt.

Toni was like a statue. Her dark, unblinking eyes never left my face. What was she looking at? I'd wiped all the flour off my face before she arrived. I'd checked. Twice.

"All right," she said, inclining her head slightly. "I'll work for you."

My shoulders slumped.

"But I want your word that you will not interfere with any of the cakes I design."

"The only time I intend to get involved is if a customer has an issue," I told her. "I'll help when asked, but beyond that, I intend to be as hands off as possible."

She nodded.

I held out my hand. "Welcome to the team."

Toni studied my hand for a moment. She eyed it like it would bite her before reaching out to shake it.

As we shook, the corners of her permanent scowl turned upward and kept going until I saw what could only be described as an honest-to-goodness smile.

"When do you want me to start?" she asked, suddenly sounding excited about the prospect.

"Is tomorrow too soon?"

The woman laughed—actually laughed—and shook her head. "No. I can be here tomorrow."

"Great. Let me show you around."

I rose to my feet and waited for her to do the same. Brooke gave me a harsh frown when I smiled at her as we passed. Then she saw the smile on Toni's face and did a double take.

What the...? she mouthed.

I just shrugged and ushered Toni into the back room.

* * *

THANK GOD FOR peaceful days. The morning rush had been hell, but the afternoon had dwindled down to a nice even pace that allowed me to get more work done. I'd just finished putting the final touches on the only cake order we had left to complete when I heard Brooke call from the front.

"Mail!"

I cast Toni a quick glance to see how the puff pastry was coming.

Her transition from employer to employee had gone surprisingly well. With the exception of one small incident with Max, she'd been flawless.

"I'll be right back," I told her.

She gave me a quick nod without looking up from her work.

Setting my things aside, I made my way to the front of the store. "Anything exciting?"

"Junk mostly. Same as anywhere else."

I rested my forearms on the counter, letting my head hang. I took a long cleansing breath.

"You okay?" Brooke asked.

I rubbed my hand across my forehead as she sat the mail on the counter.

"You sure don't look it."

"I didn't get much sleep is all."

"Something on your mind?"

I looked down at my hands, fascinated by the feeling of the tips of my nails running along the pads of the fingers.

Brooke tossed the stack of mail aside with a thud. "Talk."

I sighed. There was only one response for that tone. Offer up the information freely or let the interrogation begin.

"I got a letter from Derek last night."

Brooke stood at attention. "Really?"

I nodded.

"What did it say?"

"He mailed back his key. Apparently, he forgot to leave it behind and just kept forgetting to send it."

I'd felt hollow after reading his note the night before. The key had fallen from the envelope and clattered on the floor, my heart falling right along with it.

"It's funny," I said. "Part of me was hoping he'd kept his key on purpose. But now..."

"Oh, honey."

Brooke pulled me into the circle of her arms. I buried my face in her shoulder, and she rubbed a hand up and down my back.

"Ally," she said when I backed away, "you have got to talk to him."

I shook my head. "He wouldn't answer my calls right after he left. Why would he start now?"

"What's wrong?"

I looked up to see Toni giving me a curious look. I waved her away like it was nothing. I didn't need everyone knowing my business. Brooke thought otherwise, giving her the *Soap Opera Digest* version of my life. Toni listened quietly. The battle going on in her brain was written all over her face.

"You should go after him."

My eyes nearly shot out of my head. "What?"

"If you love him, you need to tell him. Take it from me. Living a life without the one you love is a horrible fate. I don't want that for you. Go after him, and if he won't see you, so be it. At least you did all you could."

"But the bakery!"

"Pfft." Brooke waved her hand at me. "We can hold down the fort for a few days, and if it gets crazy, I'm sure we can get Max to come in for a couple of hours this weekend."

I pulled my bottom lip between my teeth.

"Allyson." Toni laid a hand on my shoulder. Her steady gaze held mine. "Don't let this be something you regret. The best bakery in the world will never make up for not having the man you love beside you. Trust me. I know."

The truth of her statement was written all over her face. The pain of losing her husband still haunted her eyes. A pang of sympathy ran through my chest.

"Okay."

Both women stared at me like they hadn't heard me.

I took a deep breath. "I'll go."

Brooke gave a fist pump. "Yes! I'm going to go buy you a ticket."

"Thanks, Brooke."

"No need to thank me," she called over her shoulder. "I'm using your credit card."

A smile the size of the Chrysler Building broke out on my face. Untying my apron, I gave Toni the rundown of everything I needed her to do for the next forty-eight hours. She followed me around the bakery like a whirlwind, jotting down notes on a pad of paper.

"That should do it." I turned to face her. "If there's an emergency, call me, and I'll be on the next flight out."

"No, you won't." Brooke walked into my office and grabbed my boarding pass off the printer. "You're going to get your ass to Vegas and stay there until you and Derek work everything out."

I took the pass from her. "Fingers crossed." I held my fingers in front of my face.

With a few more *good lucks*, I was out the door and hailing a cab, all the while wondering what I'd just gotten myself into.

Chapter Twenty-Two

DEREK'S APARTMENT BUILDING loomed over me. It may as well have been Fort Knox, as intimidating as it was. Sweat beaded along my forehead, and my heart pounded like I had been running a marathon. I tried to step away from the curb, but my feet refused to get the signal.

I looked back down at the postcard in my hand and checked the return address against the number on the building. I was in the right place. Now all I had to do was go inside and knock on the door. Simple, right?

Is it too late to turn around and hail a cab? Maybe the airline will let me exchange my return ticket for an earlier flight. People do that kind of thing all the time, right? No big deal.

Closing my eyes, I tightened my grip on the handle of my rolling suitcase.

"You got this."

I pulled my shoulders back and forced my shaking legs to carry me to the front door, the wheels on my suitcase clicking along the concrete. A frown crossed my face when I opened the door. It didn't creak like the one back home did. I took in the main entrance and froze. I'd seen hotels that weren't as nice as this place. Was it even okay for me to wheel my suitcase across the high-shine polished floor? There were no scuff marks and scratches on the walls from kids running their toy cars across them. I bet the elevator even worked. No wonder Derek had mailed me the key.

Another wave of anxiety swept over me. My insides felt like they were vibrating at supersonic speed. I clamped my arms around my waist to keep my organs on the inside before forcing my legs to take me to the elevator.

Each floor I passed made my heart beat faster. I could practically feel it pounding in my throat by the time the ominous ding announced my arrival on the fourth floor.

Stepping out of the elevator, I checked the apartment number one more time: 4B. A quick scan of the hallway told me it was most likely on the far left. I started walking, and before I knew it, the door was in front of me.

I raised my fist to knock, but I couldn't bring myself to rap my knuckles against the door.

What was I doing? Derek didn't want to see me. If he'd wanted to see me, he would have asked me to come see him. He didn't want to talk to me. That was why he'd ignored all my texts and calls. I couldn't do this.

Spinning, I made my way back toward the elevator. This was a stupid idea. There was no way this was ever going to work. I stuck my free hand into my purse and fished for my phone. Maybe an Uber would be close enough to get me to the airport.

I looked down to find my elusive cell and collided with a solid wall of flesh and bone. My bag flew from my hand, scattering its contents across the floor.

"Oh my God!" I gasped. "I'm so sorry."

My face must have been as red as a tomato. I was too mortified to look at the person I had just tried to run down. Dropping to my knees,

I snatched my scattered belongings from the floor and shoved them back into my purse. Why couldn't I make a quick exit for once in my life? This moment couldn't get any worse.

"Ally?"

I was wrong.

I ran my eyes from the well-worn running shoes up to the bewildered face staring down at me.

"What are you doing here?" Derek asked.

I blinked up at him like an idiot. "Uh..." I tucked a strand of hair behind my ear and rose to my feet. "I came to see you?"

I thought I saw the corner of his mouth form a smirk before turning downward. He took hold of my upper arms and asked what had happened to the bakery.

"You guys just opened. Is everything all right? Are you okay?"

I stopped the tiniest sliver of hope that had taken root inside my chest at the clear concern in his voice.

"I'm fine," I told him, resting my hands on his biceps. "The bakery is great. Everything is fine."

As if he realized what he had been doing, Derek dropped his hands and took a half step away from me. His eyes narrowed.

"Then why are you here?"

I gave him a half shrug. "I told you. I wanted to see you."

Keeping my composure while Derek stared me down was torture. His searching eyes made me want to melt through the floor and slink back to New York.

His expression softened. "You came all the way to Vegas just to see me?"

I nodded.

The little half smile made its way back onto his face. "Come on. We can talk inside."

He led me down the hall and into his apartment without another word.

The apartment looked like something out of *Architectural Digest*. Everything was dark fabrics and straight lines. I couldn't imagine the Derek I knew being comfortable here. He liked mismatched patterns and well-worn leather couches with armrests wide enough to sit on. He liked his space to look lived in. This looked like a sound stage for a photoshoot..

"The company picked this place out," Derek said as if he'd been reading my mind. "It came fully furnished. Not really my style, but when somebody else is paying the moving costs..."

I shifted my weight from foot to foot and kept my eyes on anything but Derek. For the first time in my life, I felt uncomfortable in front of him.

The silence in the room stretched on for what seemed like an eternity. I'm pretty sure you could have actually seen a sundial move before either of us spoke.

"You, uh, you thirsty?" Derek asked. "All I've got right now is water and beer."

I frowned and looked at the clock. "Isn't eight a.m. a little early for a beer?"

He chuckled. "Yeah." He gestured toward the uncomfortable looking couch. "Have a seat. I'll get you a glass."

I perched on the edge of the couch and fiddled with the hem of my shirt. Despite rehearsing my speech on the flight, I couldn't remember a single word. I knew what I wanted to say. I just couldn't seem to say it.

"Here ya go."

I nearly jumped out of my skin at the sound of Derek's voice. I placed a hand over my racing heart and looked up to see him extending a small glass of water toward me.

"Thanks."

I took a sip of the cool liquid while Derek took a seat on the opposite end of the couch.

"Why didn't you tell me you were coming?"

I kept my eyes on the glass in my hands. "I was afraid you'd tell me not to come."

More silence. I chanced a glance in his direction. Derek had his lips pursed in thought.

He rubbed at his jaw and nodded. "You're probably right."

"Are you mad?"

"No," he answered, his voice low and flat. "I just don't understand what you're doing here."

"I miss you," I offered weakly.

"You could have called."

I scoffed. "Would you have answered?" The harshness in my tone made us both flinch. "Sorry. Spending five hours on a plane before sunrise apparently makes me bitchy. I didn't mean it to come out that way."

"Yes, you did."

I looked away in shame.

"But I don't blame you. You're right. I probably wouldn't have answered."

"Why are you ignoring me?"

It was Derek's turn to look away. I watched his shoulders tighten and his jaw clench. "It's too early for this." He ran a hand down his face before pushing himself to his feet. "Look, I have to go to the gym."

I looked down at the glass in my hands and nodded.

So, this was it. Five minutes together, and he was going to send me packing. I never should have wasted the money to fly out here. I knew it was pointless. Why did I let Brooke and Toni talk me into this? I should have just stayed home and let him live his life in peace.

I placed the glass on a coaster and leaned over to gather my things.

"Where are you staying?" Derek asked.

I stood. "I, uh, I don't know yet. I figured I'd just find a hotel or something. I'm not going to be in town long."

He shook his head. The grin on his face was the only thing telling me he wasn't mad.

"Why don't you go throw your things in the spare room over there?" He gestured toward a door on the other side of the apartment. "We'll head down to the gym for a bit, then I'll buy you breakfast. How does that sound?"

My brain took about half a minute to realize what he'd said. He wasn't kicking me out. A faint glimmer of hope bubbled up inside my chest. Nodding, I quickly deposited my things in the spare room before following Derek out the door.

* * *

"HOLY CRAP."

This wasn't a gym. It was a cathedral. Floor-to-ceiling mirrors. A smoothie bar. This place had everything. It was the gym in New York dialed to an eleven.

Derek chuckled at my startled gasp. "Come on." He took my elbow and guided me through the building. "We don't open for another week, but the feedback we're getting from the preview members has been amazing. The phones have been ringing off the hook with people asking about memberships. We've already blown our early membership goal out of the water."

It was impossible to miss the pride in his voice. The man was practically beaming.

"I'm happy for you."

"Thanks." He motioned me toward his office and told me to have a seat. "I have to go talk to a couple of the trainers real quick, then we'll go get breakfast, okay?"

I smiled at him and nodded, but the smile slid off of my face when he walked through the door.

My head dropped into my hands. I wanted Derek to be successful, but seeing it made me realize just how pointless my trip was. This was his dream. I'd be the shittiest person in history if I asked him to give it up now.

The sound of his deep voice broke me out of my haze.

"You ready?"

I jumped about a foot into the air, nearly landing on the floor. "Hell," I said, placing my hand over my racing heart. "You scared the crap out of me."

"Sorry."

"It's okay." I took a deep breath to make my racing heart slow down.

I followed Derek toward the front of the gym. Making a beeline for the smoothie bar, I read over the options. Were these things even food? Who in their right mind would put spinach and pineapple in the same drink? Gross.

"What are you doing?"

Derek frowned at me from the entryway.

I cast a quick glance up at the menu. "Deciding what I want for breakfast?"

He raised an eyebrow at me. "You mean to tell me that you took a red-eye all the way out here and all you want to eat is a bunch of blended fruit?"

I shrugged.

Derek chuckled and gestured for me to follow him out the front door. "Come on."

I followed Derek across the street to an old diner that looked like it had been ripped straight from a '60s TV show. I halfway expected "Happy Days" to start playing on the jukebox in the corner when the bell over the door signaled our arrival.

"Have a seat wherever you like," the woman behind the counter shouted at us as she refilled a man's coffee mug.

Derek put his hand on the small of my back and guided me to a booth. The simple touch sent a tingle all the way to my toes. I smiled. This was a good sign, right? People didn't touch someone like that if they didn't want them around.

Another waitress that looked to be about ten years younger than us walked up to our table and placed a couple of menus in front of us.

"Welcome to Tammy's Diner," she said. "Can I get you all a cup of coffee while you look over the menu?"

"Sounds great," Derek answered. "Ally?"

"Yes, please."

She flipped up the coffee mugs in front of us and filled them with the strong black liquid.

"I'll be right back to take your orders."

I gave her a nod in thanks before turning my attention to the laminated menu in front of me.

I could feel Derek's eyes on me and peeked at him over the top of the menu. He looked away the instant he saw me look up, pretending to read his menu for a minute before looking back up at me. It was my turn to look away before I got caught staring.

I pulled my lower lip between my teeth. This was ridiculous. We were adults. We should be able to handle one awkward conversation. I lifted my eyes to see a grin spreading across Derek's face.

A laugh crept its way up my throat. I tried to hold it in, but all that accomplished was turning it into a snort that sent Derek's head flying back as he broke into a boisterous laugh.

"We're idiots," I confessed through a laugh.

Derek wiped tears of laughter from his face. "As long as you remember you're the one who said it."

I rolled my eyes as the waitress walked back up to our table. A couple of minutes and a few omelet orders later, we were back to the tension that had been the hallmark of our morning.

"So"—Derek took a sip of his coffee and set the mug back on the table—"how's the bakery?"

My eyes lit up at the thought of my baby. Derek listened with a smile on his face while I prattled on about everything from opening day to the quantities of flour in the puff pastries we sold in a day.

"Oh!" I bounced in my seat in excitement. "I forgot to tell you the best part. Guess who's working for me now?"

Derek moved to take another sip of his coffee and shrugged.

"Toni."

Coffee nearly erupted from Derek's mouth. Thankfully, he got a hand up just in time to keep me from wearing it. I threw my head back in laughter.

"You're kidding?" He wiped a bit of coffee off his chin.

"Nope. She started a few weeks ago. She's actually been a huge help."

Derek frowned.

"No, seriously. Remember that talk I had with her when she came by the apartment? That really made me see her in a new light. Then, when I saw her husband's obituary in the paper, I don't know... It just sort of fit."

The waitress returned with our breakfast, and we both thanked her before I went on with my story.

"I'll admit I wasn't too sure at first. I caught her berating the girl who helps in the mornings and kind of flipped out on her, but everything's been great since then."

I dove into my omelet. The flavors of the peppers and cheese exploded on my tongue, and I gave a little moan of appreciation.

"I'm proud of you, Als."

I stopped with the fork halfway to my mouth. That name. I hadn't realized just how much I'd missed hearing it until then.

"Thanks."

Derek gave me one of those lopsided grins that turned my insides to mush. Heat rose up like a wildfire in my cheeks, and I looked away.

The conversation stalled off and on after that. Derek filled me in on the gym. It had been my turn to nearly do a spit-take when he told me about one of the new employees accidentally locking themselves in a tanning bed.

"They were fine," he told me. "I think she was redder from embarrassment than being burnt."

Derek wiped his face with his napkin and signaled the waitress that we were ready for the check. I reached for my purse to pay for my half, but he waved me off.

"I've got it." He handed the waitress a few bills and told her to keep the change.

We stood. Derek motioned for me to go ahead of him, his hand once again finding my lower back.

"Look," Derek said once we were on the sidewalk, "I hate to do this, but I've got to get back to work. Why don't I give you my key, and you can go sightseeing or something? I'll meet you back at the apartment around six or so. We can talk then?" He pulled the key off his key ring and handed it to me. "Really talk."

I took the key, careful not to let my fingers touch his.

"Okay. I'll see you later then."

"See ya."

I stood on the sidewalk staring down at the key resting in my palm. It was going to be a very long day.

* * *

MY FEET SCUFFED along the wooden floor. Back and forth. Back and forth. If I'd had a Fitbit, it would have been cheering for the number of steps I'd taken just pacing the length of the apartment.

After Derek had given me his key, I'd tried playing tourist for a while, but the jet lag and early morning were kicking my butt. I'd tried taking a nap once I got back to the apartment.

Yeah. *Tried* was the keyword.

As soon as I'd lain down, my mind had raced with a thousand variations of the conversation Derek and I would be having. One minute I was excited about the possibility of getting back together, the next I'd become convinced he was going to tell me he never wanted to see me again.

Now, I glanced at the clock. It was probably too late to go out again. It was already three. If I left now, chances were I wouldn't be able to see anything before I had to turn around and come back.

A *ding* filled the room. I reached for my purse on the small dresser and pulled out my cell phone to see a text from Derek.

On my way.

Oh shit! What would I say? *Great job planning this one out, Ally.*

I made the bed and darted into the living room.

I didn't know what I was looking for, but the path I was carving in Derek's floor was pretty impressive. If there wasn't a faded patch of wood behind the couch by the time he got home, it would be a miracle.

A sharp knock sounded at the door. I jumped.

Was Derek expecting someone? He hadn't said anything. Maybe it was Amazon.

"Ally, it's me," I heard him call from the other side of the door.

I frowned. Creeping carefully toward the door, I rose up onto my tippy toes to look through the peephole. It really was him.

"Why are you knocking on your own door?"

"I can't exactly unlock the door when I gave you my key, now, can I?"

He quirked an eyebrow, and I rolled my eyes. I unlocked the door and took a step back to let him in. Derek smiled as he kicked his shoes off by the door.

"Want a beer?" he asked as he made his way toward the kitchen.

"Sure."

I took the beer he offered me and dropped onto the couch. He sat on the opposite end, and I tried to ignore the pang going through my heart.

Taking a long pull from the bottle, I tried to muster up the courage to speak. It wasn't like this conversation would be the final word in our relationship or anything.

"So," Derek drawled, "how long are you here for?"

"Today mostly."

His head snapped in my direction.

"My flight back leaves tomorrow night."

If I hadn't known any better, I'd have thought he looked disappointed.

"Why are you leaving so soon?"

I'm not sure if you want me here.

"I can't be away from the bakery that long," I said with a shrug. "Max and Toni can hold the fort for a little while, but I can't leave them on their own for more than a few days. It just wouldn't feel right."

He nodded in understanding. Reaching for the remote, he found a ball game and turned the TV on low.

My eyes shifted from the TV to Derek's face. I couldn't help but notice the way he seemed to be looking through the TV instead of watching it.

"I'm surprised you left at all," he said after a few minutes. "I know you said things were going well, but..." Derek rested his forearms on his thighs and leaned forward, shifting his gaze to the floor. "What's really going on, Als?"

My heart fluttered at the name. I bit my lip and tried to steel myself. It was now or never.

"Why didn't you answer me?" I asked him. "After you left, I texted you. I called. Why wouldn't you answer?"

I watched in silence as he kept his eyes trained on the game. He reached for his beer, taking a drink before leaning against the back of the couch. I waited. Still, he didn't say anything. A spark of anger lit in my gut.

"I tried to talk to you over and over again, and all you could do was send me a postcard." I cast my eyes down to the floor. "You know, the day the bakery opened should have been the happiest day of my life. It was everything I've always wanted. A crowd of people. Ribbon cutting. It should have been perfect, but it was empty. It was empty because you weren't there with me."

He looked at me then, and I could see the emotion whirling in his eyes. Derek took a slow shuddering breath, but he didn't say anything. The silence stretched on for what felt like days until he closed his eyes and began to speak.

"I wanted to. God, I started to pick up the phone a thousand times. But every time I tried, all I could see was that look on your face." Derek closed his eyes like he was trying to will away the memory. "You looked at me like I was the scum of the earth, and then you just walked out." He opened his clear blue eyes and looked at me. "What was I supposed to say after that?"

It was my turn to look away. I'd been so wrapped up in what he'd done to me and how I felt that I'd never stopped to consider what my actions had done to him. Looking at him now, I could see just how badly I'd hurt him.

"I'm sorry," I whispered. "I was angry. I needed a minute to get my head on straight. When I came back and you said you were going to stay with Jackson, I…"

Chapter Twenty-Two

"We both screwed this one up, Als."

I slid a bit closer to him on the couch. "Then how do we fix it?"

Derek reached for my hand. "I don't know."

I laced my fingers with his, his thumb gliding back and forth across my knuckles. He brushed a strand of hair away from my face, his hand lingering on my cheek. I looked into his eyes and could feel myself being pulled in like a magnet.

The first touch of Derek's lips on mine was pure bliss. I wrapped my arms around his neck and pulled him closer. His fingers glided gently through my hair before he pulled away.

"I miss you, Als."

"I miss you too."

I buried my face in the crook of his neck and let myself take comfort in the feeling of his arms around me. The steady beating of his heart grounded me. It didn't matter what else happened or where we went. This, being with him, this was my home.

"I don't want you to leave," he whispered.

I lifted my head from Derek's shoulder. "I don't have to until tomorrow."

"And what happens after that?"

"I don't know."

Derek's arm fell from around my shoulders. A deep line formed between his eyebrows.

"Are you sure this is what you want, Als? This, being with me—it's not going to be easy."

I smirked. "Would I have flown all the way out here if I didn't?"

"Then we'll figure it out." He ran his thumb along my cheek before planting a tender kiss on my lips. "I love you, Als."

I couldn't help but smile. I wasn't sure what I'd done to deserve this man, but I thanked my lucky stars for bringing him to me.

"I love you too."

He smiled at me, the first real smile I'd seen all day. We had a lot to discuss in the next twenty-four hours, but we could do it. I knew we could.

Chapter Twenty-Three

One Year Later

I CAREFULLY SLID the tray of mini pastries into the display case. These new raspberry Napoleons were going to be a hit. I could feel it.

The bell over the door chimed as I slid the case closed. Putting on my best customer service smile, I readied myself to greet whoever walked in while Brooke finished her break. My fake smile morphed into a real one the instant I saw who walked through the door.

"What does a guy have to do to get a little service around here?" Derek teased as he made his way toward the counter.

I leaned forward against the display case. "For you, handsome, all you have to do is ask."

He leaned forward to place a gentle kiss against my lips.

Things had changed for us after my surprise visit to Vegas. We'd talked about the possibility of one of us just packing up and moving across the country, but we realized that we weren't quite ready to give up on our dream jobs just yet. So, we took turns going back and forth on long weekends and holidays. We video called each other every night. Some days there hadn't been much to talk about, but just being able to hear Derek's voice and see him at the end of a long day made the distance more bearable. The frequent trips he'd been making to New York for meetings with his boss didn't hurt either.

"Can I steal you away for a second?" he asked, lips still a hair's breadth from mine.

"Brooke's still on break."

As if she'd been summoned, Brooke burst through the saloon doors and into the front of the shop. She let out a loud groan at the sight of us, and Derek took a half step back. I turned to see Brooke made her way towards us with two cups of coffee in her hand.

"Aren't you supposed to be baking a cake or something?" she sassed.

Derek and I smiled at her.

"I mean, I get that he's your man and all, but could you not swap spit so close to the food? You might scare off the customers."

"Hey, I'm the boss. I can do what I want."

Brooke handed me one of the coffee cups with a mumbled "whatever" and went to work on some of the window decorations.

Derek shook his head at the two of us. He always said we were an unending source of amusement.

"Can I borrow your boss for a bit?"

"Just don't bring her back looking like she got into a fight with a lawnmower." She threw a wink at me over her shoulder before turning her attention back to the display.

My cheeks felt like the crunchy sugar on top of crème brûlée.

The last time Derek had been in town, he'd pulled me away for a lunch break. Food hadn't been on the menu that day, but I was certainly satisfied when I walked back through the door.

I hung my apron on a hook just inside the decorating floor door. "I'll take my cell in case you need me."

Brooke gave me a quick thumbs-up before showing us out the front door.

I slipped my hand into Derek's as we walked along the street.

It was moments like this that made the distance so hard. Quiet moments spent enjoying each other's company with no plans or need to hurry. Those were the moments I loved whenever we got to visit.

The sound of Derek clearing his throat pulled me out of my head.

"So Als," he began, "I—" The sound of his phone ringing interrupted his train of thought. He held up his index finger, telling me to hold on for a minute while he fished his phone out of his pocket. He paled the instant he saw the caller ID. I glanced down at the phone and was instantly on high alert when I saw his boss's name on the screen.

Their conversation had been brief, but the look on Derek's face when he ended the call spoke volumes. His boss wanted to see him. Now.

"Is everything okay?"

"We'll see."

I followed Derek to the gym and took a seat in one of the lobby chairs that were usually reserved for people filling out membership forms. My knee bounced anxiously while I waited, reminding myself that everything was fine. Derek's boss was probably just taking advantage of the fact that he was in town to go over a few things face to face instead of over conference calls. It was fine.

When Derek emerged from the office half an hour later, I felt like I'd been run through a blender. I looked up expectantly as his boss shook his hand and told him to take care. Derek nodded before making his way back to the lobby, waving to a few of the trainers he had worked with along the way.

"You ready?" he asked, offering me his hand.

Taking his hand, I summoned every ounce of willpower I had to keep from grilling him on the way out.

Derek didn't look upset. He'd been smiling when he walked out of the office. So it had to be something good right? Then again, he could be trying to save face in front of his former co-workers. What if he was just staying calm for my sake? Ugh. The suspense was killing me.

"So…" I said as we turned the corner a block and a half from the gym, "what did he say?"

Derek stopped walking. He started rubbing at his jaw with his right hand, and my heart leaped into my throat. He only did that when he was nervous about something. What could he possibly have to tell me that would make him nervous?

Derek lifted his eyes to mine.

"He wants to transfer me back to New York," he said with a smile.

I blinked. Transfer to New York? But that would mean…

"What about your job in Vegas?" I asked. "Are you going back to just being a trainer?"

He shook his head. "We're trading places."

The confusion must have been clear on my face. Derek barely took a breath before he launched into his explanation.

"His wife has family out there that she wants to be closer to. So, when I asked him about the possibility of coming back to New York, he thought it was perfect."

I nodded along as he explained everything, but it wasn't until about half a second after he finished that I actually realized what he had said.

"Wait. You asked to come back?"

He smiled. "It's kind of hard to convince a girl to marry you when you live on the other side of the country."

"W-what?"

The corner of Derek's mouth tilted upward as he reached into his pocket and dropped down on one knee.

"Als…"

My hand flew to cover my mouth. I could feel the tears making their way down my cheeks, but I couldn't hear what he was saying. Everything was moving in slow motion. My heart thundered against my chest as he opened the box to reveal the most beautiful princess cut diamond ring I'd ever seen in my life.

"Yes!" I shouted.

Derek held the ring out and laughed. "I didn't even ask yet."

"You're going to ask me to marry you, right?" He nodded. "Then hurry up and do it!"

"Allyson Marie O'Connor," he said through a cheeky grin, "will you marry me?"

"Yes!"

He slid the ring onto my finger and pulled me into his arms. I let loose a riotous laugh as he spun me around in a circle. I could barely believe it. All of my dreams were finally coming true. *Our* dreams were coming true. Life couldn't get any better than this. Especially not with that triple fudge brownie kiss.

Acknowledgment

Years ago, if someone had told me I would one day be sitting here writing acknowledgments for my debut novel, I would have told them they were insane. It is only by the grace of God and the support of an amazing group of people that I ended up here. I can't list them all, but there are a few I want to recognize. I only provided last names for fellow authors. Do me a favor and check out their work. You won't regret it.

Thank you to my Lord and Savior, Jesus Christ. Because of your sacrifice, I have the hope of Heaven. You give me a peace that passes all understanding when everything around me is chaos. Even on my darkest days, I never walk alone because you are always with me.

I never would have had the courage to start this journey if it wasn't for Kari and Rachel. The two of you were the first ones to believe in me as a writer. You pushed me to get better every day and believed in me when I couldn't believe in myself. This novel was born out of thousands of hours of the three of us chatting away about stories and ideas. I owe the two of you more than words can say.

To my Yoda, Mikal Dawn, you are the best mentor I could have asked for. More than that, you are an amazing friend. Thank you for enduring my endless barrage of questions and paranoid ravings. You are there for me no matter the situation. Our game nights have been a healing balm for my soul. Those nights full of food and laughter are memories I will cherish for a lifetime.

Shelley D Hiers, I call you sensei for a reason. I don't care how much you argue with me about it; you are wise beyond your years. From writing and business advice to paint nights and movie marathons, I can't imagine not having you in my life. I count myself blessed because I can call you my friend.

Thank you to all of my beta readers, street team members, and ARC readers. Your role in all of this cannot be underestimated. Your willingness to be a part of my journey means so much to me. You didn't have to do what you did. You chose to. That means the world.

I could be here all day talking about all the people that played a part in getting me here. Instead, I will just say a quick thank you to all the friends and family that have supported me through my various endeavors over the years. You are as much a part of this as anyone. I love you all.

About the Author

Copywriter by day, romance author by night, Erin McKnight is a sports lover, crochet nut, and dedicated foodie with a Star Wars themed kitchen. A proud employee of a local cooperative, she spends her days working to inform people about the wonderful ways they are working to improve lives. She is an active member of her church, serving in the choir, and enjoys giving back to her community.

A proud Okie, Erin grew up in the small town of Ketchum on Grand Lake of the Cherokees before moving to Norman, OK to pursue her education. She graduated from the University of Oklahoma in 2009 with a bachelor's degree in Sociology.

Batter Days is her first novel.

You can connect with me on:

- https://erinmcknightbooks.com
- https://twitter.com/emcknightbooks
- https://www.facebook.com/erinmcknightbooks
- https://www.instagram.com/erinmcknightbooks

Subscribe to my newsletter:

- https://www.subscribepage.com/z2t7l4

Made in the USA
Columbia, SC
22 March 2022